On a
Desert Shore

Books by S.K. Rizzolo

The Regency Mysteries
The Rose in the Wheel
Blood for Blood
Die I Will Not
On a Desert Shore

On a Desert Shore

A Regency Mystery

S.K. Rizzolo

Poisoned Pen Press

Copyright © 2016 by S.K. Rizzolo

First Edition 2016

10 9 8 7 6 5 4 3 2 1

Library of Congress Catalog Card Number: 2015949183

ISBN: 9781464205453   Hardcover
      9781464205477   Trade Paperback

Poisoned Pen Press
6962 E. First Ave., Ste. 103
Scottsdale, AZ 85251
www.poisonedpenpress.com
info@poisonedpenpress.com

Printed in the United States of America

For Michael, with love and thanks

At entrance Theotormon sits, wearing the threshold hard
With secret tears; beneath him sound like waves on a desert shore
The voice of slaves beneath the sun, and children bought with money,
That shiver in religious caves beneath the burning fires
Of lust, that belch incessant from the summits of the earth.
— William Blake, *Visions of the Daughters of Albion*, 1793

Part One

"A modern voyager, relating the particulars of his being cast away on a desert shore, says, 'After having walked eleven hours without having traced the print of a human foot, *to my great comfort and delight*, I saw a man hanging upon a gibbet; my pleasure at the cheering prospect was inexpressible, for it convinced me that I was in *a civilized country*.'"
—*The Mirror of Literature, Amusement, and Instruction*, 1823

Chapter One

The baby had cried for hours, a thin wail that grated on the nerves. He wished the crying would stop, but it would not let him rest when all he wanted to do was float untethered to the earth. Eventually, he gave up and came fully awake to who and where he was: Lieutenant John Chase of the Royal Navy in the hospital at Port Royal. *New-come buckra, / He get sick, / He tak fever, / He be die; / He be die.* When Chase's ship had entered the harbor, the singing and the clapping of the boatwomen selling fruits had seemed meant to give him merry welcome—that is, until he'd caught the words that floated over the water. *He be die.*

It was one of the ugly realities of the disease that the patient sometimes rallied only to succumb to the dread black vomiting—the coffee grounds, they called it—followed by the appearance of the ghastly yellow complexion, delirium, and death. Thousands and thousands of Chase's countrymen defending the British Empire in the West Indies had been lost to this fate. He'd been lucky. In his illness a host of spirits—nurses and servants—had attended him. He'd heard them chattering or glimpsed them drifting by his door as they crossed the piazza. Now the voices had stopped, and he seemed alone in the world, except for a flapping sound and its gentle breeze. Well, he thought wryly, if the fever declined to release him, he hoped the kindly hands would place his pistol within reach and leave him to put an end to the wretched work himself.

Mostly he thought about the woman called Joanna, even smiling to himself at the similarity in their Christian names. Even at the height of his fever, Chase had sensed her there, directing events. She came to poke and prod, oversee the changing of linens, or force him to swallow one of her foul concoctions. He awaited these visits, desperately, as if only Joanna had the power to stitch his sweating, puking body back to his soul. Once he had awakened to find the doctor, who reeked of brandy, standing over the bed, shaking his head to pronounce a sentence of doom. From what Chase had heard of the conventional treatments for "yellow Jack"—the bleeding and purging and the calomel, which made the saliva run like a river down the victim's face—he was not entirely sorry when the doctor went away again.

As the rank odor of his own body assaulted his nostrils, Chase grimaced, shifting his head on the pillow, and opened his eyes. Pain lanced through his skull so that he had to hold himself very still and wait, teeth gritted. But at least one question was resolved. The breeze was a gift from a boy who sat in a chair by the bed. Ten or twelve years old, he wore an oversized, striped cotton shirt rolled up loosely at the elbows and trousers of some coarse material. He had hung his broad-brimmed straw hat over the chair post and hiked up one bare foot to the wicker seat as he leaned forward, his forearm sweeping in a graceful arc to wield his fan.

Gingerly, Chase took stock. The candlelight playing over the child's curly head told him the hour was late. His fever had abated. The torment of the retching that emptied his guts had ceased, and the ache in his head, though excruciating, had receded. He felt cooler and appallingly thirsty. He tried to ask for a drink, but all that emerged from his throat was a feeble croak. Fortunately, that was enough to bring the boy to his feet. "Drink, suh?"

He nodded. With surprising strength, the boy pushed aside the mosquito net, slipped an arm under Chase's shoulders and held a glass to his lips. Watered Madeira slid over his tongue and down his parched throat. He felt a deep gratitude that brought tears to his eyes, though he wondered what the boy would make of a lieutenant of the Royal Navy crying like the infant who'd been haunting his dreams.

His gaze traveled over the nightstand, the small linen press, and the cane chair across which his dress uniform coat was draped, his black boots standing sentinel on the wooden floorboards nearby. He checked that his cutlass still leaned against the wall under the jalousies, the slatted blinds that allowed air to circulate in this hot climate. Over them, transparent curtains stirred softly.

With an effort, he summoned the memory of a dinner at the home of a local planter to celebrate the end of the recent rebellion of the free Negroes known as the Maroons. When was this party—two days ago? Three? The guests had watched him with concern as his fingers fumbled at his fork and polite conversation withered on his tongue. All that food he hadn't been able to eat: turtle soup; duck and broiled salmon; roasted plantains; cassava cakes; platters of pineapple, oranges, mango, and pomegranate; a profusion of pastry. After dinner they'd tossed the white cloth in the air to remove the crumbs, not minding when a dish left in place crashed against the wall to shatter amid gusts of laughter. By then Chase had felt far too ill to join in the fun.

They had brought him here to this house near the harbor, where Joanna had guided him to bed, her touch like balm on his burning skin. When he was lying on his back, she'd cupped her hands over his cheeks and kissed his forehead, lingering over him as she tucked the coverings around him. Then she gave commands in her musical voice.

Joanna came in again now. A supple and stately young woman of medium height, she wore a stern aspect and balanced a clay pot between her hands. It was a clever face, lacking neither sensitivity nor kindness but speaking somehow of mystery, of hidden danger. The face interested Chase. It was as if she drew the energy in the room to herself, even the candle flame bending toward her in the slight disturbance of air.

Approaching the bed, she said, "Awake, suh? That be good news."

"What's that?" Gesturing at the pot, Chase got out the words with difficulty.

"Boiled thistle seeds to stop the purgin'. Lemongrass for fever. Something more, best not to know."

"You mean to poison me, Joanna?" A feeble joke. But Chase saw in dismay that the boy had leapt back, terror in every line of his body, his chair toppling to the ground. "Joanna. *John Crow*," the boy hissed. His eyes flashed a desperate defiance. In an instant, he was out of the room and the door banged behind him. Grimness hardened Joanna's expression. Deliberately, she picked up the chair.

Chase's brain felt too thick to understand. *John Crow*, he thought. The Jamaican turkey buzzard—harbinger of death. He saw himself riding down a blinding white road, gazing at the summits of mountains, their sides profuse with bamboo and prickly yellow and sweetly aromatic logwood. A guide rode at his side, pointing up at the buzzards with their bald red heads and black feathers. The buzzards circled in the sky, perched at the tops of the cotton trees, or feasted on the putrefying flesh of horses and cows. Chase shook off this memory impatiently. "What was wrong with that boy?" he asked Joanna.

"Nothing, suh. He no trust a woman with medicines, that's all. You take what I gib you now and go back to sleep." She lifted one of Chase's hands from the bedclothes, folded it tightly around the pot, and kept her own grip in place so that it wouldn't spill. Chase began to drink, trying not to choke. The mixture was thick and bitter with an underlying sweetness that cloyed, but he drank it all down obediently.

When he finished, he said, "I've been hearing a baby cry."

"No, suh. No baby here. You dreaming." But recognition had flickered across her face, and her attention on him seemed to sharpen. She was looking deep into his eyes as if trying to see to the bottom of a well.

Stubbornly, Chase persisted. "I heard it. A child wanting its mother."

A smile tugged at the corner of her lips. "You got some good ears on you, suh. Only baby I care for is miles away from here, and she got no reason to cry, far as I know."

"Your baby, Joanna?"

"Don't you worry. Sleep now."

She was already lowering him to the bed, but curiosity nagged him. "Why are you not with her?"

"Why, she goin' to be a fine English lady, suh. Mebbe someday you be dancing with her at a fancy party."

"It would be an honor, Joanna," he said and closed his eyes, too tired for more.

She straightened the covers and lifted her pot. "Go to sleep. You soon wake and be better."

"You mean *if* I wake up?" Again, it was a pathetic attempt at a joke.

"Nah, suh. Do what I tell you. You is goin' to live."

Joanna had been right about that. But soon after his illness Chase had left Jamaica. He'd fought at Cape St. Vincent and Aboukir, where he'd been struck by the piece of metal that had ended both his dancing and his naval career. Like the hero of the fleet Horatio Nelson, he'd recuperated in Naples and, as Nelson frolicked with his mistress, Chase had enjoyed a similar relationship with Abigail, daughter of an American merchant. Abigail became his nurse and lover, got pregnant, and refused his offer of marriage. Back in her hometown of Boston, she'd borne Chase a child called Jonathan, having invented a suitably respectable dead husband. Chase had returned to London. A magistrate with a son in the navy had offered him a job working for Bow Street, charged with sticking a plug here and there in the crime that flowed through the city, as inevitable as the tides of the Thames.

But at stray moments, especially when he was tired or the filthiness of human beings weighed him down like a stone, Joanna would rise again in his memory. Chase had left the hospital without a backward look. He'd done nothing to thank a woman to whom he owed a great debt. He hadn't realized—then—that she, or rather the baby he'd heard crying in the night, would come into his life, many years later, in a different world, in England.

Chapter Two

London, 1813

There had been no marriage for the West Indian nabob's daughter that season, even though everyone knew it was her father's dearest wish to see her settled in life. Men like Hugo Garrod got what they wanted, at least most of the time. They moved their ships across the globe, managed their sugar plantations from thousands of miles away, or penetrated faraway lands, seeking beautiful things to adorn their collections or grow in their gardens. They had survived hurricanes, the yellow fever, and slave revolts. They made their fortunes and returned home to live as English gentlemen. They reveled in their wealth and secured their legacies. What they didn't ordinarily do was employ a Bow Street Runner.

John Chase, the Runner in question, was no reader of the society columns, so he hadn't heard the speculation about Garrod and his family. Chase had done several tours in the West Indies when he was in the Royal Navy, but he'd never met Garrod or had any dealings with the West India Committee, the powerful merchants who influenced Parliament, hoping to fend off any further restrictions on slavery after the British slave trade had been abolished six years ago.

On that July day the summons brought Chase to the West India Docks in the Isle of Dogs. This was a tongue of marsh and pastureland formed where the River Thames looped in its progress toward Gravesend and the English Channel. Here the directors of the West India Company had constructed their modern marvel—a sweep of wet docks and warehouses encircled by a towering wall. A fortress, in fact, complete with a military guard, constables armed with swords and muskets, and a twelve-foot-wide moat. Chase crossed the bridge over the moat and paused to study the carving of a ship atop the stone gatehouse. It was the replica of a vessel that transported the sugar, rum, coffee, and tropical woods to these docks.

"Help you, sir?" inquired the guard. Several other constables, along with a smattering of what Chase took to be customs and excise men, flanked him, all staring at him with a barely veiled belligerence. Apparently visitors to these docks were discouraged, but he had a ticket signed by Garrod. Had Chase been brought to the docks to investigate an outbreak of theft? It seemed likely and would explain the wariness of the guards. He took out his Bow Street insignia, an ebony baton surmounted by a gold crown, and unscrewed the cap. Removing the paper stowed inside, he used the baton to gesture at two nearby roundhouses. "Lockups? Doubt many thieves run their rackets here."

"A few, sir, a few," replied the guard, his expression lightening as he recognized the Bow Street emblem. "They find a way, as I'm sure you know. Excuse me a moment." There was a pause as he patted down a laborer who had emerged from the staff entrance at the side of the central arch, running efficient hands over his numbered uniform smock, checking each of his pockets, and inspecting his shoes. The laborer looked sullen but submitted, before slouching away down the pavement.

Chase handed the guard his ticket. "John Chase, Bow Street. I have an appointment with Mr. Garrod."

"Yes, sir." The constable raised his eyebrows at one of the other guards, who gave a shrug eloquent of ignorance. Obligingly, the second guard went to deliver Chase's message.

A few minutes later he was shaking hands with Garrod and being led under the portico and past a statue erected in memory of one of the merchants responsible for these docks. Hugo Garrod carried a malacca cane, which he didn't seem to need, as he set off in a long, loose-limbed stride. From his perfectly barbered head to his shiny top boots, he looked like what he was—a successful gentleman of commerce. Power defined his high-colored face, which bore the ravages of age and long exposure to the sun—a webbing of lines at the eyes and around the mouth as well as faint discoloration spots on his cheeks and a tawny cast to his skin that had yet to fade despite his years in England. As they strolled together through the teeming scene, men fell back at his approach, touching their caps or murmuring respectful greetings. Garrod waved them away, his blue eyes aflame with a zest for life.

This place was a monument to men of his kind, its scope immense, awe-inspiring, and grand. A mechanism with countless moving parts, machinery that functioned through the synchronized efforts of several thousand human beings crawling over the landscape. The works, Garrod explained, consisted of two wet docks, the import and the export, which were connected to the Thames by basins and a system of locks to control the flow of water. As Chase and Garrod walked down a wide road in the import dock, a row of brick warehouses loomed to the left, their copper roofs glinting in the sun. Next to the warehouses the iron cranes used to hoist the goods looked like monsters stretching their necks to the sky.

A breeze lifted the tails of Garrod's coat, ruffling his white hair, but he didn't seem to notice. "The Jamaica fleet has just arrived. Otherwise, we could have met at my office in Mincing Lane. I'm glad you found your way here. Come, I'll take you inside one of the warehouses."

Chase inhaled the pervasive sweetness of rum overlaid by the stench of tar and bilge water. "No problems en route?" In wartime, it was necessary for merchant ships to sail under convoy, seeking safety in numbers and avoiding enemy vessels—French or American—or, just as bad, the swarm of privateers infesting the seas.

"No, we were fortunate." Smugness warmed the merchant's tone, and Chase wondered just how much money Garrod had made from this one shipment. If he'd grown rich from his sugar plantations, he must be vastly wealthier now that he was a director of these docks, an alderman for the City of London, a former member of Parliament, and the Agent for Jamaica.

When Chase didn't comment, Garrod said, "I am interested to hear more of your profession, sir. Am I correct in thinking it one that requires a sharp wit rather than a young man's strength? A happy circumstance in your case." He pointed at Chase's knee with his cane.

How had Garrod known about his old injury? Chase had left his own walking stick home today, for the summer heat had alleviated much of his usual stiffness. Garrod's letter had asked for him by name, but this was not in itself unusual because the Runners all had individual reputations, their exploits often described in the papers. Still, Chase suspected someone had spoken of him to this man. This suspicion was confirmed when Garrod added carelessly, "At the Battle of the Nile, was it? How did it happen?"

His injury wasn't something Chase cared to discuss. "You are well informed, sir."

Garrod made a gesture that took in the busy coopers hammering at all manner of casks, hogsheads, and barrels that had been damaged in transit—a gesture that included the weighers, measurers, and excise men; the thicket of masts in the dock; and the score of lighters and barges moving goods from ship to shore. He laughed. "Don't you think I have to be?"

He had a point. Chase had noted the man's not-quite-masked assessment, as if Chase had been brought in to audition for a role on the stage. Well, what did Garrod see? A plainly dressed, beak-nosed, harsh-featured man. John Chase knew he had blunt manners and an untidy appearance. He had eyes still keen but hair gone gray after years of battling thieves, murderers, and swindlers. By his next birthday he would have lived a half century, which seemed an age to him, especially when he remembered the twenty years in the Royal Navy that had come before he ever picked up his Bow Street tipstaff. Too old to bandy words or play games; he knew that, too. "Tell me why I am here," he said.

"All in good time, all in good time. I must beg your patience. First, accompany me on a brief tour, and you will be satisfied. But I'll ask you to keep your tongue between your teeth should we encounter a small surprise along the way."

Chase stopped on the pavement. "A surprise? You are mysterious, Mr. Garrod."

The merchant turned back when he saw that Chase hadn't followed and frowned. "This way, sir."

He led the way toward the warehouses, pausing so that Chase could admire the foundation stone and its inscription, then conducting him into a brick warehouse with spiked iron windows on the lower floors. After they climbed the staircase to look over the tightly packed bags of coffee, they descended to the lower floors. Chase took a few paces down the rows of hogsheads, his boots sticking to the boards where sugar had leaked. "Impressive," he said, but he walked back to the exit and stood waiting.

They descended the stone steps together, the narrow space too close for Chase's comfort. He watched Garrod's beringed hand gliding down the banister, the jewels sparkling in the dimness.

After a moment Garrod turned his head toward Chase and smiled. "I see you have your own mind. I expect that's a good thing in a Runner, though perhaps not *always?*"

He could not mistake Garrod's meaning. Chase did his job and did it well, but he had never managed to ingratiate himself with his superiors. Often he went his own way without asking for anyone's help, and often he paid the price for that stubborn independence. He had, in fact, resigned from Bow Street recently and been reinstated. He said, "Having my own mind—and the freedom to act upon it—is one of the only things I care for in the world, sir."

"Spoken like a true Englishman, Chase."

They had reached the cellar, which reminded Chase of nothing so much as a crypt. In this confined space, the sickly smell of the spirits was overpowering, and it was difficult to see in the gloom.

Garrod spoke, his voice loud enough that several men working nearby looked up. "No fire is permitted anywhere in the docks. We must do all possible to avoid a conflagration, whether by arson or accident."

Chase nodded. Rows of casks stretched into the darkness beyond his line of sight, the dim figures of the coopers fluttering around them like moths. He noticed that Garrod stepped slowly and glanced at each face as he and Chase went by.

Still in that same lecturing tone, Garrod went on: "Several thousand pipes of rum are stored in this one warehouse, and we have built new rum sheds with vaults for the better storage of our spirits. Enough comes through these docks to make the Thames into punch."

They passed several massive columns and some enormous vats with propeller agitators that were used to amalgamate the various types and strengths of rum. "We've had some issues," Garrod was saying, "with settlement in the structure of these warehouses, so we've refitted some of the falling timber posts with cast-iron. You there," he called to a man who was kneeling on the ground, apparently engaged in examining the wood, "our guest would like to ask you a few questions."

Chase had opened his mouth to snap off a retort to Garrod's officiousness when he took a closer look at the workman leaping nimbly to his feet. He was a tiny man no more than five feet tall with a haggard, ghostlike face; pointed, elfin chin; and anxious, ever-moving eyes that missed nothing. He met Chase's gaze with glee; then his eyes slipped away.

It was Noah Packet, Chase's occasional spy, criminal world connection, and friend. Packet was a thief by profession, a pickpocket, a file, a gallows bird, a cutpurse—a thief in a fortress expressly designed to keep predators like him out.

❯❯❯

"Turning over a new leaf?" Chase asked. Packet had slipped into the corner of the administrative building, where Chase sat waiting after Garrod had been drawn away to consult with a dock official. Packet, likely breaking the rules of his employment, had followed Chase and Garrod into this area and was lucky to have caught his friend alone.

When Packet merely smirked in return, Chase went on. "You've found God? Turned respectable? Maybe you're plotting a rig to go down in the history books? Got the gentleman fooled, do you?"

"Nah," said Packet, "he's a downy one. He knows what's what."

"Well?"

"You could say it goes back to my blue coat. You know, the one that got itself ruint, thanks to you."

A few months before, while assisting Chase with another inquiry, Packet had taken a beating and spoiled his new coat. The coat had been bright blue with brass buttons. It had seemed a strange choice for a pickpocket, making its owner entirely too conspicuous, as Chase had enjoyed informing him, not to mention that it was an oddly luxurious possession for a petty thief. Now Packet, in his character of dockworker, was dressed in drab cotton trousers and a canvas jacket, a dusty, red handkerchief knotted about his scrawny throat.

Chase said, "The 'gentleman in the shipping line' you told me you did a favor for. You earned the money for that coat from Hugo Garrod?"

"I always knew you was a downy one too. Told Mr. Garrod as much."

Chase took a long pull of the grog that a clerk had served him and set the glass on the table with a thump. "What the devil does the West India Company want with a thief in its sanctum?"

"I got my uses." Packet sounded aggrieved. "I never met a bunch o' coves so mortal scared of a spot of pilfering. Spoils the perfection of their operation, see? So they bring me in to keep my glims open and report back. Easiest job I ever had. I walk around with my hammer and my memorandum book and pretends to be inspecting the floors or tapping the pillars. They's paying me a tidy sum for my trouble."

"Pilfering?"

"Don't think it could amount to much. A piece of mahogany in the trousers or a lump of sugar in the pocket."

"How would a thief convey stolen goods out of the docks? The defenses look tight."

"That's what Garrod means to know, but I expect someone's been greased in the palm to look the other way. They's to be stopped," Packer said in a pious tone.

"By you?"

"I got my eye on a few of the bastards. Never fear. I'll deliver on my promise."

"Good lord, Packet. You mean Garrod trusts *you*? He must be touched in the head."

The little thief looked hurt. "That ain't nice, Chase. He trusts me. I already told you—he pays me. Ain't I a man of honor, same as you?"

In some ways he was, Chase reflected, which was one reason why Chase had always liked him. They'd met soon after Bow Street had employed Chase in '01. Packet had already been known as a minor offender, and Chase had fully intended to see him arrested if he could. Instead they'd formed an association of sorts, which Chase had often found useful in his work when Packet ferreted out stray morsels for him. Besides being good company for a tavern carouse, Packet was a positive genius at reading men's characters, at understanding human motive and duplicity. Duplicity, Chase reflected, was Packet's specialty, and on that thought he leaned back, stretching out his booted feet, purposely avoiding the thief's eager look.

"Rather a coincidence, isn't it," he said conversationally, "you happen to be employed by the same gentleman who summoned me here today for reasons unknown? And this gentleman so well informed about my naval career and my recent problems at Bow Street? Now, who would know about that?"

Packet gave his hoarse laugh. "You told me yourself when you was half seas over one night. Well, as drunk as you ever gets."

"That's right I did. I see you've put my information to good use."

Packet's gaze flittered away and came back. "Garrod's got a job for you, Chase." When no reply was forthcoming, he went on. "Mind, I can't tell you exactly what it is, only it's something to do with his daughter. Got her for sale in the Marriage Mart, and let me tell you there's plenty lining up to take a crack, what with her governor's brass. But I hear she ain't quite the thing, somehow. Strange little bird." He tapped his forehead.

"Daughter? What's wrong with her?"

"Queers me. Rumor was she was all set to marry her cousin, Garrod's heir. But the match has gone sour, and they say Garrod ain't best pleased with his heir neither." He added succinctly, "Debts." He flicked a glance at Chase, as if to discover whether dropping further tidbits might sweeten the atmosphere between them.

"Go on."

"Ain't got much more, except that everyone is on pins and needles wanting to know how Garrod means to leave his blunt. Likes to keep them jumping, which strikes me as a risky game. Not a happy family, you might say. As for that girl—I caught a peep at her one time when she come out of a fancy party—a hunted rabbit. Traffic weren't moving. The folk in the street a-gaping at her papa's carriage, a huge thing, all over gilt with fancy paintings on the panels. 'Emblematic figures of Europe, Asia, Africa, and America,' or some such rot. You ain't never seen nothing like it, let me tell *you*."

"This girl have a mother?"

"Not one she owns to in polite company. Don't seem quite civilized, if you ask me."

"She is Garrod's natural daughter?"

"You might say that." Packet pursed his lips and made a little tsk of disapproval. "The mother was a slave on one of Garrod's plantations. He set her free. Left her behind in Jamaica and brought the girl over here when she was this high." The arm he extended from his hip ended in delicate fingers with dirt caked under the nails.

Digesting this, Chase chose not to be sidetracked. "None of

which explains why you blabbed your mouth about me or how Garrod found you in the first place. It doesn't fit." He frowned.

"Why get your dander up? You've helped me out now and again, and here's me returning the favor. I put a word in his ear, see, and not just for you but for that gentry-mort friend of yours."

Chase drained his grog and stood up to rest his hands on Packet's slight shoulders, pressing hard and squeezing. "I must be touched in the head too, for I can't recall why I ever kept company with you. You mean Mrs. Wolfe? What has she to say to this?"

Packet peered up at him owlishly. "Don't be like that, Chase. I thought you'd be glad to see me on the square."

"Mrs. Wolfe?" said Chase, squeezing harder.

"I told you. I done a turn for her. You told me she ain't been in high fettle since that husband of hers took hisself off. How's a poor female to get her bread, I ask you? All I done is show Mr. Garrod that pamphlet she wrote, and he recalled the stories about her in the papers. He thought of the rest."

Having endured a brush with notoriety and a royal scandal, Chase's friend Penelope Wolfe had fought back by publishing a pamphlet to set the record straight about her father's dealings with a certain courtesan and the son they had conceived— Penelope's brother Lewis. Chase thought the pamphlet well done, but he wouldn't tell her that. He knew she had needed the money, a woman alone with a daughter to raise and now a young brother to establish in a career. She had defended Chase's conduct in the last inquiry, attacking his critics.

Penelope had written a new kind of account of a sensational murder—one that sought to do more than raise the hairs on the back of readers' necks, one that tried to locate the heart of a crime in understandably human motives. And, as a result, she had made powerful enemies in government and the press. But, knowing her, Chase feared that the success of this pamphlet would inspire her to write others that would only draw her further into hazardous territory. She would look at him with those brown eyes and insist that justice had been denied, or that a truth had been hidden that only she with his help could uncover. He doubted whether their other friend Edward Buckler could restrain her either.

Before Chase could elicit more, Garrod entered the room. Catching sight of Packet, he rapped out, "Get back to work, you fool. Do you want to be seen talking to him? You'd be no use to me anymore." His face had darkened.

"Sir." Packet shook off the grip on his shoulders, winked at Chase, and was gone.

"Will you have a seat, Mr. Chase?" The color staining Garrod's cheeks faded, and he was again the polished gentleman. He conducted Chase into a comfortably furnished office.

As they arranged themselves in two armchairs, Chase considered telling Garrod something of Packet's history, then rejected the idea. It was nothing to him, after all, if the West India Company chose to employ a thief, and if Packet was to be believed, Garrod knew what he was about. "You've suffered some thefts here?" he ventured instead.

Garrod stiffened. "We've struck at the root of the plunder, but must be ever vigilant. Terrible, the losses we once endured. Brazen females used to come on the quays and carry off sugar and coffee in their aprons. We've nothing like that to contend with these days."

"You yourself were a prime mover behind the construction of these docks? I am told they were financed through private subscriptions."

"I got involved soon after I returned from abroad. Now you've seen what English ingenuity, the advancement of science, and the public spirit of men can accomplish."

It was more than time to push Garrod to the point. Chase said, "I'm told you require my services. It was Packet who mentioned my name to you?"

"True enough. He showed me a story in the newspaper about you and Mrs. Wolfe. She has caught my imagination, you know. I wholeheartedly admired your defense of her—true chivalry on the part of you and that barrister who won her brother his freedom." He slanted a quick look at Chase. "I understand

Mrs. Wolfe's husband is still playing least in sight?" His smile deepened.

Again, the man was well informed. Jeremy Wolfe had fled London to escape debtors' prison. Because the sudden gleam in the merchant's eyes when he pronounced Penelope's name raised Chase's hackles, he changed the subject. "You are a busy man, Mr. Garrod, as am I. Tell me about your problem."

Garrod took the watch from his fob pocket and sat fingering the chain. He took a few breaths and rubbed his chin. At length he said, "Your friend Packet will have told you something of my daughter's history? She has everything, Chase. Scores of beautiful gowns, jewels, fashionable parties, a phaeton to tool around the park, and yet she spends her days hiding in her room. I had thought her future assured but now—"

"A betrothal?"

"To her cousin Ned. Or to any one of the young sparks I've paraded in front of her. As I said, she has everything, but I've never seen a girl so miserable."

Inhaling another sharp breath, Garrod continued. "Her chaperone—the daughter of an earl to whom I paid an exorbitant fee, mind you—couldn't control the girl. Why, Ned's sister Beatrice took to the fashionable set far better for all she is above thirty! Marina's behavior caused comment. She either lurked in the corners at parties or hid in some ladies' withdrawing room until time to go home. I thanked God when it was over."

"Perhaps she is shy or homesick," said Chase, his interest caught. "She was born in Jamaica, sir?"

"This is her home. Marina has been properly educated to fill her station. She remembers nothing of her life on the island."

Chase was unconvinced. The past did not release its hold so easily. He wondered if Miss Garrod resembled her mother and whether this resemblance set her apart in English society. He wondered too at the closed expression on Garrod's face when speaking of his child. It seemed unnatural somehow. "Are you sure of that? It may be she misses a mother's care."

Garrod recoiled, closing his eyes. He opened them again and said, "Do you believe me when I say I loved her mother and desire only what will make our daughter happy? Do you believe me, sir?" Urgency vibrated in his voice, yet Chase thought the man exaggerated for effect.

"If it is not Miss Garrod's past, her troubles must be of more recent date."

Garrod pressed one thick finger against his cheek and studied Chase with a hooded gaze. "You might say Marina suffers from a delusion."

"A strong word, sir."

"Well, yes. You will laugh," warned Garrod and laughed bitterly himself. "This delusion has gained a powerful hold on her mind. She's said very little to me, but I am told she fears…a curse."

Chase felt a chill pass over him. The ordinary office faded away, and he leaned forward. "Curse?" he demanded.

"A young girl's fancy, nothing more, but I must be sure." Garrod's eyes wandered to the window through which could be seen the looming hulks of the cranes, tiny boats trailing toward the dock, and a glimpse of brilliant sky. He was silent for a moment, as if seeking the right words.

Then he said, "I'm worried, Chase. Marina claims someone has been playing tricks on her. One of her favorite shawls was slashed with a knife. An expensive trinket, a ring I had given her, vanished, then suddenly reappeared in her jewelry box. She said she saw a light in the garden at night, but we found no one. She put some dirt and other rubbish in Ned's bed and refused to explain why. Worse, she has taken to wandering in her sleep. Once we could not find her for several hours. We were about to call in the authorities and damn the scandal when she turned up, wet through from the rain and sobbing as though her heart would break. We've been at our wits' end with the girl. None of us can understand why she would behave this way and invent such stories."

"What's your theory?"

"I don't know. To make herself important? My sister Anne says that Marina doesn't want to be married, so perhaps that accounts for it."

"Surely Miss Garrod is very young? Why not wait a few years until she is more mature? Allow her to outgrow her fancies."

Garrod shook his head. "I'm getting on in years. I intend to leave my affairs in good order. I've labored too long, and there will be no playing fast and loose with my fortune after I am gone. And yet I'm afraid I've been hasty and don't wish to be unfair to anyone. I want to see my daughter honorably wed—and so I've told Ned. He's as bad as the rest at managing the business. No, what she needs is a devoted husband to look after her. This is particularly true for a girl like Marina, whose background is…unusual."

Unusual? She was the daughter of a slave, carrying the blood of Africa in her veins, and the potential heiress to vast wealth. She'd been born into slavery, though no doubt she'd been formally manumitted. She would be seen as foreign—not English. There were some who might consider Garrod himself to be something less than an English gentleman with his flamboyant displays of wealth, his whiff of the exotic—especially now that many thought the institution of slavery a blot on the national character. It may be that some would not be willing to overlook his daughter's heritage, no matter how large a dowry Miss Garrod could boast.

"Let's settle this." Garrod reached into his pocket for a bank draft, which he held out imperiously. "Can you start tonight?"

Chase ignored the outstretched hand. "There is one possibility we have not discussed, which is that Miss Garrod has told you the truth. You're afraid this may be so, and that's the reason you called me here today. Otherwise, you would consult a priest or a doctor rather than a police officer. I am hardly the best person to play nursemaid to a young girl. Why did you choose me, sir?"

"Joanna." The name dropped from Garrod's lips, almost unwillingly. "You knew her."

Astonishment held Chase speechless. Finally, when he had his emotion under control, he said evenly, "The nurse from Port

Royal." His thoughts whirled in chaos for a moment, and then he understood. Good Lord, Garrod's daughter must be the crying baby all grown up. "Joanna is Miss Garrod's mother?"

He nodded. "When I went to say goodbye to her before we left the island, she told me about saving your life. She was quite taken with you and so pleased you'd survived. All these years later I thought of you when Marina's troubles started. I had seen your name in a newspaper article, which told me the Bow Street men can be found at the Brown Bear tavern. So I went in search of you. You weren't there—"

"But Packet was." Chase shook his head in disbelief. "Why didn't he tell me?"

"I bade him keep quiet. I had changed my mind. Marina was about to have her season, and I feared the gossips would get wind of my having hired a Runner. So I decided to wait. I thought she would be so distracted by her pleasures that she'd forget her worries. I was wrong."

"And Joanna?"

He shrugged, looking away. "She is well, as far as I know. We've not been in contact. She'd caused a deal of trouble on my estate before I manumitted her. She was said to be an Obeah woman—a native doctress. Most of my people were afraid of her. I did my best for Joanna, gave her a chance in life. But nothing is ever simple in this world, is it?"

"Look, if your daughter is in danger, you were very wrong to wait. What exactly do you wish me to do?"

A muscle twitched at the corner of Garrod's eye; his mouth worked as he struggled to frame a reply. "Watch over her for a week or two. That's all."

"I'll need to interview her."

Garrod shook his head. "I don't want her upset. She's fragile, Chase." He extended his bank draft a second time. "Your retainer. I will require your escort this evening for a few hours. Will that suit?"

Glancing at the amount, Chase took care not to show his reaction. It was a fabulous sum, four times the fee a Runner usually commanded. He decided he would take this job, though it wasn't because of the fee, as welcome as it was. It was because he wanted to meet Joanna's daughter.

Chapter Three

Penelope Wolfe emerged from a darkened passage into paradise. Innumerable globes of fire burst upon her vision, sparkling from an avenue of trees. The scent of greenery mingled with the perfumes of the guests; laughter and the sweet strains of music struck her ears; at the end of the Grand Walk, a flaming obelisk beckoned. All was spectacle, all illusion, but that hardly mattered. She felt lighthearted, younger in spirit, ready to put aside her cares, as she and her brother Lewis joined the stream of people flowing toward the orchestra. When Penelope saw that his face wore a look of wonder that must have been reflected on her own, she smiled, happy to see his pleasure.

"Isn't it lovely?" she cried, pressing Lewis' arm in her excitement so that he narrowed his eyes at her. But at least he didn't pull away, as he would have only a few weeks ago. Progress, she thought, and looked around with fresh delight.

This was Vauxhall Gardens on a summer's night, a magical place of illuminated temples and pavilions in Kennington on the south bank of the Thames. She must find Edward Buckler in this crush, for he was the one, she was sure, who had dreamed up this expedition, and she hoped their mutual friend John Chase would also be present. Part of her delighted in the nonsense. Another part—the sober Penelope responsible for a household consisting of a five-year-old daughter, Sarah; her brother Lewis; her nursemaid and friend Maggie; and Maggie's two children—had resolved to be on her guard. It wasn't that Buckler could ever mean her harm. She knew he loved her and was almost convinced she loved him. That was the trouble. The more time they spent together, the more convinced she was, and the harder they struggled to stay within the bounds of propriety. But, absent husband or no, Penelope was a married woman.

Buckler's invitation had instructed her to use the silver entrance token attached to her card by a ribbon threaded through a loop; she was to proceed to the Grove to meet her party. The token showed three Cupids, two of whom supported a flower garland while a third played a lyre. Who was the "Mrs. Wood" whose name was engraved on the reverse of the medallion? Had she come to Vauxhall sixty years ago at the height of its glory to stroll the walks with her husband—or perhaps a lover? Whoever she was, Penelope had inherited her season ticket. The man at the entrance booth had accepted the older token without question, though he'd informed her that these days the gardens issued ordinary paper passes.

Penelope and Lewis found themselves in a large quadrangular space ornamented by a range of pavilions. Under a fanciful Gothic structure, musicians played. Hundreds more lanterns of every hue decorated the arches and the branches of the trees. People sat in supper boxes in the alcoves of the colonnades, their happy chatter rising in the night air, the lamplight illuminating a sea of eyes. At first Penelope was confused, and her gaze darted here and there, seeking a familiar face. They had just begun to make a circuit when John Chase appeared at her side. He was neatly dressed, but as usual a few gray-brown strands had escaped his queue. His expression was grim.

"Mrs. Wolfe."

"John! I thought you'd be here. Must I remind you to call me Penelope? Don't you see the absurdity of formality among friends?"

"Penelope, then," he said, his eyes conveying appreciation for her appearance, which was a comfort, considering she'd been forced to surrender her more expensive gowns to the bailiffs to satisfy some small portion of her husband's debts. Her ensemble had likely cost a fraction of those worn by many of the women here—some of whom strutted so boldly she thought they must be prostitutes—but at least her muslin dress was becoming. It was true that any formality between her and Chase had become absurd. He had proved her father's innocence and, with Edward Buckler's help, saved her brother from the gallows. She relied upon Chase's good sense, acrid humor, and uncompromising integrity. She knew he would tell her the truth, even when she didn't want to hear it, and would always be loyal. In recent months, she'd noticed him watching her and Buckler with a faint air of skepticism, as if he thought she needed an older brother to protect her, behavior that Penelope had found both irksome and oddly comforting. But why did he look so disapproving tonight?

"Where's Edward?" Penelope smiled at him, extending her hand.

There was no answering smile. Chase took her hand and nodded a greeting at Lewis. "You've misunderstood. It wasn't Buckler who invited you, though he's here too."

"Was it you?"

"No." Chase would never be called a talkative man, but he tended to get monosyllabic when in a temper. He had been especially terse recently, even with her. She thought him a good deal troubled by the lack of word from his son in America, but didn't like to raise the subject.

Before she could ask another question, a stranger approached to bow courteously. A tall man with white hair arranged in a style too young for him, he had nothing in common with the elderly gentlemen who sometimes clung to their old-fashioned wigs and heavy buckled shoes. This man was dressed in skin-tight evening breeches, fashionable coat, and snowy cravat from which a diamond sparkled. He raised Penelope's hand to his lips, his lined face creasing in a practiced smile. "Greetings, ma'am." He bowed to Lewis. "And Mr. Durant," he hazarded. He cocked his head at Chase. "What are you waiting for? Make the introductions."

At his most expressionless, Chase murmured, "Mrs. Wolfe, may I introduce Mr. Garrod?"

◇◇◇

They made their way to a booth where Edward Buckler sat with a young woman. Jumping to his feet when he saw Penelope, he greeted her and stepped back as Marina Garrod rose to make her curtsey. She was a lithe figure garbed in the conventional white muslin gown of the debutante. It shimmered in the glow of the many-colored lamps, which played over the warm skin of her face and throat. She had large, brown eyes set under winged brows, sculpted cheekbones, and an arrow nose pointing toward an elfin chin. Lewis, gazing at the girl in admiration, barely recalled himself in time to make his bow. Miss Garrod gave him a frank look of interest, and a smile wavered on her lips before her expression settled back into more remote lines.

Penelope seated herself next to Buckler, who shrugged when she sent him an inquiring glance. She took out the silver token with its Cupids and pushed it across the table to Garrod. "I believe this belongs to you, sir."

He didn't take it. "For you, Mrs. Wolfe. A gift. You may wish to return to the gardens on another occasion. Keep it."

"Very kind. But I cannot accept it." She didn't understand what was happening here. Buckler seemed uncomfortable, and Chase had apparently decided he would leave Garrod to make his own explanations. She wasn't sure she liked what she had seen of her host thus far, nor did she appreciate the arrogant note in the man's voice when he spoke to Chase.

Garrod launched into an explanation. "I'm glad you were able to join me this evening, ma'am. I have wanted to make your acquaintance and for a particular reason."

"Indeed?" Penelope shot a look at Chase, who was seemingly absorbed in the performance of the singer who had just taken the stage, but she saw that the nonchalance was a pose.

Garrod had observed Penelope's glance. "Before you take Chase to task, I must tell you that he knew nothing about my little plot until he arrived tonight." He grinned at her. "Forgive me, ma'am. I intended only your pleasure. You will excuse an old man for saying you look lovely tonight, the perfect foil to the beauty that surrounds us." Softly, he quoted, "*Can any mortal mixture of earth's mould / Breathe such divine enchanting ravishment?*"

This was the inscription printed at the bottom of her invitation, the one she'd assumed came from Buckler. Penelope blushed, which only increased her embarrassment. Then she saw that Lewis, still gazing with all his eyes at Marina Garrod, had apparently decided she was the more fitting recipient of this poetic tribute. Penelope gave him a gentle nudge with the toe of her slipper. He started and shot her an annoyed glance.

Setting down his glass of arrack punch, Buckler spoke into the silence. "Milton's *Comus?* You quote a villain, sir, a sorcerer who happened upon an innocent in the forest and entrapped her."

"Ah, but her virtue and fiery intelligence protected her," replied Garrod, unperturbed.

Penelope broke in. "I thought my friends had arranged this gathering."

Garrod laughed joyously. "As I intended you should, ma'am. Are you truly sorry? For you see your friends *are* here. I wanted you to become acquainted with me and my family." He paused. "In short, I hoped this evening would give me an opportunity to convince you to accept a further commission, one that would do me an enormous service."

Penelope felt Buckler tense. He and Chase were two bristling dogs standing at attention, ready to snap at anyone who might threaten her. Her sense of the ridiculous stirred. Had Buckler been brought here tonight by a similar token and engraved card? If so, she assumed Mr. Garrod had selected some less effusive quotation for him.

After a moment, Garrod continued. "I've employed Chase to provide security at my house in Clapham for a week or two. It will be just the family in residence since my daughter needs rest, but I have planned a party in celebration of the full moon. I thought you and your brother might like to come to us for a week."

Penelope stared at him in bewilderment. "You brought me here to invite me to a party? Why should you, Mr. Garrod? I'm a stranger to you."

"As I said, I have a commission for you, Mrs. Wolfe. A certain magazine has approached me to request a sketch of my life, but I have stipulated that I wish to choose my own interviewer. I happened upon some work of yours, namely the piece you wrote about Mrs. Durant. I must say I thought it marvelous."

Under the table, Penelope's hand went out to find Lewis', and he allowed her to clasp it for a moment. After all the lies in the papers, Penelope had wanted to tell the real story of his mother's life. Though she had written the piece under a pseudonym, her own identity had been thinly veiled, so she was not terribly surprised that Garrod knew of her authorship. "You wish me to write an honest account of your life, sir?"

"I'd rather you wrote a puff piece, to tell you the truth. But I will put no restrictions on your muse. I guarantee that, ma'am, and can assure you a handsome fee. You will find promising material to amuse the public in the entertainment I have planned." Garrod turned his courteous smile on Buckler. "I also entreat you, sir, to attend my small evening party. Tomorrow night? Nothing elaborate."

"Short notice for Mrs. Wolfe," said Chase, and Buckler began to utter a scarcely more polite excuse that seemed intended to speak for both of them.

"I will answer for myself, thank you." Penelope had already decided to accept the invitation. Buckler and Chase knew how she was placed. It shouldn't be hard for them to understand that if she had a chance to earn some money, she must take it. Making a living from her pen had proved a precarious existence at best.

Garrod's voice intruded on her thoughts. "May we count on you, Mrs. Wolfe?"

"Do come, ma'am," urged Marina Garrod, a statue coming to life. "We shall have such fun. Nothing formal: riding, driving and taking long walks. I'd be glad of a companion." She smiled at Lewis. "Do you enjoy riding, sir?"

He smiled back. "I've never had much opportunity."

Chase leaned forward. "You draw Mrs. Wolfe into matters that don't concern her." His eyes flickered in Marina Garrod's direction. "Private family matters."

"Nonsense. Clapham is lovely at this time of year. She will enjoy it. Let us discuss the details later. There's the bell for the waterworks. Mr. Buckler, will you escort Mrs. Wolfe while Mr. Durant and I take Marina? Let us make haste. Mr. Durant, will you come with us?"

"Mind your pockets," said Chase sourly. "The thieves will be busy."

Garrod jumped from his seat and grabbed his daughter's hand. Together, they ran off into the surging crowd, Marina Garrod laughing like a child. As Lewis followed, a new worry occurred to Penelope. She'd feared that Lewis might fall into bad company among the young men who haunted taverns and coffee houses, but it had never occurred to her to fear other kinds of entanglements. Her brother, who had worked for a time as a junior teacher, was a scholarly young man who had heretofore shown little interest in women. She shook off this concern and looked at Buckler.

"You heard him," said Buckler. "Let's go, Penelope. Chase?"

"I'll sit here and finish my punch." He sat back, frowning at the painting on the wall of the supper box. It showed two Mohammedans gazing, awestruck, upon the beauties of the garden. Chase looked considerably less pleased.

When the curtain rose on the mechanism of the waterworks, Penelope and Buckler exclaimed with everyone else. She pretended more enthusiasm than she felt for the mill with its revolving wheel and foaming cascade, smiling dutifully as Buckler pointed out the mail coach with its tiny passengers and the hunters accompanied by a pack of hounds. His shoulder against hers was a distraction, and though he kept his face resolutely forward, she knew he felt the same hum of awareness between them. After a time and without any discussion, they wandered into a more secluded walk among lofty trees in which nightingales sang.

She had been afraid Buckler would raise the subject of Garrod's invitation, but he seemed content merely to stroll, drinking in the glamor of the night and listening to the sweet strains of the music that mingled with the birds. Penelope forgot Hugo Garrod and his daughter. She forgot John Chase and his disapproval of her decision to accept Garrod's commission. She forgot her resolution to keep Buckler at a distance. Something of the magic she had felt when she stepped into these gardens returned.

When he was sure they were alone, Buckler pulled her under the sheltering branches of an elm. He stripped off one of her gloves, bending to kiss her hand, a lingering pressure. She didn't move. He straightened to kiss her lips, and she was dimly conscious of the louder trilling of a bird whose clamor seemed to increase in volume as if perched very near. There was a moment when she could have moved away, but she didn't, instead opening her mouth to him. Then he pulled her even closer, and she felt herself sinking into a dark place of pure sensation. Buckler had kissed her like this only once before, soon after Jeremy had left her. She had warned him the experiment could not be repeated. As she struggled to summon the will to stop him, the birdsong abruptly broke off. They heard a cough.

Buckler reared back, striking his head on a low branch. He voiced a curse, which he immediately stifled with a horrified look at her. He strode to the shrubs lining the path. Reaching in, he hauled out a man in a dark coat, dark breeches, and soft-soled shoes. Blinking as Buckler lifted him up and thrust his face into the glow of a lantern, the man broke into a flood of apologies. Penelope had never seen Buckler so angry, and she was belatedly appalled at her own behavior. Quickly, she tidied her hair and smoothed her gown, not looking at either man.

"What the devil do you mean by this, sirrah?" Buckler thundered.

"No harm, sir. No harm. Doing my job."

"Your job is to skulk in the bushes like a blackguard?"

"Hush, Edward," Penelope said. "Someone may come by. You'll only make it worse. Let's go."

His expression softened. Nonetheless, he said mutinously, "He'll explain himself first." He released the scruff of the man's coat.

The man stumbled back a few paces. "My deepest apologies, sir and madam." He kept his eyes respectfully averted from Penelope's face. "It's just that we don't get so many birds of late since London's grown so big and smoky. So they pay me to sing." He inclined his head at Penelope and added discreetly, "The ladies like it, you see."

Penelope couldn't help it; she began to laugh, and after a moment Buckler had to smile too.

The bird-singer smiled back in relief. "You won't be lodging a complaint against me, will you, sir? I need the money."

"Take yourself off."

After the man had slipped into the shadows, Buckler said, "I'm sorry." He was still angry at himself, maybe even at her. Her amusement faded. She often pictured him in his chambers, copper hair standing on end as it was now, lean face alive with interest, drinking endless cups of tea and paging through his legal books to seek an arcane reference and settle a dispute with his clerk. Their mutual friend Ezekiel Thorogood had once told her that she and Chase were good for Buckler—they had drawn him from his habitual solitude and frequent melancholy into the bustle of life. He was a gifted barrister, his career finally on the rise, but a career was not enough for a man.

"We'd better get back." Clasping his hand, she led him to the path. What need to say more? No point in thinking ahead or trying to solve an unsolvable problem.

They retraced their steps, their pleasure in each other's company gone. After a moment Buckler said, "You don't really mean to accept that fellow's invitation? I had a word with Chase before you arrived. There's something up with that girl that he needs to investigate. Tell Mr. Garrod you've changed your mind."

"I haven't. What about Lewis and Sarah? I must take this chance for them."

"I don't trust him. What's more, Chase doesn't either."

"He and Lewis will be there, and you will come to Mr. Garrod's party. I'll be perfectly safe." She spoke in a reasonable tone, but an edge had crept into her voice. Though she didn't want to argue with him, she was conscious of a spark of resentment. It seemed that every man in her life thought he knew what was best for her: her father, Chase, and even Buckler. The next thing would be Lewis assuming his right to pronounce dictates. There was only one man whose authority over her she was bound to recognize, and he had long ago abdicated this role.

"You don't need to tell me I've no right to interfere," said Buckler.

"No, you don't." Misery descended, and she increased her pace.

"Penelope, you're not thinking. Chase will agree with me. You're too impulsive. If you'd only let me—"

"Let you what, Edward?"

"Help you. Advise you. Be a friend to you since I cannot be more."

"I cannot and will not accept your financial assistance, as I've told you many times. Nor will I be treated as a child or a half-wit." She turned her face away, a lump coming into her throat.

After they rejoined the others for supper and fireworks, Penelope conversed brightly with the Garrods. But her mind continually drifted to the letter she had received from her father. Eustace Sandford had married the Catholic daughter of a Sicilian shopkeeper and raised his daughter on the island after his wife died. Penelope didn't think he would ever return to England. Now he had reported that, the political situation remaining chaotic, he could not at present return home to meet the son he had abandoned as a baby. He had sent instructions to his bankers to provide a sum of money but said nothing about reestablishing his daughter's allowance. Instead he'd written that she and Sarah were to return to Sicily to live under the parental roof as soon as they could find safe passage, while Lewis was to remain in England to prepare for the Oxford entrance exams, a proposal her brother had refused. Penelope would not leave him and did not wish to go abroad. But what was she to do?

Chapter Four

John Chase had been sitting in the supper box, bored by the necessity of making polite conversation. So this was Joanna's daughter. Marina Garrod played the role of pampered English beauty well. However, she tried too hard to please, chattering to her father and turning like clockwork to include Lewis Durant. Something about her nagged Chase, and after a while he realized what it was. It was as if she sought to disarm criticism, deflect any watching eyes, so that they only saw a polished surface. Sometimes she seemed to forget her role and sink into silence, her face closing up like a flower in the evening.

He could detect no signs of mental instability. He'd expected a silly, fearful child of seventeen; instead he found an intelligent and poised young woman who would have no trouble asserting her own will. For the first time he felt a qualm about his own fitness for this task. What could he know about girls of this age? Not much, he decided, as he watched her flirt with Lewis Durant, a handsome young man with naturally good manners, though not accustomed to doing the pretty with a society heiress. Garrod didn't seem to mind Lewis' attentions to his daughter, probably because he thought the boy so far beneath her as to be insignificant. Chase was seeking a way to end the festivities when Marina reached into her reticule to offer Lewis a sweet from her comfit box.

She placed the white lace bag with pink silk ribbon on the table in front of her and loosened the strings. Her hand slipped into its mouth. She froze, an exclamation of disgust erupting from her lips. Something spilled out, but Chase couldn't see what it was.

"Marina?" said her father sharply, breaking off his conversation. She turned toward him in fear.

"Is something wrong, Miss Garrod?" Lewis reached out a hand toward the reticule, but she snatched it away in a panicked motion that strewed its contents across the table. Everyone looked at her, then down. She sat, turning alternately crimson and white. One hand went out in a blind, groping way.

With a muttered apology to Buckler, Chase leaned around him. "Wait a moment," he said and touched her arm to stop her. Her dark eyes flashed resentment, but she complied. The ordinary items of a lady's reticule were there—the comfit box for her breath sweets, the small coin purse, the embroidered handkerchief, and the small mirror. But Chase plucked up a smooth, white object that he at first thought a piece of ivory. Then he found another faintly translucent piece similar to the first and realized it was bone. Among these bones and other rubbish was a single black feather, which Chase also inspected, running a finger down its spine. It might have come from a rook.

Penelope had several fragile, white shards in the palm of her hand. Holding them out, she said, puzzled, "Eggshell?"

"What nonsense," scoffed Garrod. "Marina, did you leave your reticule outside?"

"No, Papa, I did not," she said in a low, angry tone.

"What is it you've got there, Chase?" asked Buckler.

"Fish bones, I think, and eggshells mixed with earth. And a feather." He pointed at Marina's gold and sapphire comfit box, which was coated with a dark, moist soil. When he lifted her handkerchief, more was dislodged. He took up the reticule and inserted his own large hand into its delicate folds. Dirt and more fragments of shell and bone crumbled between his fingers.

Penelope brushed off the box. "Your comfits are not spoiled, Miss Garrod."

Helping her, Lewis hastened to agree. "Yes, see, I've dusted your linen. Have it washed, and it'll be fine."

"Marina," said her father in warning, as she swung a distracted gaze at Lewis.

"Who would do that and why?" she cried.

She hit a shrill note that set Chase's teeth on edge. "Do what, Miss Garrod?"

"Put that filth in my reticule."

"You know nothing of how it got there?"

"I do not. It was meant to distress and humiliate me. I may be only half an English lady, but I know that much."

It was an extraordinary thing to say, and shock registered in the faces around the table. Did she refer to her youth, her breeding, or her race? Chase studied her. It was difficult to imagine what the motive could be for such a trick unless it was to unnerve the girl—but why these particular items? Memory stirred but refused to come into focus. Where had he seen such a thing before? Abandoning the effort to remember, he upended the reticule and dumped out the rest of the dirt, shaking the bag vigorously. He handed it back. With trembling hands, Marina began to restore her property. Is it possible, thought Chase, that this girl could have put this rot in her reticule herself for effect or to make herself the center of attention? If so, she had succeeded. "Who would wish to distress you?" he said, trying to speak gently.

She didn't answer. As she reached for her coin purse, her arm jerked, and her glass of punch spread a stain over the tablecloth. "Oh, how stupid of me!" She seemed about to burst into tears.

They all gaped at her. Lewis grabbed a napkin to mop up the stain. "It's nothing, Miss Garrod. Don't distress yourself."

"I'm sorry, Father."

"You worry over nothing, my dear." Despite the easy words, his disapproval showed. He raised a hand to summon the waiter, who hurried to mop up the spill. Seeing the pile of dirt, the waiter seemed about to ask a question, but Garrod stopped the man with a peremptory gesture. The cloth was removed, a fresh one laid.

"We mustn't let our evening be spoiled," said Garrod. "It's almost time for the fireworks." Obeying the hint, Marina turned again to engage Lewis.

Chase shook his head. "I wouldn't call it nothing, sir."

"Leave it for now," said Garrod curtly.

Amid the buzz of forced conversation, Chase found an opportunity for a whispered conversation with Penelope. It had not escaped his notice that something was amiss between her and Buckler. They had returned from their stroll behaving like two strangers, Buckler lapsing into a gloom he barely troubled to conceal and Penelope talking too much, entirely too friendly with their host. She looked striking tonight—her dark hair becomingly dressed, her lush figure outlined by her gown, her brown eyes shining. Chase could see Garrod thought so, at any rate. Now Chase said to her, "You see I was right. There's something wrong in Garrod's household. Decline his invitation."

"It's only for a few days, John. You know why I must go."

"Take care, or your brother will fall in love with that girl. Do you really want him to pursue the acquaintance?"

She looked uncertain but, as usual, chose to disregard his warning. "Is someone playing tricks on Miss Garrod?" she said instead.

"Possibly."

"Why?"

"I don't know, but I intend to find out."

After that they went to view the fireworks, which were no sooner over than a shower of rain descended on the revelers. Chase made his farewells and joined the crowd shuffling toward the exit. In front of him was a matron who held a shawl over her head. The complaints of her husband, coat buttoned to his chin, floated back. Chase knew there would be a long line of coaches awaiting those traveling by road, so he followed the husband and wife down the water-stairs to the landing, where a uniformed bailiff strove to keep order amid the confusion. The boatmen's cries of "Oars, oars" assaulted Chase's ears. The foul odor of the Thames invaded his nostrils. Moonlight bathed the scene in a cold glow that didn't touch the black water. Fatigued from his long day, Chase leaned heavily on his walking stick. He ignored the mudlarks offering to procure a boat for him.

When it was his turn, he stepped into a wherry with three other people to make the journey across the river. He disembarked near the Adelphi and walked the short distance to his lodgings, brooding as usual about the lack of word from his thirteen-year-old son, a captain's servant aboard an American privateer. The war between Britain and her former colonies ground on; American privateers continued to inflict their humiliating losses upon British shipping; the mails grew ever more erratic; and Chase had grown ever more impatient for news of Jonathan.

He arrived home to another kind of war. As he put his key in the lock, the sound of raised feminine voices reached his ears. He groaned. He wanted his letters, a brandy, his newspaper, and his bed—in that order. He would have to send word to Bow Street about his upcoming absence too. But when he opened the door, it was to find his landlady Mrs. Beeks and the household's only other tenant, Sybil Fakenham, ranged like duelists on opposite sides of the dimly lit entry hall. Looking on, Mrs. Beeks' son Leo wore a rapt expression on his deceptively cherubic countenance, though his younger brother, William, was nowhere in evidence. A shy, bookish sort, William would have retreated to his room. Leo gave Chase a little grimace and pantomimed terror.

Sybil looked relieved to see him. "Mr. Chase! You're home."

"As you see, but I'll be going out of town tomorrow. Any letters?" He addressed this question to Mrs. Beeks, attempting to sound casual.

Some of the anger faded from his landlady's face. "Now, Mr. Chase, you'll be hungry and wanting a bite of supper. A mutton chop with potatoes? There's a steak and kidney pie as well as a fruit tart. Shall I serve you upstairs, sir?"

"I've eaten. My letters?"

"No word from Jonathan, sir," said Leo.

The boy drew breath to ask a question, but Mrs. Beeks interrupted. "As to your correspondence, sir, there's nothing much that seemed important. I put it in your room."

Chase glanced from one tense face to another. Could he avoid inquiring into the cause of this uproar? No, Mrs. Beeks was practically choking on her spleen, and Sybil was clearly determined to retaliate at any cost. The contest would only rage the hotter as soon as his back was turned. He said, resigned, "I heard your voices from the street. Is there a problem?"

Mrs. Beeks snorted. "You might say so, sir. You know I've always kept a respectable house, and I'll not allow Miss Fakenham to bring scandal down around our heads." A woman with raven eyes and fleshy, red cheeks set off by a crisp widow's cap, Mrs. Beeks prized respectability above all else. Chase must assume there had once been a Mr. Beeks, but he had only rarely heard his landlady speak of him. These days her one consuming aim in the world was to ensure the proper establishment of both her children.

Chase elevated an inquiring eyebrow at Sybil, who flushed and avoided his look. "Meaning what precisely?"

The landlady folded her arms, swelling to her full but inconsiderable height. "Ask her. Tell her that if she can give a proper account of herself, we'll say no more."

"She can hear you, you know. Is there a particular reason you inquire, ma'am?" This quarrel came as no surprise to Chase. The fact was that Sybil Fakenham had long harbored a secret, and secrets were intolerable to women like Mrs. Beeks.

"Nasty rumors," replied the landlady. "It's the outside of enough when I can't even go to the baker to purchase my bread without hearing my lodger's name on everyone's lips."

"I've a right to my privacy the same as anyone else," said Sybil. "She'd better mind her own business; that's what I have to say. And you too, Mr. Chase."

"Oh?" said Mrs. Beeks. "Then you'll leave this house first thing tomorrow, miss. That is, after you've paid the rent." She pulled one work-worn hand from her apron pocket and thrust it out, as if daring Sybil to produce the coins on the spot.

Chase sighed. "How much?" he said to Mrs. Beeks and fumbled in his greatcoat pocket for his purse.

Sybil flushed an ugly color. "Charity, sir? I won't trouble you. Go back to sniffing after your thieves. Leave my poor affairs to me."

Knowing her a bit better than he once had, Chase chose not to be offended by this piece of rudeness. Sybil Fakenham was not an easy woman to like, but he did like her. She was a wan young woman, an impoverished seamstress liable to cause offense wherever she went. But Chase had learned that she often stayed up all night sewing to earn her few miserable pennies. He pitied her, even though she aggravated him profoundly. He often sat talking with her late into the night while she labored to stay awake over her work. He sometimes gave her coals for her fire or shared his plum cake with her. Of course, Mrs. Beeks knew none of this.

"Miss Fakenham and I can agree on that much," the landlady said. "Why should you, sir? I'm sure it wouldn't be right. Well, miss, if you're prepared to honor your word, we'll say no more. I'll thank you to leave your room in good condition when you depart."

He observed the flash of fear that crossed Sybil's face. She said, "Don't worry, Mrs. Beeks. You'll have your money and your room. By tomorrow." She flounced up the stairs. Chase lingered in the hall to talk Mrs. Beeks out of this unceremonious eviction and quietly made good on the money over her objections.

A glass of brandy in his room soon revived him, and after a while Sybil came in with her sewing. By now they were well enough acquainted that the silence did not trouble them so that both could be comfortable. Pensively, he watched her needle darting in and out of an emerald green silk gown draped across a table placed at her side. Intent on her work, she was quiet.

"Are you going to tell me?" he asked. When she did not at first reply, he added, "For heaven's sake, be sensible. You have nowhere to go. You must make your peace with Mrs. Beeks."

This won him a twitch of her lips, and it occurred to him that their intimacy could prove risky, even beyond the fear of Mrs. Beeks catching them sitting alone together at night, albeit with the door left decorously ajar. At first, Sybil had seemed so like a scrawny stray that liked to spit at him that it had never occurred to him to see her as a woman. He didn't find her in the least attractive, except for occasionally when she would make one of her vinegar remarks while looking at him knowing he would share the joke. That was the trouble. Prickly, arrogant, and foolish as she was, Sybil Fakenham possessed a sense of humor and an innate dignity that appealed to him.

She set aside her needle and studied him for a long moment before she said, "Why should I? If I'm to be put on the street, it will do no good to humble myself."

"You humble, Miss Fakenham? Don't make me laugh. Come, you must tell me. Perhaps this sniffer after thieves can be of some use."

The quirk came again. She took a pull of her own brandy, set the glass down, and picked up her work. "You cannot help me, Mr. Chase," she replied, her tone cool.

"Try me." He paused. "I can guess part of it. You were turned out of your place? You were once a lady's maid, I should imagine."

If he'd wanted to startle her, he failed. Sybil merely nodded her thanks as Chase leaned over to trim the wick of one of the candles that had begun to smoke. Then she said, "Clever of you. You don't need *me* to tell the story. Tell it yourself."

"Accused of theft?"

"No, insolence. My employer Lady Danbury had a ball. I was called to assist one of her friends who had had too much to drink. I helped the lady to a withdrawing room where she was vilely sick down my dress. Then she started ranting about my lady." Sybil bit off a thread, keeping her gaze averted.

"What did she say?"

"Called her a whore. She implied, with good reason, that my mistress bestowed her favors too generously—on the drunken woman's husband in particular."

"I assume the drunken woman regretted her indiscretions?"

"The very next day. All it took was a word in my mistress' ear that I had treated her friend rudely, and I was dismissed. The lady I had assisted claimed I had been the one to disparage my mistress, seeking to gain a new place in her household."

"Lady Danbury refused to give you a character?"

She gave him a contemptuous look. The needle flew. Sybil's fingers were so skilled that she seemed to need very little of her attention on her work, but Chase noticed that her white, clenched hand stood out against the brilliant green. Seeming to realize this, she loosened her grip, absently smoothing the creases in the silk.

"How did the neighborhood tabbies get wind of the story?" asked Chase.

"Who knows? Servants' gossip, I expect. Or they don't know anything and are merely raking me over the coals for fun."

Chase had long wondered why Sybil seemed so alone, so friendless. He said, "Have you no family to assist you? No one to help you?"

"I've told you before. My father died. There's no one. An aunt and uncle who have made it quite plain I'm not to expect anything of them. I go my own way."

He sighed. It was often said that women were the more pliable, the gentler, the weaker sex—but that had certainly not been the case in his experience. He was an old bachelor, but was it possible that a wife would be any easier to manage than the women in his life? Somehow he doubted that. He found himself telling Sybil about the invitation Penelope Wolfe had received from Hugo Garrod.

"It's a chance for her," said Sybil. "She is quite right to go unless...you think?" She raised her brows.

"You mean Garrod? It would not surprise me if he had something of the sort in mind. A rich man. A young and beautiful woman with no husband in evidence and an unconventional background to make her fair game. She won't see that." He scuffed one toe against the carpet and took a long pull of his brandy, emptying the glass. He rose to pour himself another measure from the decanter on the mantelshelf. "Penelope sees the good. She finds a way to trust people and believes in her own luck. It's a weakness, I think."

"Or a strength. You worry too much. But I do understand that Mrs. Wolfe is your particular friend." She wasn't looking at him as she stabbed delicately with her needle, but Chase understood her.

"It isn't like that," he told her, suddenly awkward. "Mrs. Wolfe and I—she's in love with another man, and I have become interested in her wellbeing as a friend or an older brother. She drives me mad half the time because she never thinks before she acts." Actually, he thought it strange that Penelope was willing to leave her daughter with the nursemaid for a few days, unprecedented in his experience. Penelope and her little girl were inseparable, of necessity Chase supposed, considering that damned Jeremy Wolfe's frequent antics.

As if in echo to his thoughts, Sybil commented, "She's a married lady. She won't like to learn what happens when the world condemns you." She gestured at the gown that would keep her up most of the night.

"Oh, she already knows that. The question is whether that will stop her."

He related Marina Garrod's story, including his own connection to her mother, and was surprised when Sybil expressed sympathy. He would have assumed she would see Marina as that most fortunate of beings: one who never had to worry about her next meal. But she said, "Mr. Garrod left her mother in Jamaica? Poor girl. She never asked to be what they've made her."

It was late and but for his fatigue and the two glasses of brandy, he would never have uttered his next thought. As it was, the remark, which seemed imprecise and sentimental, embarrassed him: "If she is anything like Joanna, she will be no weakling. Joanna was a kind of native doctress, grand and rather terrifying. Something has…dimmed Miss Garrod's luster. I mean to know what it is."

"How do you interpret the feather, fish bones, and eggshells?"

"Not standard equipment for a lady's reticule?"

"Hardly. Let us hope her maid is not dismissed as a result."

They shared a smile. Chase said after a moment: "Miss Garrod is better off in England. There is less open prejudice, and she would have only one choice in Jamaica: to become the plaything of a white man in order to uphold her caste. The mulattos and quadroons do not mix with the blacks. Here she can be decently wed."

"And inherit her father's estate?"

"Presumably. Listen, when I return from this job, I'll call on Lady Danbury and persuade her to give you your character. In the meantime, can I rely on you to stop antagonizing Mrs. Beeks?"

"Under one condition, kind sir." Her lip curled with such outrageous scorn that Chase had to grin.

"What's that?" he said warily.

She reached down to rummage in the basket at her feet. "Something I've been wanting to do for months. The sewing scissors won't do. Let's see. Do I have them? Yes." She pulled out a pair of shears and brandished them so that they gleamed in the candlelight. "No proper lady's maid would be without these."

Pushing aside her worktable, she advanced upon him.

Chapter Five

"Don't worry, mum," said Penelope's friend and nursemaid Maggie. "Miss Sarah and I got big plans, don't we, love?" Over the child's head, Maggie observed a tear trickling down Penelope's cheek and fixed her with a stern look from narrowed blue eyes. Practical to the bone, Maggie approved of this excursion, insisting her mistress would be "daft" to reject this opportunity. It might even lead to a step up for Mr. Lewis, which the Lord knew, would be welcome, his future having been a frequent topic of discussion among them. Maggie, who possessed a wandering husband of her own, had no patience for squeamishness when it came to a woman making her way in the world.

It was too late to turn back, for there, pulled up at their front door, was Mr. Garrod's gleaming barouche along with a pair of elegant, matched grays. Maggie's sons, Frank and Jamie, danced with excitement on the pavement. Sarah pushed her mother's clinging arms away and joined the coachman, who hoisted up each child to pet the horses.

So Penelope kissed her daughter goodbye and climbed into the carriage beside Lewis. As the carriage wound through the traffic-clogged streets, they drove with the top folded back, the warm air lifting their hair. Mr. Garrod had told her that his estate, one of three along with his townhouse in Wimpole Street, lay only four miles from Westminster Bridge in Clapham, an ancient parish in Surrey. Once a woodland where the wild boar and red deer had roamed and still surrounded by farms and fields, it had become an exclusive suburb for the merchant classes, including, Garrod had said with a grin, "a pack of evangelicals and abolitionists." Bankers and merchants had built their villas around the Common, a large tract of land that had been well drained and improved with turf, trees, and ponds. Set behind a carriage drive, Mr. Garrod's mansion fronted the north side of the Common, his extensive pleasure grounds stretching back to the main road. The house, erected about sixty years earlier, had a symmetrical façade of yellow brick and a pillared entrance porch.

"I call it Laurentum," their host told them after they'd trooped through a series of gardens, greenhouses, graperies, and peach houses until Penelope felt almost drunk with beauty.

Lewis looked about to explain this remark, but Penelope said, "A city near Rome, wasn't it? Site of the imperial villa." Garrod seemed surprised, and she smiled to herself. All those years her father had kept her chained to her books could sometimes pay unexpected dividends. They resumed walking down the graveled path, the afternoon sun warming the top of her straw bonnet. It was a frivolous confection decked in knots and ribbons, which she had trimmed herself with Maggie's help.

"Laurentum—suitable for one who wears the laurel wreath," added Lewis in a neutral voice. Penelope read his thought: there was something exquisitely pompous in the idea of naming one's house after the wreath awarded to victors. She sent him a quelling glance and put her hand on Mr. Garrod's sleeve. They entered the hothouse.

It was a house of glass with straight sides and rounded ends. The air felt wet, a mist beading on the shiny surfaces of the leaves and swirling around her face. As the mingled scents of sweet and spicy flowers teased her nostrils, Penelope gazed at the riot of blooms outlined against foliage in every shade of green. She was reminded of the summers in Sicily before her mother's death when she used to play out-of-doors for hours, the ripe fruit from the trees in their garden dropping willingly into her hands. She released Mr. Garrod's arm and went on alone.

Ornate benches and chairs, placed at intervals along the walkway, beckoned invitingly, but she continued past a reception area where tables had been set up around a dais, then paused to admire a lily pond with delicate pink blooms afloat on green pads. Here she stood, craning her neck to see the tops of the palm trees, their majestic crowns just brushing the iron skeleton roof. She could not see the far walls, which were screened by trellises and stages decorated with colorful shrubs.

Pleased by her appreciation, Mr. Garrod called out a litany of names: pelargoniums and hostas and heaths and begonias. But Penelope scarcely listened. She stepped into the alcove formed by the half-moon end of the structure and contemplated a shrub growing in a large tub with wheels. About five feet high, it flaunted cream-white blossoms nestled in a bed of blue-green.

"Beautiful, isn't it? Protea Lacticolor," said Garrod, coming up to her, his face a-glow, his voice hushed as if they were in church. "I introduced it to this country from the Cape and have now in my houses twenty-four different varieties of the genus Protea. They are very rare. Indeed, I know of no other horticulturalist in England who has them in cultivation. The world is small and getting smaller, Mrs. Wolfe. England has built a vast commercial empire that benefits us all and brings goodness and culture and leisure to our daily lives. Our lives are enriched both materially and otherwise."

Before Penelope could think to guard her tongue, she blurted, "But not the lives of your slaves in Jamaica?"

Garrod shook his head, smiling. "You are an abolitionist? That will no doubt add a spark to our work together."

"I am indeed, in spirit at least. I cannot claim to have aided in the campaigns."

"I look forward to educating you more on this subject, ma'am, for there are many ill-informed views floating around these days. The West Indian colonies are yet the jewel in the imperial crown."

Penelope stroked one silky, cup-shaped flower. "I cannot think it right that any person be held in bondage, sir."

He stepped closer and spoke in a low, insistent tone: "Do you not see that Africans are natural inferiors born in a savage land? It is our duty to bring them to enlightenment. They will gradually evolve toward freedom. Their lives are no worse and often better than those of the industrial classes in England."

"If not now, when?"

He shrugged. "You must acknowledge the danger of rushing to extremes. Have you heard what happened in St. Domingue? Not a hundred miles from Jamaica, the blacks rose up, and horrifying bloodshed was the result. We must do all we can to prevent that tragedy from being repeated."

Penelope made no attempt to hide her anger. "It will happen again if you treat these people so cruelly."

At that moment Lewis called out to ask what was behind the drapery on the dais, and Mr. Garrod hurried over, his arm raised to block him from peeking behind it. "No, Mr. Durant, be patient. You must wait until tonight to see that particular treasure." Abruptly, Garrod bent over and scooped up a shiny object that had been obscured by the hem of the curtain. "Why, look at that. You've done me a service, sir. I had misplaced my ring of keys. It must have fallen out of my pocket when I visited the hothouse yesterday, and there it was all the time. Strange I didn't notice. My valet was certain he'd seen the keys in my dressing room last night. Entirely too sure of himself, that fellow." As he spoke, he detached a single key, then stowed the ring in his pocket. He excused himself to disappear behind the curtain, apparently to attend to some neglected business.

Emerging a few minutes later, he rejoined Penelope. When Lewis had wandered off again, Garrod returned to their earlier conversation. "I suppose you think yourself untouched by slavery, Mrs. Wolfe?"

"Your meaning, sir?"

He looked up from fastening the little key to his watch fob. "Just this. I know for a fact that your family has interests in the West Indies. Your uncle Ralph Sandford, whom I have encountered in my business affairs, is an investor in several shipping concerns, part of a combination that owns three or four plan-tations in Barbados. Your father, Mr. Eustace Sandford, draws upon his stake in the family concerns to pay for his Sicilian retreat." He spoke gently, not as if he wanted to triumph over her but as if he wanted her to understand.

This could be true. It probably was true, considering that her father had lived comfortably for years on an allowance provided by his older brother, an allowance that allowed him to pen his massive histories and political treatises about the rights of man. Eustace Sandford had, in turn, used this same wealth to provide for his daughter. The thought filled her with shame.

"Our conversation has strayed beyond my intent," said Garrod, his eyes still on her face.

She nodded, but something prompted her to say, "You have explained all this to your daughter?"

Garrod's brows shot up, but he said, "Let me show you some-thing, Mrs. Wolfe." He reached into his waistcoat pocket and extended his palm. He held a gilt-framed miniature about three inches wide. It showed a dark brown, liquid eye with impossibly long lashes. Penelope shifted it in her hand, and the sun picked up flecks of gold and green in the painted surface.

Garrod said, "I had it painted soon after Marina's birth by a miniaturist who had come to the island, hoping to make his fortune. It's good work, isn't it, ma'am? I rely upon you to tell me, as you are the wife of a talented artist yourself. I regret I didn't have Joanna's full portrait painted. She was a lovely creature. Marina is much like her."

"Miss Garrod's mother is dead?"

"No, I don't think so. She works as a nurse in Port Royal. I used to show the miniature to Marina when she was a little girl. It comforted her, her mother's eye watching over her." His voice thickened. "In truth, it comforted us both. I've been rather lonely, Mrs. Wolfe. But it is years ago, and I have my daughter to concern me. We must put these matters aside."

Penelope wondered whether it was as easy as that for him, but she shook off the thought and tried to enjoy her surroundings.

They wandered down the paths for a while, exchanging comments, until, unluckily, Lewis posed a question about the heating mechanism. Garrod's face lit up. He led them out a side door and toward the rear of the building, where he indicated a large water pipe. It split into two pipes, one leading into the hothouse, the other terminating in a valve beside a window at ground level.

"This pipe brings water from a nearby stream, Mr. Durant," Garrod explained. "One channel nourishes the greenhouse plants through tubes controlled from within."

"And the other?" Lewis asked.

"Let me show you."

They approached two cellar doors with ornate brass handles. Garrod pulled them wide, revealing stairs that led down to a room beneath the hothouse. He and Lewis descended, and Garrod looked up mischievously at Penelope, daring her to follow. With some reluctance, she went down the steps to be hit by a wave of hot, stale air. A brick furnace with an oblong cast iron boiler mounted above it dominated the tiny room. Next to the furnace sat a coal bin. Garrod reached out a hand to assist her to stand at his side.

Garrod said, "My greenhouses are heated by steam from this boiler. We once used smoke from coke fires, but the odor and filth were a nuisance. Steam is cleaner, not to mention more economical and gives more regularity of temperature. The smoke from the stove is vented through a flue, and the steam rises through a pipe and carries radiant heat to the floor and walls of the house. At any time, we can throw open a valve in the hothouse, and my tender plants are bathed in warm moisture. The furnace uses coal or even plant clippings to boil the water, which is fed to the boiler from the cistern by means of another valve. As the water in the boiler dissipates in steam, a float descends, opening the cistern's valve to replenish the supply. When the level rises again, the valve shuts. Simple and ingenious."

He indicated a large metal cistern that sat high on the wall. There was a small window placed above it; next to that, a pipe disappeared into the ceiling. A ladder leaned against the side of the reservoir, which Lewis climbed to peek over the rim.

Garrod watched him complacently. "The level in the cistern can be checked from the window and refilled without entering the cellar. The ladder allows access for service."

"No danger of fire?"

"None, Mr. Durant. The boiler is maintained to avoid undue stress. There is an added safety valve as well as a valve for admitting atmospheric air to equalize the pressure. In fact, steam heating requires less attention from the gardeners. They may go eight or ten hours together without a drop in temperature requiring their attention to the apparatus."

Sighing inwardly, Penelope attempted to show an interest. "It seems a marvel."

He turned toward her in the confined space, and she took a step back. He stood too close, seeming to loom over her in the half light. She put a hand to her brow to brush away the sweat that trickled down the back of her neck and dampened the neckline of her gown. Distracted by his inspection of the reservoir, Lewis hadn't observed her uneasiness.

"I've thought of everything," said Garrod. "Chaos ever threatens in life, but a farseeing man may often prevent it. We had terrible losses from hurricanes in Jamaica, but always we rebuilt, stronger than before. Let's just say, I protect what is mine. I have labored too long to see it wasted or destroyed."

She wondered if this philosophy helped him manage his daughter and somehow doubted it. "Tell me more of this work you wish me to do for you. I am to relate something of your history? Offer an outline of your business affairs?"

"Something like that. You must understand, Mrs. Wolfe, that we West India merchants are engaged in a war against those who would discredit us in the court of public opinion and destroy our way of life. I've been honest with you. I am certain you will represent me fairly." He fixed her with his intent gaze, and Penelope thought with a sinking heart that John Chase had been right to discourage her from accepting Garrod's commission.

To change the subject, she said, "I hear voices."

He started. "What? Oh, yes, sometimes you can hear people talking in the glasshouse through those ventilation grills set above the boiler. It must be the gardeners making their rounds." They heard footsteps as the voices moved away. Garrod's eyes were still on her face, uncomfortably probing.

"We should continue our tour," she said.

"Of course, ma'am." He motioned her to the stairs.

Penelope and Lewis hesitated on the threshold of Garrod's drawing room. Though still thin and pale after his ordeal in Newgate prison, her brother wore an air of easy confidence. With their father's gift of money, Penelope had sent him to a tailor, so she was pleased with his evening gear. This was the first time they had appeared together at a formal gathering, and the sight of his upright form in a skin-tight tailcoat, white waistcoat, and black breeches created a lump in her throat.

"Ready?" he said with a grin, offering her his arm.

The room was hung with crimson and gold satin. Gilded columns supported a painted ceiling where mythological figures lounged at perpetual ease. Windows, which opened to a terrace and flower garden, covered one wall. Occasional tables, sleek sofas, and a grand pianoforte basked in the evening sun. This same glow glanced off the mirrors and bathed the room's occupants, making them into a living portrait, a *tableau vivant* of beings from another world. Contrasting her surroundings to the barren lodgings she shared with Lewis, Penelope felt her pulse quicken. Courage, she told herself, and pasted a smile on her face.

"Mrs. Wolfe," said Hugo Garrod. "Allow me to make you known to my family." Garrod drew them further into the room, pausing first before an older lady, whom he introduced as his sister Anne Yates.

Mrs. Yates curtseyed, holding out her hand. "Welcome to Laurentum, Mrs. Wolfe, Mr. Durant. Beatrice, Marina. Come greet our guests."

Beatrice Honeycutt rose from a sofa against the wall. About thirty years old, she was the niece Garrod had adopted after her own parents died in Jamaica. Unlike him, she'd guarded her pink-cheeked complexion from the rigors of the West Indian climate. She would never be described as beautiful—her nose was too thick and decisive, her eyes with their sparse eyelashes too faded—but she was a woman of obvious breeding. As she greeted Penelope and Lewis, she revealed an awareness that seemed at odds with her rather bovine appearance.

"Where's Marina?" said Beatrice, looking around.

"Here I am," said the girl, who'd been poised at the far end of the room. She came forward. Tonight Marina Garrod wore a gown that made her appear a wood sprite. Her greeting was subdued, delivered in a barely audible voice, but she directed a searching look at Lewis, which he could not fail to observe. Remembering the laughing, vital girl who had dashed off on her father's arm to see the waterworks at Vauxhall, Penelope was puzzled.

"That's an interesting bracelet, Miss Garrod," she said, unable to think of anything to say. In truth, the ornament warred with the delicate greens of her dress; the black spots on the garish red beads were shiny like onyx. Penelope moved closer to get a better view.

"Like eyes watching you, isn't it?" Marina said in a clear, carrying voice that caused Beatrice to break off in the middle of her sentence. "I wear it to watch those who look at me."

Beatrice's fingers closed around the girl's wrist. "So that's why you hid your arm behind your back when we came down for dinner, you naughty girl. Where did you get that? I thought your bead necklace had been broken."

"I restrung some of the beads to make a bracelet. Some were lost, thanks to my maid's clumsiness when she pulled on the necklace too roughly and snapped the string. Leave it alone, Beatrice. It's mine."

"Of course it is, my love. Only it clashes."

"You don't like it because it reminds you of my bond with the poor black slaves. That is just why I do like it. I've no objection to being ranked with my brethren."

Everyone froze. Anxious to smooth over the awkwardness, Mrs. Yates broke into a flow of chatter. "Marina, I did tell you that the ornament is inappropriate. Dear Beatrice understands what is fitting and elegant in dress." To Penelope, she said, "Indeed both my girls—for I call them such and play no favorites—would put no mother to blush for their manners or appearance."

"You've no children of your own?"

The cordial smile faded. "No, Mrs. Wolfe. My husband was killed in the first American war. I don't know what I would have done without Hugo all these years."

The moment passed, but Penelope began to notice a growing tension in the room—the feeling they all waited for something. Clearly annoyed, Hugo Garrod kept looking at the door. Occasionally, a fuming silence overcame him, and there was a distinct edge in his voice as he initiated a hushed conversation with Mrs. Yates.

At length he addressed Penelope and Lewis: "My sister can be relied on to help me make your stay a pleasant one. She knows my ways well."

"I am housekeeper here, ma'am," said Mrs. Yates, smiling affably. "I would have welcomed you earlier, but Mr. Garrod has his own notions. What you must have thought of me I cannot imagine." She peered at Penelope out of a round face dissolved in wrinkles and tilted her head, sending a wreath of gray curls bouncing under her cap.

"Nonsense, Anne," Garrod said. "You are far more than housekeeper here."

"I fancy I know my place." Her smile robbed the words of offense. She bustled off to attend to the needs of the other guests, about a dozen in number, most of them business associates, judging by the conversations Penelope overheard. Some were very young gentlemen, the sons of planters sent to England to be educated. As he presented her to several of these boys, Garrod explained that it was part of his duty as Agent for Jamaica to watch over the young people in their parents' absence.

Penelope took a nervous sip of her sherry. "Where is Mr. Chase? Has he arrived?"

Her host nodded toward the window, where John Chase stood, surveying the company. In his good-humored way Garrod said to Beatrice and Mrs. Yates: "What do you think of our genuine Bow Street Runner?"

"He looks quite fierce," said Beatrice, making a comical face. "I don't think he approves of our grandeur."

"Mr. Chase?" Penelope said. "You won't easily read his thoughts in his face, but he is not likely to bite you, Miss Honeycutt." She excused herself to approach her friend.

"What?" he said when she had inspected his appearance.

"Why, it's marvelous, John. It suits you. Why did you do it?"

"A managing female got her hooks into me."

The managing female—whoever she was—and Penelope had to repress a surge of curiosity on that score—had cut his hair quite short so that it emphasized the bones of his face, making him appear a decade younger. His straggling, gray queue had seemed such a part of him that she had never imagined he might actually chop it off one day, but she wasn't lying that the new hairstyle suited him. The gray was mixed with the remains of brown so that Chase appeared quite distinguished. He was also wearing a coat she hadn't seen before, and there was the faintest hint of extra color in his cheeks.

"You're very fine." Her eyes quizzed him. "Where have you been all day? I've missed you."

"Familiarizing myself with my surroundings and attempting to make the acquaintance of my charge. And you?"

"Lewis and I enjoyed a tour of Mr. Garrod's domain. Our pleasure extended even to an introduction to the marvels of the boiler room that keeps his plants warm. Lewis was far more taken with the perfections of the machinery than I could ever be."

He snorted. "You'd better go do the pretty. I'll speak to you later."

"Aren't you dining with us?"

"Do you think our host would sit down at table with a Runner? I'm here to play watchdog; that's all."

"That's the outside of enough. As if you weren't as much the gentleman as Mr. Garrod. More, I'd say."

"Stubble it, Penelope," Chase recommended.

Chapter Six

Dinner was announced, and Penelope went into the dining room on Hugo Garrod's arm. The dining room was a large chamber paneled in mahogany and dominated by a huge table covered in snowy damask. Two chandeliers hung from a richly decorated ceiling. Along one side of the room opposite the wall of windows, a long sideboard displayed Chinese porcelain and plate. The meal was an elaborate affair with three courses, all offering an array of dishes, including a turbot, a sirloin of beef, and two haunches of venison. Garrod had included some exotic dishes for his guests to sample: spears of pineapple; pepper pot, a meat and vegetable soup; and cassava bread, made, Penelope was informed, from a starchy root that formed a portion of the slave diet on West Indian plantations.

Penelope was seated next to her host with Lewis placed at the foot of the table next to Marina. Garrod's daughter sat, her food untouched. Her other dinner partner, a portly merchant, tried to draw her out, but she did not respond. Garrod, though engaged in conversation, watched his daughter. They all did. Penelope had noticed this attention in the drawing room too: Garrod constantly calling upon Marina to step forward and assume her role of hostess. But the girl had hung back, and she hung back still, answering in monosyllables and addressing most of her attention to the food she wasn't eating. Was she shy? No, it was more than that. Somehow she made everyone at the table feel her presence and exerted a kind of power from withholding herself. One time, and one time only, Penelope saw her look up at the sound of Lewis' voice speaking to Beatrice Honeycutt, and for an instant the mask cracked. A different young woman peeked out. Then Marina went back to her plate.

Garrod poured the claret. "A glass of wine with you, Mrs. Wolfe?" He gave one of his wide, disarming smiles.

She lifted her glass. "Thank you, sir."

"Would you oblige me by coming to my study tomorrow morning?"

"Certainly. I am eager to start work."

"No, indeed, ma'am. You misunderstand. There is not the least urgency. I mean for you to enjoy yourself while you are with us. An hour or two spent discussing our task, nothing more. You shall give yourself over to leisure." He paused. "I have something planned for this evening that I hope will please you. A small surprise."

"You are too kind," said Penelope firmly. "You have done quite enough for me and Lewis already."

She was not sorry when it was time to address the neighbor on her other side, a man about forty years old with a sharp nose, pronounced brow, and inquisitive eyes. Just in time she recalled his name: the Reverend Samuel Tallboys—the local vicar, a noted West Indian scholar, and Mr. Garrod's old friend. Even though Mr. Tallboys had greeted her politely in the drawing room, she'd noticed that Lewis was accorded nothing more than a nod and a distant bow. Granted, her brother was the illegitimate son of a courtesan who'd had the poor taste to get herself murdered, but that could not excuse ill manners.

Now Tallboys addressed Penelope. "Hugo tells me you have a daughter, Mrs. Wolfe. You've left her in the city. Not too hot and uncomfortable for the child at this season, I trust?"

"No, sir. Sarah enjoys daily exercise in the park with her nursemaid. The heat rarely troubles children."

He nodded, seeming to cast about for a new topic. "Your father lives in Sicily? I hear there's been rather an uproar there."

The clergyman referred to the struggle to implement the new Sicilian constitution adopted under the direction of the British envoy, this despite the opposition of Ferdinand, the exiled King of Naples, who had fled to his other domain in British-protected Sicily to escape the reach of Napoleon. Unfortunately, the various factions of Sicilians could not agree to finance the fledgling government. They were steeped in feudalism, so her father always said of his adopted home.

"My father seems to despair of the new constitution even as he works to prop it up."

"Is that why he hasn't come to your aid in your recent troubles? Forgive me, ma'am, but I read about you in the papers."

Penelope lifted her chin. "My brother and I have managed on our own, sir."

Tallboys remained unconvinced, his gaze following Penelope's brother, who had engaged Marina Garrod. The girl's velvet eyes smiled into Lewis' as she toyed with her fish. Lewis looked a little flushed, Penelope thought. She hoped he was not overindulging in the free-flowing wine.

Mr. Tallboys' placid voice called her back. "I hope you'll excuse me if I was too pointed in my remark." He paused. "Do you mind my asking how long you intend to stay in this house?"

"A few days only, sir," she said in some surprise. "Mr. Garrod has asked me to compose a report on his evening party along with a sketch of his life that will be published in a magazine."

"I myself have written such trifles for him in the past when I could spare the time from my own work." He regarded her speculatively. "You must have much to occupy you in your husband's absence, since you are charged with establishing your brother in some respectable profession. I wish you every success, ma'am, though I fear you've been saddled with too heavy a responsibility. My friend Hugo means well but does not always think how things may appear."

The clergyman's utterly self-assured and rational tone took her back to her girlhood. How many times had her father spoken to her thus? And this from a man she'd met only five minutes before! She said, "Forgive me, sir, but allow me to be the judge of what is best for Lewis."

"Now I know I've offended you. But you must have sensed that this is not a happy house. Did you not see the way that young woman reacted to the reminder to remove the heathen bracelet? I do pity them all. The girl is uncontrollable."

"If Miss Garrod was wrong to disobey her aunt, her cousin was equally so in reminding her in front of everyone."

But Tallboys objected to this. "Miss Honeycutt? No, ma'am, you've mistaken her. She is devoted to her family, a model for her young cousin. She is worthy of our warmest admiration. I know Hugo thinks so too. She had opportunities to marry but has chosen instead to help him train the girl to fill her position in society. We must all hope Miss Honeycutt can be persuaded to grace her own hearth one of these days."

The man's eye had grown positively moist with his fervor. Penelope said tentatively, "Are there plans to that effect?"

"I spoke hypothetically. Mrs. Yates is getting on in years. Miss Honeycutt's duties at home will no doubt increase, not diminish."

Uncomfortable with the conversation, Penelope was cudgeling her brains for another topic when the door to the dining room was thrown open. The guests looked up to see a gentleman on the threshold, the butler hovering at his elbow. Unlike Garrod, whose face was rather sun-browned, this man was fair and had a sickly yellowish tinge to his complexion, as though he'd spent one too many nights carousing. He had guinea gold hair and weary blue eyes. Fine lines of discontent were etched about his mouth, which had a sulky cast that marred his otherwise agreeable features. It took Penelope but a moment to identify the familiarity that swept over her as she and everyone else gazed at him. He reminded her of her husband Jeremy: dissipated, dissatisfied, and disinclined to exert himself. He stood, staring back at the company with a faintly amused expression on his face. Rising from the table, Beatrice hurried to greet him, their resemblance apparent, though the brother had received most of the good looks. This was one of Hugo Garrod's presumed heirs, Ned Honeycutt.

"There you are at last," said Garrod with heavy sarcasm. "I'm pleased you could join us, Ned." He lifted one finger to the butler. "Lay another place for my nephew."

◇◇◇

Edward Buckler made his way through the crowded reception rooms. He had arrived after dinner with the other guests invited to hear a well-known harpist and drink tea. He soon found Penelope seated in a spindly gilt chair next to a gentleman in clerical dress. Her face wore a set expression, as if her companion was not to her taste. She smiled in relief when he approached her, and Buckler felt some of the depression that had been dogging him lift.

"You're the barrister who defended Mr. Durant in court?" inquired Mr. Tallboys when greetings had been exchanged.

Buckler bowed. "I am, sir."

"I'm sure Mrs. Wolfe is infinitely obliged to you."

"It was a close-run thing. I was never more relieved in my life when Lewis was released."

"Indeed, Mr. Buckler has been a very good friend," put in Penelope. "I owe my brother's freedom to him and Mr. Chase." She addressed the clergyman. "I will introduce you to Mr. Chase, sir, if he can be spared from his duties."

Looking a trifle askance, Tallboys merely nodded, and Buckler, bridging the silence, said, "I'd like a word with Chase myself should opportunity present. He was interrupted the other day when telling me a story about nearly dying of the yellow fever in Jamaica. I'd like to hear the end of that tale." He addressed Tallboys politely: "Chase was a lieutenant in the Royal Navy until an injury cut short his career."

"A shame," was the noncommittal reply. Buckler took a seat at Penelope's side, and the remaining time until the music started was filled with a discussion of Britain's recent victory at Vittoria in Spain.

The concert over, Hugo Garrod announced, "It is far too lovely an evening to remain indoors." He swept out an arm. "We'll take tea, and I will show you my surprise. It is as rare as any work of art in my collection. Rare and far more ephemeral." They went into the garden, which was at this hour, suffused with the last of a golden light tinged with gray-blue twilight. Buckler stopped Penelope on the walk. "Is something wrong? Where's Lewis?"

"I wish I knew. I didn't see him and Miss Garrod during the concert, and I'm afraid that wretched girl is going to get him in trouble. Oh, Edward, Mr. Tallboys thinks there will be more gossip if I stay here."

"Are you wishing you hadn't come? I have a rented coach. Return to London with me tonight."

"That would only lend credence to any rumors. No, I'll finish my work as quickly as possible and then go. It is not easy to be apart from Sarah." Her voice faltered.

"A bad business," muttered Buckler. Though he knew Penelope to be capable of handling her own problems, his instincts were chivalrous. He hated to see her in difficulties and be unable to solve them. He tried to unclench his jaw and smile at her reassuringly.

"I know," she said. "You don't need to tell me I told you so."

He squeezed her hand and released it. "Don't worry about Sarah. I'll take Maggie and the children out for an ice or to the Tower menagerie tomorrow."

She smiled her gratitude. They went on through the flower garden. Lanterns had been hung in the trees that lined the path. The path began to rise as they approached the hothouse, whose position on elevated ground commanded a view of the surrounding country and, in the distance, the sprawl of the metropolis.

Inside, girandole lamps burned in wall sconces, their glass pendants reflecting myriad beams of light, which mingled with wisps of steam that curled from the floors and walls. A small orchestra played softly in one corner under a canopy of greenery. Tall shrubs in pots created shadowy corners in which benches had been placed under makeshift arbors, and the high windows had been thrown open to admit the night air. The company walked around, viewing the brightly colored flowers and climbing plants, some of which wound through ironwork trellises and trailed down to brush a cheek or shoulder. In the reception area, maids dressed as shepherdesses served the guests. But before taking their seats at the tables that surrounded the dais, people filed up the steps, paused a moment, then came down again, though Buckler, peering through the mist, could not see what they looked at. The clatter of teacups arose. Some of the shepherdesses carried plates of cakes or offered wine, while others hoisted the trays that held the steaming cups.

Buckler forced himself to attend to Tallboys, who, having turned back to continue their conversation, waxed enthusiastically about the Protea flowers. "The name comes from the god Proteus," Buckler was informed, "the changeable god of many forms, which seems rather appropriate for Mr. Garrod, doesn't it?" Tallboys pointed out that the large, brilliantly colored flowers of pink and red and orange were actually composed of smaller tubular flowers inside a frame of petal-leaves. Though Buckler smiled and nodded, his mind remained on Lewis. He agreed with Penelope that the boy should not pay such marked attentions to Marina Garrod. Chase was not in sight, but Buckler hoped his friend did not find his task too onerous. It was not uncommon for the senior men of Bow Street to be invited to attend fashionable parties to guard the nobs and their valuable jewels. This job, however, was out of the ordinary.

It was Buckler and Penelope's turn to ascend the steps of the dais, where Garrod stood next to an urn set in the center of the stage. As an overpowering scent of some perfume wafted toward them, Buckler paused to draw in a breath. But Garrod's broad back blocked his view, so he glanced instead at Tallboys' profile. Wonder had softened the clergyman's stiffness.

Tallboys stepped aside. "Look at this, Mr. Buckler. It really is quite extraordinary."

When Buckler would later recall the details of this evening, more than anything else it was that hushed, expectant look on Tallboys' face that had stuck in his memory.

Annoyed that Marina Garrod had given him the slip, John Chase negotiated the path, avoiding the curious stares of the guests. He had seen Penelope and Buckler entering the hothouse, but where had the girl gone? He'd kept Marina under his eye during the concert but had lost sight of her in the confusion when the music ended. He increased his pace, his boots sending a spray of gravel into the air.

As Chase passed a lady and a gentleman promenading arm-in-arm and bantering in cheerful fashion, he felt his irritation mount. The woman sent him a haughty glance, and Chase realized he was scowling. If he'd done his job and gained Marina Garrod's trust, this wouldn't be happening. The truth was that he hadn't handled her well thus far. He'd glimpsed her with Lewis during the exodus to the gardens and had expected to find her in the hothouse with everyone else. She must have turned off somewhere, he decided, retracing his steps. This time he spotted a door in the wall and opened it.

He found himself in an orangery with tall windows on three sides, a roof lantern, and a stove at either end. Tubs of orange trees as well as pots of myrtles, olives, and cactuses filled the space. There were blank spots where some of the orange trees had apparently been removed to summer outside in the garden.

Ned Honeycutt had Lewis backed up against one of the glass windows while Marina tugged ineffectually at her cousin's arm, tears of distress shining on her cheeks. Honeycutt brushed her off and tightened his hold, his hands pressing against the boy's collarbone. No match for the older man, Lewis managed to land a kick on Honeycutt's shin as he twisted to one side. None of them noticed Chase's approach until he reached out an arm to drag Honeycutt away.

The boy gave Chase one look out of flaming eyes and renewed

his attack, his fist landing a sharp blow to Honeycutt's cheek. Honeycutt reared back, snarled something, and closed again.

"No, damn it," Chase said. "Leave off, you idiots." He hadn't realized that Penelope's brother had such a temper. He thrust Lewis behind him and stepped between them. "What are you doing?"

Honeycutt snarled, "I followed them. This young sprig needs to be taught a lesson. He's not fit to touch the hem of my cousin's gown."

"And you are?" said Lewis, panting with rage. "Let's settle this, sir. Name your time and place."

"I fight with gentlemen. You are a bastard and a low worm. I'll oblige you with a good thrashing if that's what you want."

Marina flinched as if she'd been struck. "You say that in front of *me*? How could you, Ned? If Mr. Durant is a bastard, what, pray, am I?"

"I didn't mean that…I wasn't referring," stammered Honeycutt, aghast.

"At least I don't tyrannize over women," interrupted Lewis. "She doesn't want to talk to you. Leave her alone."

Marina turned a frightened face to Chase. "My cousin is a regular at the boxing saloon," she whispered. "He'll hurt Mr. Durant. Don't let them fight, Mr. Chase."

Chase thought Honeycutt was more likely to be a fighter who started strong but quickly lost his wind and his science, whereas Lewis was intelligent enough to correct any mistakes and persist doggedly. But he said, "Don't worry, Miss Garrod. There will be no brawl today."

Catching these words, Lewis held himself very straight. "He has insulted me and frightened Miss Garrod, Mr. Chase. I demand satisfaction."

Chase wanted to shake the boy until his teeth rattled, though there was something in his bearing that commanded respect. "Look," he said quietly, "why care for his opinion? Your sister will be wondering where you are, Lewis."

"Yes, go find your big sister, Lewis," said Honeycutt, sneering.

Marina said, "Oh, do be quiet, Ned. You are being tiresome. Mr. Durant is right. I don't want to talk to you, not when you're in this humor. Besides, we have nothing to talk about."

Ned Honeycutt contemplated her. "But we do. Marina, you know we do," he said, pleading.

She shook her head. "As usual, you think only of yourself. It's your own fault if my father is angry with you, not mine. Speak to him."

Lewis put a hand to his disordered hair and straightened his cravat. "You're right, Mr. Chase. We'll go." He offered his arm to the girl. "Miss Garrod?"

She accepted Lewis' escort and went off without another look at her cousin, who stood gazing after her, his expression enigmatic.

Chase said, "Was there a particular reason you wished to see Miss Garrod?"

Honeycutt's eyes dismissed him. "No concern of yours, is it?"

"Her welfare is my concern," said Chase mildly. "She doesn't seem to like you much."

Honeycutt strode to a bench against the wall. He sat down, stretching out his long legs and leaning his shoulders back. Slowly, the anger drained from him to be replaced by calculation. "I've known that girl all her life," he said at last. "My uncle intends for me to wed her. How can you think I could ever harm her? Durant annoyed me and I only wanted to protect her. How do I know whether he might be a rogue or a fortune hunter? I doubt Uncle Hugo would have invited him had he known his hospitality would be abused." He raised his brows. "Besides, isn't it your job to watch her?"

Chase sat down next to him on the bench. "I am talking about you," he said as if commenting on the weather. "Garrod not willing to pay your shot anymore?"

"Something like that."

"So you mean to make all secure with the heiress before he tosses you out, or a rival gets in your way."

Honeycutt gave a bitter laugh. "Rival? Do you think my uncle would allow that insolent puppy within ten feet of Marina were Durant in earnest? She'll never marry against her father's wishes. Don't you know a good marriage is the only way to wash the blackamoor white and carry on the family line? Here I am, a willing sacrifice, ready to do my duty."

"You will speak of Miss Garrod with respect or not at all." Disgust welled up in Chase, and his fists flexed at his side.

Honeycutt's color rose. "You don't have to tell me that. I'm fond of her, always have been."

Chase had encountered men of Honeycutt's stamp among the Creoles of Jamaica. Proud and vain men, they lived indolent lives, primarily occupying themselves with whoring, drinking, and gaming. They kept their slave concubines and allowed the children of these unions to tumble about their plantations. The Creoles sometimes subsided into an early grave after their bodies sank beneath their excesses and gave out. Chase supposed it could be said in their favor that, in their natural setting, these men were often hospitable to an extreme and elegant in their manners, not that these particular qualities drew his approbation. It occurred to him that Ned Honeycutt might be just as out of place here in England as his cousin. Certainly, he lacked his uncle's energy and powerful will to direct complex business interests.

"Tell me about your debts," said Chase.

"What of them?" Giving a shrug, he crossed one foot in its black pump over the other. "Hugo always forgives me in the end. What choice does he have? You should have seen him trying to match Marina with London's finest. What a joke! The girl couldn't string two words together, let alone bring the more eligible gentlemen up to scratch."

An enormous estate was at stake. What would Ned Honeycutt do to ensure he received what he no doubt deemed his rightful portion? It suddenly struck Chase as surprising that Honeycutt had gone after Lewis Durant with so little provocation. This hadn't endeared him to Marina; if anything, his tactics would only throw her the more into the boy's arms.

Either Honeycutt was an immature fool—evidently more than possible—or he had another reason to pick a fight during his uncle's evening party.

Chase got to his feet. "Debts aren't the only thing I'll lay to your account. You've been playing tricks on Miss Garrod to frighten her and stop her from marrying anyone else."

"You're mad." Honeycutt's face had gone white, but Chase could have sworn the man had not been surprised by this accusation.

When Chase started to walk away, Honeycutt called after him, "Do you mean to tell my uncle about our little chat? Don't bother. I'll tell him myself."

"Leave Durant alone, and stay away from Miss Garrod," Chase said over his shoulder.

Before he could reach the door, he was brought up short by a sudden racket. He heard the shrieking of many voices and a loud clatter, as of several dozen chairs being drawn back at once.

Chapter Seven

Velvet curtains had been drawn back to expose a centrally mounted trellis. Penelope could see what everyone had been looking at: a tangle of thick vines that snaked around the lattice, climbing fully eight feet. The tip of each vine bore great white flowers at least a hand's breadth across with stamens of bright yellow. Perhaps a dozen of these flowers glowed like a cluster of jewels on the vine, and an intense scent wafted toward her as she approached. Hauntingly fragrant, it was both innocent and cunning in the way it teased her senses, initially strong and then slipping away.

"This plant blooms only once each year during the full moon of high summer." Hugo Garrod's outstretched finger hovered close to the white petals but did not touch them. Softly, he recited, "*Queen of the dark, whose tender glories fade / In the grey radiance of the noon-tide hours.*" He smiled at her evident admiration, adding, "Night-blooming cereus. It will bloom a few hours and wither at first light."

Tallboys said, "In Jamaica it is thought that the strong odor of this plant may attract spirits or, as the slaves call them, the duppies. Some say it should not be placed too close to a house."

Obviously much moved, Garrod paid scant heed to this remark. After a moment he said in a more natural voice, "I have a special blend of Pekoe and Congo to share with my guests of honor." He looked around peevishly. "Where has my daughter got to? She was to help me serve."

Mrs. Yates seemed unconcerned. "I believe she conducts Mr. Durant on a tour of the orangery. Ned has gone to fetch her and will bring her along shortly, Hugo."

"We won't wait for them." He smiled at his sister. "You won't object, my dear, if I call upon Mrs. Wolfe to assist me? I know you are already familiar with my teapoy. I think it would amuse her to view its interior."

Mrs. Yates acquiesced graciously, but Penelope, enduring another glance from Tallboys as well as an indrawn breath from Buckler, tried to think of an excuse to refuse. None presented itself. With extreme reluctance, she went to stand next to a three-legged mahogany table, which was topped by a built-in tea caddy. Garrod used the key from his watch fob to unlock the caddy. As he lifted the lid, a painting on the interior was visible, showing Roman captives with cropped hair, kneeling. Penelope saw that the cut-glass bowls of the velvet-lined tray held a miniature sugarloaf wrapped in blue paper next to a pair of sugar nippers. A second glass bowl contained a larger loaf of a slightly darker variety, unwrapped. On another table next to the teapoy, a teapot, a dish of lemon slices, a cream jug, an urn of hot water, and a slop basin waited.

Finished blending the tea, Garrod warmed the pot, then poured water over the leaves, as Mrs. Yates supervised the footman to arrange the chairs and set up at each guest's side simpler teapoys with octagonal tops, each designed to hold an individual service. As she busied herself, Penelope found that Garrod compelled her attention strangely: his tall and elegant figure; his ruddy skin that glistened in the lamplight; his prominent nose and wide-set, glittering eyes.

She forced herself to attend to her task. Finally, Garrod broke off in the middle of a humorous story about Jamaican duppies to demand, "Where can your brother be, Mrs. Wolfe?"

"He'll be here shortly. He'll want his tea."

About to add sugar to the cups, Penelope hesitated over the two varieties. Seeing her difficulty, Garrod said, "Use the sugar wrapped in blue paper. It is royal sugar, Mrs. Wolfe, the finest grade available. It has been melted with weak limewater and clarified three times, passing it through a cloth coated with the very best clay. The result is a sugar whiter than snow. Hold up your hand to the thickest part of the loaf. It is so transparent you can see your fingers on the other side."

"Not for me, thank you, sir," put in Tallboys. "You know I always take the refined instead. The royal is far too rich for a clergyman, sir. The refined will do well enough for me."

"Your principles do you honor, sir," said Beatrice Honeycutt.

"Nonsense, Tallboys," said Garrod. "I'll not indulge your beggarly whims on this occasion. Take your tea and be thankful. Now to work, Mrs. Wolfe."

Two spoons of sugar went into Garrod's tea; one into Miss Honeycutt's, Tallboys', and Buckler's. Into her own, Penelope put a dollop of cream. She handed Buckler his cup without a word, avoiding his eyes. She also looked inquiringly at Anne Yates, who smiled her thanks but approached the teapoy to add her own sugar and cream. Feeling unhappily self-conscious, Penelope carried around the rest of the cups.

Later she would tell Chase that Hugo Garrod had drunk his tea to the bottom, as if so thirsty he could not wait for the liquid to reach a more comfortable temperature. Tallboys, too, seemed to relish his but drank only about half, as he consumed several cakes. Beatrice Honeycutt took a few sips, folded her hands in her lap, and put aside her cup to engage Penelope in a stilted conversation. Still feeling anxious about Lewis, Penelope nibbled a cake and drank her own tea to the dregs. She noticed that Mrs. Yates, who had moved away to attend to one of the other guests, did not drink her tea, nor did Buckler, still absorbed in contemplation of the night-blooming cereus that seemed to have caught his imagination. After a while, without asking, she took his first cup away, emptied it in the slop basin, and used the tea strainer to fix him a fresh one. He smiled his thanks.

Penelope felt her nerves stretch almost to the breaking point. Finally, she said, "Mr. Buckler, will you find Lewis and tell him I'm waiting for him?"

Buckler bowed. "Of course, Mrs. Wolfe." His eyes began to scan the crowd.

Hugo Garrod glanced up, seemed as though he meant to speak, and vomited over the side of the stage, the liquid striking one of the shepherdesses. The maid jumped and emitted an involuntary sound of disgust. Quickly, Mrs. Yates moved from her position by the urn to help her brother, who was bent over, clutching his gut. She wrapped an arm around his shoulders to support him. "You are ill, Hugo," she cried in a high, frightened voice. "Come, we'll return to the house."

Tallboys clutched at his throat, choking on a morsel of cake. Appalled, Penelope looked at Buckler. His attention still focused on the crowd, he hadn't noticed anything wrong.

"I see Lewis and Miss Garrod. They're in that alcove over there," he said. "I'll fetch them." Buckler got to his feet and raised his cup to his lips, about to take a hurried sip. Obeying an instinct, Penelope jerked out of her chair to leap toward him. She dashed the cup from his hand, and liquid spilled down his shirtfront. He gave a yelp as it scalded him. "Penelope!"

She shook her head and went to kneel by the Reverend Tallboys' chair. "What's wrong? Can you speak, sir?"

"I don't know. I feel so strange. The tea—it tasted too hot, like pepper, maybe." His eyes seemed to bulge. He gripped her arm so hard she winced.

Penelope looked around wildly. "Someone help us, please," she called. She approached Miss Honeycutt, who sat in her seat, moaning and pressing her hands against her abdomen. The woman's face was so white it seemed she must faint, but, though she slumped, she managed to keep her seat.

Around them the voices stilled and erupted again, louder. Spectators surrounded the dais, holding their hands to their mouths, radiating incredulity and dismay. For a moment no one moved. Then Lewis was there with Marina, their faces perfect pictures of horror.

Buckler's terrified eyes searched Penelope's. "What is it?"

"There's something very wrong here, Edward."

Groaning in pain, Hugo Garrod looked up at them piteously while the Queen of the Night continued to breathe its sweet scent over them all.

◇◇◇

A cacophony of voices met John Chase when he entered the hothouse. A string of faces suspended in the murky air flashed by his eyes as his feet pounded down the walk. He stepped around a turbaned woman sitting on the gravel next to a toppled cane chair and paused briefly by a round-faced, pimply boy emitting spasmodic screams. Maids dressed as shepherdesses huddled under an archway bursting with flowers. Ladies and gentlemen streamed past, heading toward the exit; other guests blocked Chase's way, goggling at the illumined stage where figures milled about. Someone shoved at him with both hands, and Chase's arm snaked out to steady a hollow-eyed man.

"Out of my way," snarled the man. He yanked his arm out of Chase's grip.

Garrod's butler, whose name was Niven, lingered nearby, wearing a look of utter bemusement. "No one is to leave," Chase told him. "Station someone at the door. Gather all the manservants to assist me."

The butler blinked. "Yes, sir." He hurried off.

Ned Honeycutt was suddenly at Chase's elbow. "What the deuce? What's happened here?"

"I am about to find out." Chase ignored the steps to the dais, which were congested, and jumped up the side, his knee giving a protesting twinge. He went to Penelope, who held a clergyman's head over a basin, her hands wrapped over his cravat to shield it from the vomit. She looked up.

"You're not hurt?" He felt a tug at his heart when he saw her look of fear fade to be replaced by trust and relief.

"I'm fine, John. But Mr. Garrod, Miss Honeycutt, and Mr. Tallboys have taken ill."

Buckler approached them. "I don't like this, Chase. You'd better call a doctor, and get these people out of here."

Ned Honeycutt was helping his sister toward the stairs. Mrs. Yates crouched over Hugo Garrod's prostrate form, guarding him. A few feet away Marina Garrod stood, irresolute, under a guttering lamp that cloaked her expression. Then she moved out of the shadows, and Chase glimpsed a gem-like hardness that jarred him. But as she knelt at her father's side, her face crumpled with distress.

Chase faced Buckler. "Escort Penelope and Miss Garrod to the house. Lewis must go with you. Take statements from the guests. Have the footmen help you."

"Consider it done," said Buckler grimly.

Chase moved to the edge of the dais, pitching his voice to carry over the hubbub. "Is there a doctor here?"

A man bending over the hysterical boy straightened. "Here, sir." He made his way to Chase's side, a gaunt, balding figure in an old-fashioned black coat. "I am Aurelius Caldwell, surgeon."

"What's wrong with that boy?"

"Nothing, so far as I can tell. Thinks he's been poisoned."

"Leave him. What must we do to help the sufferers?"

Caldwell had already gone to support Tallboys, who was racked with nausea, his eyes rolling in his head as he tried to speak. The surgeon said, "We must get these patients to bed so that I can examine them. Send a servant to my house in the village to fetch my bag."

"Is it a poisoning?"

Somber gray eyes met his. "That would be my guess with several people taken so violently all at once. That is unless they have all been struck down by tainted food." He threw a glance at the teapoy and tables and the litter of abandoned cups. "Do not allow anybody to clear the debris. I must collect samples."

"You attend to the patients. I'll get your samples."

Caldwell seemed to assess Chase but gave a curt nod.

A row of sturdy footmen and several gardeners had assembled in front of the stage. Chase sent a footman to fetch the surgeon's kit and instructed others to start urging the guests back up the path toward the house.

"They call for their carriages, sir," said a servant.

"No carriages yet," said Chase. "Take the guests into the drawing room with the overflow to wait in the library."

He took possession of the teapoy, instructing Niven to lock it up in the pantry along with the plates of cakes, the saturated tea leaves, the urn, the waste basin filled with vomit, and all the crockery. Next, he accompanied Mrs. Yates and Niven to confront the tearful cook in the basement kitchen. The cook had retrieved the household's stores of sugar and flour, which were added to the stash of suspect items. More than half convinced she was under suspicion and would be hauled off to prison forthwith, the cook sobbed, crying out repeatedly that there was nothing wrong with the food when it left her kitchen. Finally, Chase rapped out an exasperated rebuke, and the sobs subsided into gulps.

"Anyone else been ill recently? Any food that had turned or spoiled?"

"No, sir," she said, sniffling.

"What poisons do you have on the property?" Chase asked. "Arsenic? Corrosive sublimate?"

"None in the kitchen," said the cook.

"Shall I inquire of the head gardener?" asked the butler.

"Do that." Chase reached into his pocket for the hastily written note he had prepared. "Have this delivered to Bow Street. I have requested the assistance of additional constables. When they arrive, they will need to search the house and account for every medicine vial, pill box, and cosmetic bottle."

Niven took the letter and bowed. "Sir."

The next few hours were a blur. Further consultation with the surgeon brought little reassurance. Had there been only one sick person, Caldwell said, they might suspect an attack of the English cholera, common in the summertime, or perhaps a bloody flux, but for three people to fall into sudden and severe affliction pointed to a contaminating agent. "An irritant poison administered either accidentally or deliberately, most likely arsenic," he said.

"What's the name of the local magistrate?" said Chase.

"Why, it's the Reverend Tallboys. He's in no condition to speak to you now, sir."

"Will he survive?"

"I think he will, he and Miss Honeycutt both. I understand that neither of them drank all their tea. As for Mr. Garrod, that, sir, seems much less certain. He is advanced in years, which must make a difference."

When Chase went to check on Edward Buckler, he found that his friend had followed his instructions. The guests waited in the drawing room with footmen helping Buckler keep order while he conducted interviews. It would be wise to release these people, Chase decided, for their complaints and lamentations grew to deafening levels. He couldn't blame them. It was getting late, and everyone was tired.

Buckler shook his head in response to Chase's terse questions. No one had seen anything in particular, no stranger lurking, no convenient solution to the problem of who could have tampered with the tea, the sugar, or perhaps the cakes. "You must seal up Garrod's papers for the lawyers," Buckler said.

Chase nodded; it was a timely reminder. "The rest of the staff awaits you in the servants' hall, Buckler. Start with them and I'll take over shortly. The shepherdesses are girls from the village. I've asked them to stay until you can speak to them."

"Garrod?"

"Vilely ill. Penelope helps tend him until nurses and a physician can arrive to assist the surgeon."

Buckler lowered his head to flip idly through the pages of his pocketbook. He spoke quietly. "I could easily have drunk that tea if Penelope hadn't stopped me. She leapt up and swept the cup from my hand. My God, she had drunk the tea herself."

The thought of Penelope and Buckler and that tea had been a thorn at the back of Chase's mind that pricked him with his own incompetence, his lack of foresight, which might have brought him a terrible loss he couldn't bear to think of even now. But he said merely, "That's why I think the poison was in the sugar."

"You may be right. Penelope doesn't take sugar. And I saw her eating one of the cakes. Nothing wrong with them, it seems."

Suddenly Chase's anger erupted. "I should have been there. Instead I was running that girl to earth and playing games with Garrod's nephew."

Buckler's forehead creased with concern. "Not your fault, John. Poison is an ugly, sneaky attack. I had a word with Lewis, and he deeply regrets causing trouble for you. I told him what I'll tell you too. You couldn't have prevented what happened." Changing the subject, he asked, "How is Miss Garrod?"

"Deeply shocked. Mrs. Yates is with her. I've asked Lewis to remain within reach. Honeycutt is in his room, drinking himself under the hatches from all accounts. Best he stay there for the present."

"Just as you say. Don't worry."

One of the guests came up, breaking into bitter complaint, and the two friends separated.

Chapter Eight

Buckler saw off the last of the carriages before going upstairs to check on Penelope. A servant having directed him to the bedchamber where the Reverend Samuel Tallboys lay, Buckler rapped at the door.

It edged open, and Penelope stepped into the corridor, a rank smell compounded of sweat, feces, and vomit following in her wake. Buckler's hands reached out for hers. She was swathed in an apron far too large for her and stiff in patches. There was a yellow streak on her forearm. Her hair confined in a tight bun, she looked at him with eyes that were huge in her strained face, but she seemed calm. It occurred to him that she was like a soldier ranged for battle.

"Tallboys?" he asked, squeezing her hands gently and drawing her a little closer so that she could rest against him.

She spoke into his shoulder. "The vomiting has eased, though he has burning pains in his stomach. I must go back. We are giving him castor oil and a solution of egg whites in cold water every few minutes."

"Is there anything I can get for you?"

Reaching into her apron pocket, she retrieved a crumpled sheet of paper. "Send this letter to the vicarage. It's a note for Mr. Tallboys' housekeeper. Oh and Edward, send word to Maggie. I don't want her to read the news in the papers tomorrow."

He took the note from her and used his handkerchief to dab the vomit or whatever it was from her arm. "Don't worry about

Maggie and the children. Take care of yourself," he said, feeling helpless. With a brief smile for him, she vanished, closing the door with a click.

He was about to descend the stairs when the surgeon emerged from a bedchamber at the end of the hall and moved toward him down the darkened corridor, the only light provided by a lamp that burned on the landing.

"How does your patient, doctor?" said Buckler.

The surgeon, whose look of gloom sat oddly on his pleasant features, balanced two sealed containers in his hands. "Which one? If you mean Mr. Garrod, he's in dire straits, I fear, sir."

"Is such variation usual?"

"Quite. Any poison's effects would be unpredictable, depending on the amount ingested as well as the general health and age of the patient."

"Is there any way to know whether the poison was in the sugar?"

"Tests may tell us." Caldwell held up the containers. "I'm on my way to deliver these samples to the Runner. I've cut out fragments of the clothing stained with effluent to add to the samples." Shaking his head, he turned to go. "I must oversee the preparation of a concoction that may be of help in binding and bringing up the poison. Moreover, I have a message from Mr. Garrod—against my advice, I may add."

"I'll deliver your message, sir."

The surgeon set the containers on the parapet for a moment and rubbed his tired eyes. "I should be obliged. Mr. Garrod labors under a degree of inquietude that can only worsen his state. He insists upon seeing the legal man in the house."

"Legal man? He means me, I suppose. I am Edward Buckler, a barrister of the Inner Temple. But surely Mr. Garrod should summon his own counsel?"

"It may be too late. Will you go to him? Reassure him if you can, but try not to tax him further." He took his jars and descended the stairs.

When Buckler entered Garrod's room, an exhausted and disheveled maid looked up. She had a cloth in her hand, which she was using to wipe the patient's face and neck. A basin of water sat on the table next to her along with a vomit and blood-soaked cloth. Garrod's arm was bandaged where the surgeon had bled him. The room was close, the stench hitting Buckler like a blow as he approached the bed. He considered asking the girl to open the window but decided he shouldn't, in case the doctor had ordered otherwise.

"Sir?" said the maid.

"The doctor asked me to step in." His eyes were on the bed, where Garrod writhed in his sheets, moaning and thrashing his limbs. Shocked, Buckler thought that any attempt at coherent conversation was likely to be fruitless. Death already hovered, setting its stamp upon the sick man's recumbent form.

"He has a terrible thirst on him," whispered the maid, seeming glad of another human presence. "I keep giving him a drink, but it does no good. He just brings it up again." She held a cup to his lips, but he rolled away from her, his claw-like hands plucking at the bedclothes.

"Let me try." Taking the cup, Buckler leaned over. "Mr. Garrod, I am sorry to see you suffer. What can I do? Take some of this, sir."

Garrod opened his mouth and tried painfully to swallow. "Buckler?" he said in a hoarse whisper.

"He don't see you proper-like," said the maid. "His eyes ain't right, gone dim or some such."

Buckler said, "Shall I summon your solicitors, sir?"

"You may be…chamber counsel. Need you to act." Getting out the words with difficulty, Garrod moved his head on the pillow restlessly. Then he seemed to realize that the maid watched them with avid interest, and his eyes glittered with hostility. "Get rid of her."

The girl looked affronted. "The doctor bid me stay. I am to keep him cool and watch for any change."

"Withdraw," said Buckler. "This won't take long."

When she had flounced to the window, the sick man seemed to gather himself, drawing upon reserves of strength that would not last. "A foolish and insane impulse...why did I—?" he said in a lather of torment and self-punishment. A spasm contorted his features, and it was a full minute before he could resume. "That...codicil. Must make a new one."

Buckler's heart sank. This would set the cat among the pigeons with a vengeance. Though he had no experience with estate and trust law, he knew that deathbed alterations to a will could be tricky—very tricky. If it could be shown that the dying person was not in his complete senses, such a change might lead to endless litigation in the Chancery court. "Let me fetch a paper and pen," he said, backing away from the bed. When consulted, the girl directed him to Garrod's dressing room, where he kept a writing desk. But by the time Buckler returned to the sick man, a new pang of agony had overtaken him so that any opportunity for further speech was lost. Hastily, Buckler summoned the nurse. And at that moment the surgeon came back into the room and waved him off in no uncertain terms.

"What do you think he was trying to tell you?" asked Chase.

"I don't know. He was delirious. I think he regretted some recent change to his will and wished to reverse it. Poor devil. I doubt he will rally enough. But you'd better send for his lawyers."

Chase uttered a groan, his hand groping at the back of his head for the queue that was no longer there. "It only needed that. Packet told me Garrod likes to keep the family guessing. Played one too many rounds of his game."

"A codicil or a new will won't hold up in court unless he had it properly drawn. I'll ask around among the servants to see if Garrod mentioned any plans to alter his will, shall I? You can bet the lawyers will be close-mouthed on the subject."

Chase opened his mouth to argue, then gave a reluctant nod. "Tomorrow morning will be soon enough. I imagine you'll be staying close by. You won't want to leave Penelope here on her own even with me."

"No, I won't. I thought I'd take a bed at the local pub until this matter is resolved."

They were in Hugo Garrod's immense library, which opened from the picture gallery. The man owned as many books as costly *objets d'art* and botanical specimens. Many of the expensive volumes had actually been read, their pages cut and markers placed in their pages, the books left lying about in stacks on the tables. Gazing up at the high shelves, Buckler reflected that if Garrod should die, the task of cataloging his possessions prior to his estate's being settled would be massive. This task would likely fall to his secretary, a thin, sensitive young man now sleeping off the worst of his nerves.

All the secretary had been able to tell them was that, despite the press of business on the prior afternoon, his master had sent him away for an hour to see Mr. Honeycutt. No, Mr. Garrod hadn't mentioned wishing to alter his will, though he'd met with his solicitors several times in the last week. Yes, in addition to the desk and cabinet in his study, he had a portable writing desk. Yes, Mr. Garrod sometimes forgot to secure this desk since he kept it in his private dressing room. This was the writing desk where Garrod stored his personal ring of keys, including the key to the teapoy, when not carrying them.

The box in question, a rectangular mahogany traveling desk with brassbound corners, sat on the table between Buckler and Chase. They'd lifted its lid to display the baize-covered writing surface and emptied its leather pockets of their papers. Its drawers, including four "secret" compartments concealed behind a spring-operated panel, gaped wide. Next to the box Chase had stacked and restacked the letters, pens, sealing wax, and inkbottles, as if they could tell him something. Three of the hidden compartments had been empty; the fourth held only a signet ring, a few seashells, and a lock of dark hair tied up in faded ribbon.

For the last half-hour Chase had been pacing the carpet in the library, his cup of coffee left untouched on the mantelshelf. Now he went to the window and thrust the curtains back, allowing the feeble light of a gray dawn to trickle into the room. Worried, Buckler studied his friend's rigid shoulders. Neither of them had closed their eyes that night. He'd never seen Chase, a man of inner stillness and absolute focus, so restless. The focus was there, but Buckler, having learned to know his friend better, could see that he was profoundly disturbed.

"Garrod's will could be a motive for the murder," said Buckler. "I've been thinking…why attack him now in the middle of an evening party with two score witnesses on hand?"

Chase let the curtain drop and turned around. "To prevent him from changing his mind if someone wished to preserve the will's current arrangements? It could be any of them. Honeycutt is a wastrel in no good odor with his uncle. Miss Garrod continually worries and disappoints her father, and I would not trust her mental state. Mrs. Yates and Miss Honeycutt—who knows how they are left in the will? Though we could be on the wrong track entirely, and the motive has nothing whatever to do with inheritance. In that event, I suppose the poisoner might even have been one of the servants or guests."

"Unlikely. A successful poisoning must be premeditated and carefully planned, the poison purchased in advance. The culprit chose this moment, perhaps counting on the screen provided by many people even though he or she had no way to know who else might die. Brazen—the poisoner was not deterred by the presence of Bow Street. You're certain Garrod was the target?"

"I can be sure of nothing," Chase said heavily. "Never mind that now. I must trace the purchase of the poison. Garrod has gone to the City and out to the West India Docks a few times in the last two weeks and Honeycutt has had social engagements in town, but the ladies of the family have been here in Clapham for the most part. Surely anyone wishing to escape detection wouldn't buy a poison locally? I'll check, of course."

"No, you'd think the villain would go further afield. But it's likely the druggist didn't record the purchase even if you can find him."

Chase threw himself into the armchair and lowered his head to peruse the witness statements for the third time. "Get some rest, or you'll be of no use to me," he told Buckler.

He was right. Buckler decided he would take himself to the inn, sleep for a few hours, send to his chambers at the Temple for a change of clothes, and eat a fortifying breakfast. Then he'd be back. He opened his lips to suggest a similar course of action for his friend and closed them again. Instead Buckler said, "You'll look in on Penelope?"

"Every hour," Chase replied without looking up.

Chapter Nine

The next day John Chase was relieved by reinforcements. He instructed the two constables from Bow Street to search the house, cautioning them to be discreet and asking them to compile an inventory of any potentially suspicious substances. They were to avoid the sickrooms but explore the rest of the house and grounds. And at mid-morning, two of Garrod's lawyers arrived from the City, but though they spent the day outside the patient's bedchamber, he was too ill to see them. Cagey, suspicious men, they gave only vague replies to Chase's inquiries.

When the constables had finished their search, Chase took the lengthy inventory and sought the housekeeper Mrs. Yates. With him, he carried Garrod's antique key ring of Italian workmanship that was decorated with a nobleman's coat of arms. He found Mrs. Yates supervising the maids as they put the ground floor in order. She took him down to her private room in the basement and offered him a seat. Gratefully, he lowered himself into one of her overstuffed armchairs. He knew he would have to sleep soon as he didn't want exhaustion to dull his wits, but the tea the housekeeper served from a freshly purchased supply soon revived him. As he sipped, she perused the inventory. Donning a pair of spectacles, she turned the pages with an age-spotted hand.

At length, she shook her head. "I see nothing unusual here."

"Miss Garrod has been prescribed a composing draught?"

"Yes, Mr. Chase. Her rest is often disturbed. It helps her to sleep."

"Laudanum?"

She glanced up. "I take it myself on occasion and keep another bottle of drops among my stores in case someone gets the cough or some other ailment. But it wasn't laudanum that sickened the victims surely?" Mrs. Yates didn't wait for an answer but returned her eyes to the list. She sat in her chair, her face grave, her back very straight. On her head rested a starched bit of lace, and she wore a black silk gown covered by an apron, which was embroidered in white silk sprays of flowers, twining stems, and leaves. The hand not occupied with the inventory smoothed this apron continually, a motion that seemed only half conscious.

Chase said, "The constables found a full bottle of some sort of tonic in the rubbish. It had most of its label scraped off. Can you explain why someone might have discarded it? Medicine is expensive. It seems unlikely a prescription would go completely unused."

"I suppose the purchaser changed his mind. He or she distrusted its purity or potency."

"The label doesn't match the others we've found. Who is your chemist, ma'am?"

"We get our prescriptions from the apothecary in the village. A Mr. Willis." She put aside the inventory and pushed her spectacles back up her nose. "Have you found the source of the poison, sir?"

Chase set the ring of keys on the table between them. "Not yet. But I have some other questions. You know Mr. Garrod hired me to inquire into a series of malicious acts destroying his daughter's peace of mind?"

"Yes, Hugo told me."

"What can you tell me about these incidents?"

"Oh, sir, she's young. She likes a bit of fun, though she goes too far for my tastes. Don't think for a moment there's anything more to it than that."

"Are you telling me Miss Garrod herself carried out the tricks?"

Mrs. Yates broke into an agitated speech, though all the time her eyes remained steady on his face like twin beacons. "You must understand how trying the season was for her. That must be some excuse. She was a good deal exhausted and overwrought. Parties and balls and trips to the opera—she didn't seem to enjoy herself in the slightest. I often wondered whether Hugo was wise to demand this heroic effort of her when she'd be happier living a quiet life. The dear girl wanted to please her father, of course. But it was all too, too much. Is it any wonder—?"

"Ma'am?"

"It was a fearful struggle for a girl like Marina. Many and many a time I came upon her crying when she'd said a wrong word, forgotten the proper form of address for a viscountess, or some such thing. She's of a retiring disposition, sir. Who can be surprised that her appearance in society should often raise these fears? All those eyes on her, waiting for her to make a mistake and deem it a flaw in her breeding that could never be erased for all her father's wealth. Who can blame the child? Not I, Mr. Chase. But Hugo—he is a man and would have it his own way. I understand him well, but love is blind, do you not agree?"

"Mr. Garrod is blind to his daughter's faults?"

She lifted her teacup and took a small, precise sip. "We all have them, don't we? I find human nature so interesting with its glorious inconsistencies, its foolish pride and petty concerns. Poor Hugo. None of it can matter to him now. I do pray for his recovery, Mr. Chase."

"You've lived with your brother for some years?"

"Since my widowhood. I had married Major Yates out of the schoolroom, but when he died at Saratoga, I was left destitute. Hugo took me in despite the fact that we hadn't seen each other in years. After the major's death, I went out to Jamaica."

"An adventure."

"I had never thought to see foreign parts. But I tried to repay Hugo by being of use to him, especially with the children. First Ned and Beatrice. They are the children of our sister, whose husband had been a merchant in Kingston. Poor things—they were orphaned quite young. Then came Marina. I've been a lucky woman, Mr. Chase."

It seemed plausible enough. But had Mrs. Yates grown tired of being a dependent, forced to work for her own bread while Garrod's niece, nephew, and daughter enjoyed a life of luxury? Why did he sense that under all her busy compassion for Marina—her excuses and justifications for the girl's conduct—lay a stagnant pool of dislike? Chase finished his tea and said, "Speak plainly, ma'am. Of what do you accuse Miss Garrod?"

But she would by no means go further. The flow of confidences dried up. Folding her lips together, she said, "You misunderstood me, sir. I accuse her of nothing."

"Tell me this. Do you know of a reason why anyone should wish harm to your brother or the other victims?"

"Oh, none," she replied. And when he asked her whether she was aware of her brother having made recent changes to his will, she denied any knowledge of such matters. "That's for the gentlemen, isn't it, sir?" she said comfortably. "All I can tell you is that Hugo is a man to do right by his family. He's mentioned to me that I can expect a small annuity to warm my declining years."

Chase nodded. "I need to ask you some questions about Mr. Garrod's teapoy. When was the last time he brewed tea from these stores?"

"The night before last. He usually brewed a pot for us in the drawing room after dinner. He'd been out, but he fancied a cup when he came home."

"He used the supply in the teapoy?"

"Why, yes, and locked the caddy when he was finished."

"Which variety of sugar did he use?" inquired Chase, consulting his notes. Penelope had described the scene in the hothouse with admirable detail.

"The royal."

"So there was nothing amiss with the sugar the night before," he mused. Chase isolated the relevant key on the ring and showed it to her. "Where did your brother keep the ring that holds this key?"

"In the writing desk in his dressing room or sometimes in his pocket."

"The writing desk he sometimes neglected to lock?"

She looked surprised. "I couldn't say."

"When was the teapoy carried into the hothouse?"

"Yesterday morning after breakfast, around eleven o'clock. Hugo had given me my instructions, and we were making preparations for the party. I myself accompanied the footman who placed the teapoy. But it was locked. I can verify that."

"Where was the key at that point?"

There was a pregnant pause. Then she said, "That's just it. I don't know. I wanted to check the stores before the footman delivered the teapoy, so I asked Hugo for the key ring. He was on his way upstairs to wash his hands around ten o'clock. He said he'd fetch it for me, but then we had a fuss when he couldn't find it. Later he told me he'd discovered the ring on the floor of the dais when he was taking his guests on a tour and had taken that opportunity to open the teapoy and make sure everything was right and tight. I got so busy with my other work that I never gave the matter another thought."

"Could someone have taken the keys from Mr. Garrod's dressing room and later left the ring on the dais to make it appear it was dropped accidentally?"

She frowned. "Possible, I suppose. But I don't know when that could have happened. My brother rose early to attend to some correspondence in his room. He went down to breakfast around half past nine and then to his study to see a messenger from the City on some business."

"The key was missing for several hours, until around three when Mr. Garrod found the ring in the hothouse? Could it have been taken from the dressing room earlier, say the prior night while he was sleeping?"

"I doubt that. I saw him put it in his pocket after we drank tea, so he carried it up with him. Hugo is a light sleeper, Mr. Chase. Yesterday, when he challenged his valet as to where the ring could have gone, Fimber reminded him it had been in the writing desk at bedtime the night before. The servants and I looked everywhere for it. I myself checked the downstairs rooms."

"Who has access to Mr. Garrod's dressing room during the day?"

"Why, anyone. Fimber told me Marina had been in. She often enjoys a chat with her father. Occasionally Beatrice puts her head in. Ned is generally a slug-a-bed."

For all this woman's readiness of tongue, Chase felt she fenced with him expertly, parrying his questions and telling him little, though implying much. "Was anyone else in the house that morning? Any delivery men or groundskeepers, for instance?" The beacon eyes met his. "Just Mr. Tallboys. He called to discuss a charitable project with Beatrice."

◇◇◇

Beatrice Honeycutt confirmed this account when Chase stopped by her bedchamber. He could see the surgeon was correct in thinking she would soon recover. A decade younger than Tallboys and over thirty years younger than Garrod, she possessed the elasticity of youth they lacked. Though her face was drawn, he found her sitting up in bed and eating gruel as her maid hovered in the background.

"I am pleased to see you looking so well, ma'am," he told her.

She pushed away the bowl with a languid hand. "I feel very fortunate. How is Mr. Tallboys?"

"Much better today. Mr. Caldwell hopes he will continue to improve."

"That is a great relief."

"Don't let me interrupt your meal," said Chase.

"I was finished. How is my uncle? Dare I hope he has improved too?"

"No, ma'am. He grows weaker by the hour."

"God help him in his struggle," she said fervently. "That it should come to this after all his wanderings."

"Did you return with him from the West Indies?"

"I did and cannot tell you how grateful I was. How shall I describe the moment when we stepped onto land? My first impulse was to kneel and kiss the earth of England, giving thanks for having been brought safely through all our perils. We'd been pursued by pirates and were terrified out of our wits with the fear of encountering enemy vessels. Uncle Hugo was magnificent—nothing could daunt him." She smiled at the memory, then looked grave. "Is everything possible being done for him?"

"Yes, ma'am," he said, feeling again the guilt that this crime had occurred on his watch. "Mr. Caldwell has called in a physician to give a second opinion, and a competent nurse has arrived."

At his request, she dismissed her maid. When they were alone, Chase asked her about her movements on the day of the party. She had breakfasted downstairs with Marina and Mr. Tallboys, who had come to discuss his scheme to improve the religious education at a local seminary for young ladies. Beatrice had known nothing about the misplaced key ring until her aunt told her about its loss when they went to the hothouse to arrange the tables. This had been about eleven after Mr. Tallboys' departure.

"Did Miss Garrod accompany you?" Chase asked.

"No, sir. I believe she went for a ride before luncheon."

He studied her. According to Garrod, she had enjoyed a minor social success during the season, or perhaps she had merely shone in comparison to her reclusive cousin. Now he caught a glimpse of that charm when she raised her gaze to his, the blue of her eyes deepening and taking on the richer color of her dressing gown. An interesting countenance with its strongly marked features, he thought, one that spoke of some substance. It would not do to underestimate her. Many women would have hurried into further speech, but she waited patiently for his next question. He said, "Miss Honeycutt, in the drawing room last night you expressed disapproval of your cousin's ornament. Mrs. Yates had asked her to remove it?"

Her face worked; a tear trickled down her pale cheek. "Poor Marina. I was rough with her. I am sorry for it. But she is obstinate, Mr. Chase. She doesn't understand we have her best interests at heart."

He heard the note of falsity and was suddenly convinced that Beatrice liked Marina no better than Mrs. Yates did. He felt a pang of pity for a young girl who seemed to have no real allies, but he suppressed it. He must keep an open mind, he reminded himself. He pressed Beatrice. "But the bracelet, ma'am, why so strong a reaction?"

"It's like this, Mr. Chase. My cousin develops enthusiasms that we don't feel are good for her. We think that wearing that ornament will only feed an unhealthy preoccupation with the past. It's of West Indian make."

"Where did she get it?"

Beatrice looked perplexed. "I've no notion. My uncle has a collection of Jamaican artifacts."

Now this was interesting. Hugo Garrod had reported that Marina harbored irrational fears associated with her background. Her family's attempts to distract and shield her could explain the household's simmering tensions. What if she wouldn't cooperate? What if the behaviors had worsened? He was remembering the dirt and eggshells in her reticule. He addressed Beatrice again. "Would your cousin hoard such things for some purpose of her own? Beyond the bracelet, I mean."

"I very much hope not," she said, her mouth prim.

"Did anything in particular happen during the season to distress Miss Garrod?"

"No, sir, not to my knowledge. You will have heard that her debut was not a success, but, as to why, we none of us have a clue."

"Not even your brother, Miss Honeycutt? I'm told he aspires to the lady's hand."

"If you mean to suggest that he may be responsible for her conduct, you are out there, sir. He has been a model gentleman. None of this is Ned's fault, I assure you."

Chase said, "But your brother has been at odds with his uncle? Mr. Honeycutt told me about his debts."

"I'm afraid that's all too true, Mr. Chase," she said, sighing. "And yet I do not entirely blame Ned. His wildness started with our mother who doted on him excessively and gratified his every whim. By the time she died, the seeds of his character had been planted." Her eyes fell to her hands, which lay across the bedcovers. "Perhaps I am lucky to have been less favored."

Next Chase went in quest of the model gentleman himself. At first unable to locate Honeycutt, he was eventually directed by a servant to walk through a second conservatory, which led off the drawing room. On the other side was a billiards room, where he was surprised to find his quarry at play with Lewis. Wearing a pair of Turkish embroidered slippers with curled toes and smoking a Havana cigar, Honeycutt looked annoyed at this interruption.

Chase said, "A word with you, sir?"

Lewis leaned his stick against the table. "Shall I go, Mr. Chase?"

"For a few minutes. I won't keep him long."

Lewis drew him aside to tell him that Penelope was resting in her bedchamber since a professional nurse had arrived to care for the patients. "She asked me to take note of anything that might prove of interest," confided Lewis in a lowered tone. "That's why I sought Honeycutt's company. I thought you'd want me to make all smooth so that I could keep an eye on him. I still don't like him much." He wrinkled his nose to indicate his disapproval of the expensive Spanish cigar and cast a scornful look at the Turkish slippers.

Just what Chase needed: a would-be conspirator who could be trusted to complicate rather than simplify matters. "Avoiding fisticuffs with the man is one thing, Lewis, but don't strain your good nature. I'll be glad when you and your sister are out of this mess. It won't be long if I can help it."

Lewis caught this note of irony. He chose to ignore it. "How is Miss Garrod today? I've not seen her. She must be deeply upset about her father."

Chase considered his reply. From the moment he'd first met Penelope's brother, he'd liked the young man, found in him a combination of integrity and quixotic ambition that reminded him of Penelope. But he couldn't have Lewis interfering with Marina or coming between him and the girl. "Did Miss Garrod say anything to you last night about what troubles her?" he asked sternly. "I need to know."

Lewis hesitated, obviously unhappy, then said: "Ask her, Mr. Chase. You won't expect me to betray a lady's confidence."

"By God, Lewis, this is a serious inquiry. Your sister would be the first to tell you to cooperate. What if Miss Garrod should be in danger?"

"Truly, she didn't say much, but…you see, she made me promise."

Chase moved away. "You'd better hope she'll talk to me."

When Lewis had closed the door behind him, Chase rejoined Honeycutt, who said with some constraint, "I couldn't think of anything useful to do, other than entertain our guest. Mrs. Wolfe has been an angel in the sickroom, so I thought smoothing things over with Durant was the least I could do."

"Good of you. Answer a few questions, sir. Where were you between nine o'clock and about three yesterday?"

Honeycutt lifted his brows at Chase's tone and blew out a cloud of smoke before replying. "Asleep. I'd had rather a night of it with some friends the prior evening. I don't think I climbed out of bed until after eleven. Had my chocolate, ate my rolls, growled at my valet, as I'm sure he'll tell you."

"The rest of the day?"

"I saw my uncle in his study and, at about two o'clock, went up to town to see about a horse. Stopped at my club, where I was detained rather longer than expected. That's why I was late to dinner."

His account could be verified. None of it mattered much, Chase judged, except for the period when the key ring had gone missing. Honeycutt could easily have slipped down the corridor and taken it from his uncle's dressing room, though he'd have risked an encounter with other members of the family or Garrod's valet. "Who do you think did this, sir?"

"I wish I knew. Look, I'm eager to assist with your inquiry, Chase. We must do everything we can to catch the villain responsible for this heinous crime. You should look into my uncle's business affairs. One doesn't achieve what he has without making lots of enemies. It could have been one of the guests at the party, for instance."

"It was someone who had access to Mr. Garrod's teapoy. Most likely a member of the family."

Anger flashed across his face, but he said evenly, "No. It can't be. Whom would you suspect? Me perhaps?"

"No one in particular yet. Tell me one thing. At the party why did you go in search of Miss Garrod instead of into the hothouse for tea?"

"I was with my aunt and Beatrice during the concert. Afterwards, we saw my cousin slip into the orangery with Durant. Hardly proper, was it? She was unchaperoned."

Chase opened his occurrence book and flipped to the appropriate page, thankful again for Buckler's detailed notes. "Describe the meeting with your uncle in the study earlier in the afternoon. What was the argument about?" He quoted, "'Raised voices were heard. Mr. Honeycutt left in a temper.'"

"I'm sure you can guess. Word about a few post-obit bonds had come to my uncle's ears."

A post-obit bond was money borrowed on the expectation that it would be repaid with substantial interest when the borrower came into an inheritance. It seemed that Ned Honeycutt had got himself into the clutch of moneylenders. Chase had always found post-obit bonds to be peculiarly distasteful, depending as they did on the ghoulish expectation of stepping into a dead man's shoes. And what if the borrower angered the person who had the power to bestow the money in the first place? Casually, he said, "Not content to wait until the body is cold, eh?"

Ned Honeycutt winced at this deliberate insolence, his amiability falling away like a cloak. "My uncle was angry, yes, and I can't say I blame him. Nothing new, Chase. Uncle Hugo and I have had this conversation many times over the years. You can't think I would—"

"Poison your uncle if you thought he meant to alter his will? I admit it's a possibility that has occurred to me. At the moment

I can see a motive for you, or for your cousin Miss Garrod. The ostensible heirs."

Honeycutt regarded Chase with a glint in his eyes. "So that's the way the wind blows. Marina's a child, incapable of harming anyone. While I know you won't believe the same of me, I can assure you of my complete innocence in the matter."

"Did Garrod say anything about his financial arrangements?"

He tapped the ash from his cigar in a dish that sat on the edge of the billiards table. Leaving the cigar burning there, he said, as if suddenly weary, "Nothing outright. My uncle likes to play games. He's had us dancing to his tune for years. If someone did kill him, it will be because of that. But it wasn't me, and it wasn't Marina. I told you before that she and I are as good as affianced."

"Mrs. Yates seems to suspect Miss Garrod of trickery and malice."

"Nonsense. The trickster will prove to be one of the servants with a grudge. Do your job and find out who it is, Chase. This person may be your poisoner."

Chase had already considered the possibility. Either the poisoning had nothing to do with the malicious tricks, or there was some relationship between the two that eluded him, unless their motive was to discredit Marina. But the attack on Garrod had to be about money at the bottom. So what was he left with? A mentally unstable girl who could have poisoned her own father? Or another person acting for reasons of his or her own?

Garrod's nephew had nothing more to offer, so Chase went upstairs to check on the sickrooms. As he passed his employer's bedroom door, his eyes slid by the lintel—and stopped. With a muttered exclamation, he thrust up his arm, swearing as his finger snagged on something sharp. Chase worked his hand back and forth as he tried to yank out an object stuck above the door, and in an instant he had it free. It was a black feather that had been held in place by a rusted nail.

Chapter Ten

John Chase wrapped the feather and rusted nail in his handkerchief and put them in his pocket. He went downstairs to eat some cold meat and cheese in the servants' dining hall while pondering his next step. He'd been able to tease a memory of his time in Jamaica to the surface. It had bothered him ever since Marina Garrod had emptied that pile of rubbish from her reticule at Vauxhall Gardens. Then the significance had eluded him; now a glimmer of understanding dawned.

Finished with his meal, he glanced at his watch and saw that it was past two o'clock. He ascended to the ground floor and made his way to the morning room, which was tucked behind the drawing room. He thought about knocking but changed his mind, instead putting his head around the door. He saw an ordinary room, less grand than the more public areas he'd seen. A print of Nelson presided over the mantel. A low table held several books, a quick scan revealing that these included the Bible as well as works of history and botany.

Dressed in a simple blue cambric gown that pooled around her on the hearthrug, Marina Garrod sat on a low stool by the empty grate. Today she wore her hair loose, letting it tumble about her shoulders in a mass of dark curls. Mrs. Yates would not approve of Chase seeing her alone, but he could not summon the will to care.

"May I speak to you, Miss Garrod?"

"Come in, Mr. Chase. Have you come to give me a report of the patients?"

"Miss Honeycutt is on the mend, and the doctor believes Mr. Tallboys' strong constitution will prevail. But I won't lie to you. Your father is seriously ill."

"Will he die?" She cast him a melting look that made his throat tighten with emotion. Light filled the room so that the shadows had been banished; her face seemed open and vulnerable.

Chase took her hand, bowing over it. "I don't know, but you should prepare yourself for the worst. I must talk to you. If something—or someone—has been troubling you, Miss Garrod, tell me now. It's my responsibility to ensure your safety and discover the poisoner."

Marina appeared to listen to the silence. "I'm not sure what I can tell you, but I'm willing to try, especially if I can help you find the person who has done this terrible thing. My aunt always wants me to take the air. Shall we go for a short drive in my gig, that is unless you object to being driven by a lady?"

"I've no objection." He stepped back.

She rose to her feet in a graceful motion. "I'll get my bonnet and join you in the stable yard."

A quarter of an hour later he went outside. Marina was already seated in a pony-chaise that was hitched to a sweet-mouthed gray that looked fresh and eager to depart. Chase eyed the girl's arms with trepidation, but he needn't have worried. She proved an excellent whip, controlling her horse effortlessly as they bowled down a green lane and took the carriage road through the Common, passing poplar groves and a pond with a pagoda and pleasure boats.

Marina snapped her wrists, and the chaise picked up speed. Chase thought of telling her to slow down; instead he bit his lip and gripped the seat. The breeze carried a pleasant coolness, and from somewhere cows lowed. On the hillside above their heads, laundry maids stretched out garments to dry in the sun. Marina pointed out the elm trees her father had planted to beautify the Common and indicated the parish church of Holy Trinity. Here, not far from Garrod's front door, stood the modern brick church where the Clapham evangelicals had worshiped and prayed for the day that ended the British slave trade.

She checked her horse as a drover with his herd of cattle came into view. Chase gave her time to negotiate the obstacle; then he retrieved the feather and nail from his pocket. "I need to show you something. Do you know what this is?"

Her hand yanked back on the reins so that the chaise veered toward some trees at the side of the road. "Where did you get it?" she said, correcting course.

"Someone nailed this feather above your father's door. I didn't see it last night, and the constables didn't notice it when they came through this morning. Who can say when it was put there, but I do know that it's an Obeah charm." Chase watched with amazement as she quickly masked her surprise.

Marina sent him a quick, sidelong glance. "Why ask me if you've already written your own story?"

"I let the facts—the evidence—dictate the story."

"Don't you see that facts can lie like truth?"

"I'm right, aren't I? This is an Obeah charm." He knew a bit about Obeah but wanted to hear what she would say. It was an African spiritual practice, which had been adopted by the Jamaican slave population and which the planters were determined to eradicate. Obeah men and women were rumored to have the power to inflict curses, issue protective charms, or communicate with the dead. Despite the intervening years, Chase recalled the young boy with the fan, who had been in the room when he lay ill of yellow fever. Joanna—Marina's mother—had frightened this boy. *John Crow*, he had whispered to her before he fled after Chase had unwisely joked about poisons. The Jamaican vulture with its black feathers was associated with Obeah, as was the use of poisoning to strike back at enemies. So now Chase wondered: had Joanna once been suspected of being an Obeah woman? Did someone take advantage of that connection now?

Marina replied, sounding reasonable, "Here? Impossible, Mr. Chase."

"What would be the purpose of such a charm?"

"I suppose it would be intended as a key to the world of spirits, a protection from evil or a curse."

He studied her profile. "Charms? You don't believe in such stuff?"

As if reciting a memorized lesson, she said, "Belief is an ever-shifting thing. We have our beliefs in the light of day, as well as those arising from darkness. These are equally, sometimes more, potent. They can do harm or good."

Chase's head pounded, and frustration built within him like a storm. "We speak in riddles. Who's been telling you these tales, Miss Garrod?"

This time she answered without evasion. "The Reverend Tallboys. He is quite knowledgeable on the subject."

"I don't think your father would approve of your interest."

"No, but I was curious."

They continued along the graveled road that traversed the Common to a clearing, where the elevation of Clapham above the Thames laid before the viewer the gray and smoky city. It seemed incredible that the metropolis, that endless expanse of pavement, could be a mere few miles away from this verdant suburb.

"Pull up here," he said roughly. When she'd brought the pony to a halt, he set the feather and nail in her lap. She couldn't hide her instinctive recoil, but she did not remove or touch them.

"This feather is a message," Chase told her. "I saw the John-Canoe dancers once in Jamaica. They decorate their headdresses with the black feathers of the John Crow vulture. And feathers and seeds, as well as fish bones and cats' teeth and other such things, form the bundle of an Obeah man—or woman. Did you know, Miss Garrod, that these native doctors are also suspected of murdering with plant poisons?"

She sat upright on the bench, gazing out over the Common. Chase put a hand to her cheek to turn her face toward him. Marina confronted him proudly, though Chase could see the fear behind the pride. It was there in the tight chords of her delicate neck and in her frozen look.

He cleared his throat but somehow couldn't remove the hoarseness. "I met your mother in Jamaica. She saved my life when I was ill. I intend to repay that debt by helping you. That's why your father chose me to protect you."

The blank look fled, and light flooded into her eyes. She said, "You astonish me, Mr. Chase. My father didn't tell me you knew my mother. What is she like? I don't…remember her."

"I didn't know her well, but I can tell you that she used her great skill with plants to cure disease." He hesitated, struggling to find the words to describe Joanna. His memories of that time were fragmented, but he could recall one thing plainly. "When she was busy with the other patients, I used to wait for her to come back into the room. I believed she would not allow me to die because she was a staunch ally of life, Miss Garrod. Or perhaps just stubborn."

Tears spilled down her cheeks. Chase handed her the handkerchief that had held the feather and nail. She mopped her tears, gave a sniff, and offered him a tremulous smile. "No one has ever spoken of her to me as if she were a real person, who might enjoy the company of a friend, lose her temper, or take a walk in the sun—no one except my father sometimes when the mood was on him. I won't forget what you said, sir."

"Then help me find your father's attacker. Have you been dabbling in superstition? Playing a game? I could understand that you might have wanted to return some of the insults you've received. Were you upset with your family?"

She pulled away. "Don't be ridiculous. In Jamaica, to possess an Obeah charm would bring the penalty of transportation at the least. Not so long ago a slave might have been gibbeted alive or burnt by a slow fire. In England this charm means nothing."

"Even when left above the door of a dying man?"

She stared at him woodenly. After a moment she said in a small voice, "You think I put it there. You think I invent stories and do harm to others." Her hands were clenched on the reins. "You think I was the one to put the poison in the tea."

He tried to reassure her, but it was no good. The truth was that he didn't know how to talk to a seventeen-year-old girl. She was right to question his belief in her innocence. But was she disturbed enough to murder the father who had used her as a pawn? Poison was often considered a woman's method, a devious way of exerting power. This thought brought him to Beatrice Honeycutt. She had lived for years on her uncle's bounty. How might she benefit from his removal and the chance to make a life for herself? He supposed the same could be true of Anne Yates. Where did her loyalties lie?

And Chase knew that a man could poison as well as a woman. There was Ned Honeycutt, at loggerheads with his rich uncle and fearful he would be cut out of his inheritance should the heiress wed someone else. There was also the Reverend Samuel Tallboys. Chase had learned that the clergyman was to be one of Garrod's executors and a trustee of the estate. Should Garrod die, he would be in control of a massive fortune. But Tallboys and Beatrice Honeycutt were ill from the poison. Surely this must exclude them from consideration, though Chase could not be sure of that.

On the way back to Laurentum, the doubts and worries circled in his brain. When they pulled up in the yard, a groom came out to take the chaise, and Marina went upstairs to remove her bonnet, leaving him without a backward glance.

Chapter Eleven

Penelope had been dreaming of the hothouse and those steaming cups of tea. In the dream she'd known what was about to happen but could not utter a word of warning. She stopped in front of each guest to dispense a cup of death, her face a smiling mask, until at last she approached Edward Buckler. This time he tossed the tea down his throat as if it were nothing, despite the fact that he knew its contents too. To acknowledge this courage, she kissed him there in front of everyone, watching as he crumpled to the ground. Then her dream-self drank the tea and collapsed with the others into a pile of corpses to be wept over by a single, motherless child. *Sarah*—a pang of anguish pierced Penelope's heart. *But I didn't take any sugar*, she objected, and came awake with a start.

She could tell from the angle of the sun on the curtains that she'd slept only a short time, perhaps an hour. She splashed water over her face, then penned a chatty note to her daughter, relating as many light anecdotes as she could muster, including the story of John Chase's new hairstyle. Penelope hoped Maggie was guarding her tongue and hiding her own worry so that Sarah need never know what had happened in Clapham. Since Penelope's husband, Jeremy, had left without a word three months ago, her daughter had been nervous and sometimes withdrawn. Penelope told herself again that she should not have come here. Her letter finished, she changed her gown and studied her face in the mirror. The shadows under her eyes could not be helped, she decided, though she pinched her cheeks to give them more color. Downstairs, she handed the butler her letter and asked if he knew Lewis' whereabouts.

"He and Miss Garrod are in the garden, ma'am," the butler said with stone-faced disapproval. "Go out the library doors and follow the path through the shrubbery. No doubt you'll come upon them." She kept her irritation from showing. Blast it, Lewis, she thought. The girl's father suffers in agony—hardly the time for youthful amours. But it seemed Nature did not agree with her. Outside, the earth's clamor was hushed, and all was still in the perfection of the summer's day. She hurried along the path, which wound past a folly and several vantage points, finally locating her brother and Marina Garrod in an arbor, where a statue of Apollo overlooked a small stretch of water and green fields beckoned beyond the ha-ha fence. Lewis and Marina sat, heads close together, on a bench under shady trees.

"Am I intruding?" said Penelope.

The rest of the day was long and cheerless. Penelope endured a strained dinner followed by a vigil in the drawing room as everyone waited for word from Garrod's sickroom. Mrs. Yates conversed too loquaciously with Ned Honeycutt, who listened with only half an ear as he watched Marina, a frown in his eyes. Penelope, seeing that Lewis and Marina now avoided each other's company, felt her uneasiness grow. She didn't trust that limpid innocence.

Buckler had also dined with them, obviously ill at ease to be foisted upon the family at so difficult a time. But Penelope thought his feeling went deeper, for his eyes seemed dulled, and he was less energetic than usual. She knew he was despondent about the future of their relationship. For that matter, he sometimes seemed to reject the promise of any human happiness at all, an attitude she could neither understand nor approve. Watching him make desultory conversation with Garrod's family, she hoped he wasn't punishing himself for that kiss in Vauxhall Gardens.

After dinner she suggested they take a stroll in the garden. The sun hung low in the sky, its fading warmth touching the shrubs with gold. Buckler and Penelope paced the laurel-walk in silence, their shoulders just brushing. Assessing Buckler's mood, she decided he looked weary and sad, but she didn't know how to help him.

At length, he spoke. "Chase says Mr. Garrod won't last the night, poor devil. If something should happen, if you need me for any reason, you'll send word?" He had paid a boy to fetch him a clean shirt from his chambers and had taken a bed for another night at the public house.

"I don't see why you should remain here," she said for the second or third time that evening. "You must have your own affairs to attend to."

He stopped, seized her hands, and turned her toward him. "Do you mean to drive me mad, Penelope? I'm sure that must be your intention."

Suddenly, her temper rose. "What I said is true, isn't it? You sacrifice yourself for my sake, and I can't think of a single reason why you should. I can see that our…friendship lowers your spirits, and no wonder. What do you get out of it, after all?"

"I do not view friendship—the real kind—in that light," said Buckler tightly. "It's not a commercial transaction."

She gazed up into his face, which seemed to her dearer than it had ever been before. She read fire in his tawny eyes, steadfastness in his nose and chin, anxious love on his lips—and felt a powerful grief.

"I know that," she answered.

"I don't stay just for you, Penelope. There's John. Don't you see how worried he is, how beset by doubts that he ought to have prevented Garrod's death? He is my friend too."

"Of course, he is, but you know very well that wasn't what I meant."

"Yes," he said with some bitterness and released her hands, "you want to end it, don't you? I suppose you've decided, all on your own and without consulting my wishes, that it would be best for both of us."

"And so it would," she said, pleading now, though the desolation was keen and she found it torture to deny him when she wanted to throw herself in his arms. "All I do is drag you into turmoil and scandal at every turn. What can I give you in return? Nothing but sorrow and frustration and loneliness. How do you expect me to live with that? You deserve a woman with bright and fresh hopes to share with you. An entire life to share with you, not a half-life." Her voice sank lower. "And children. When I see you with Sarah, I wish with all my heart that she were yours. But it cannot be."

"I suppose there's nothing more to say. I will not add to your troubles, Penelope."

"You seemed determined to misunderstand me. I am thinking of you."

He shook his head, his expression turning remote. After kissing her hand, he went away without another word. She watched his upright figure retreat down the path to the gate and thought her heart would break.

In no good humor she returned to the drawing room, sitting next to her brother on the sofa. "Lewis," she said in an undertone, "we must help Mr. Chase and leave as soon as possible. We don't belong here. If Miss Garrod has confided in you—"

"We can't go. There will be an inquest. You will be asked to testify. As for Miss Garrod, I'm not a fool. I know she needs to speak to Mr. Chase—and soon."

"Why hasn't she asked for help? Can't she see that her secrecy only encourages others to think ill of her?"

"I've told her that. Give her a little longer. She's had no one for so long, Penelope. She's grown used to acting for herself. You see, I know what that feels like."

She put her hand in the crook of his arm and leaned against his shoulder. "Yes, I know you do. Still, I don't want you involved in this. It's not your affair. People will say—"

He grinned down at her. "Say what? That bad blood will tell? That I saw a chance to take advantage of a troubled girl?

Maybe even that I conceived a plot to murder her father and elope with the heiress?"

"It's not a joke!"

"Since when do we care what people think, Penelope?" He pressed his hand over hers, but she saw he would not be swayed.

"John Chase deserves better than this from us, Lewis," she said.

Eager to escape, she went early to bed and fell into a dreamless sleep to the company of a gentle patter of rain on the window. Some hours later a thump from the corridor brought her fully awake. Her ears caught the rustling of cloth, soon followed by a bang on the wall. Startled, she sat up to listen. Thinking it was probably the nurse on some errand to the kitchen or someone in quest of one of Mr. Garrod's fancy water closets, she was about to lie down again when she heard a low murmur that sounded so close it might have been in the room with her. Her pulse quickened with fear, but then she realized the sound came from just outside in the corridor. It came again, and this time the voice started low and rose to a high pitch.

She swung her legs over the side of the bed, donned her dressing gown, and slid her feet into slippers. Padding to the door, she edged it open to peer into the corridor. It must have been very early in the morning, several hours before sunrise. Though the house seemed peaceful, Penelope distinctly heard uneven breathing and hushed footsteps on the thick carpeting. Then she saw a flash of movement and caught sight of a figure moving away from her.

The figure was slight—that of a woman, or rather, a girl—and Penelope knew at once it was Marina Garrod. Penelope watched her list to one side and stumble into the wall. In the moment before she righted herself, something dropped from her hand. She went on, more quickly and surely, until she reached the stairs and disappeared, a white blur in her nightgown.

Penelope set off in pursuit. She considered fetching John Chase—he'd told her where his room was on the floor above—but didn't want to lose Marina. She did pause to fumble for what the girl had dropped, her fingers grasping a round, smooth object. A bead? Stowing it in her pocket, Penelope followed Marina down the stairs.

About twenty feet ahead and gaining, the girl passed the landing between the first and ground floors. Here she stopped to glance over her shoulder, and for the first time Penelope saw her clearly in the square of moonlight framed by the large window. Her face floated in an unearthly way, her eyes like two holes. *Ay but their sense is shut*, Penelope thought, and she understood with a shiver of fear that Marina Garrod was not aware of her surroundings. The girl raised one hand, and a second object fell from her grip. Then she slipped lightly down the rest of the wide, curving staircase, her hand on the banister. Hard on her heels, Penelope retrieved the object Marina had dropped—another bead like the first—but there was no time to do more than snatch it up and hurry on. Marina reached the ground floor, where a light burned in the entrance hall, and turned left.

The girl entered one of the rooms, closing the door behind her. Penelope reached the door and put her hand to the knob, wishing she knew more about the geography of this house. She recalled that the picture gallery, dining room, morning room, and drawing rooms were all at this level. This was not the main drawing room, where they had assembled before dinner; she knew that much. She opened the door and paused on the threshold. The curtains at the long windows opening onto the terrace were not drawn so that a stream of moonlight washed the room in a serene glow. This glow illuminated a desk, bookshelves, and two easy chairs that looked like beasts crouched in front of the hearth. A masculine room: an office or study.

Marina stood in the center of the hearthrug near an ornate marble chimneypiece, her back to Penelope. The girl stood quietly, as if she listened to a melody played only for her, and when Penelope reached her side, Marina turned an empty gaze upon her. Penelope hesitated, uncertain what to do. Hadn't she read somewhere it was unwise to awaken a sleepwalker? She must guide Marina back to bed.

She took the girl's arm, but Marina shook her off and moved to the French doors. A instant later she was outside, running in her bare feet down the terrace, her hair streaming behind her, her nightdress hiking up so that her bare limbs were visible. Penelope kicked off her own slippers, not wanting to risk tripping over her feet on the rain-slick stone. She negotiated some shallow stairs to stand on an expanse of lawn, which formed a smooth carpet under her feet. Flowerbeds sprouted from this carpet, and a path stretched off into a shrubbery. The flowers were uniform gray ghosts, some in indistinguishable masses, some bending on their stalks and stirring in the breeze. What did Marina intend?

Penelope had her answer when the girl ran past a large tub on wheels and halted at an ornamental vase to caress a large bloom. Penelope froze, caught in the beauty of the moment. She knew she must persuade Marina to return to the house before she injured herself, but she couldn't help but stare in fascination at the girl in the shadowed garden that seemed to welcome her as if she belonged here under the cold light of moon and stars, among the sweet night scents. Marina lingered over the bloom with a butterfly's touch; then her hand plunged down in a sudden motion that made Penelope rear back in shock. Marina had the flower in her grip, and earth was spilling down the front of her nightdress. Her hand descended to rip up another bloom.

"Marina, no," said Penelope. There was something indescribably horrible in this destruction.

Before Penelope could react, Marina ran to stand over a bed of roses. She ran her fingers over the petals, the sleeve of her nightdress snagging on some thorns. Without warning, she made one of those wrenching motions and yanked out a fistful of tendrils and flowers, the petals fluttering down around her. Now there was blood on her nightdress and hands as a dozen thorns tore her flesh.

>>>

Chase snatched a few hours of rest, expecting to be called to the dying man's bedside. He had discarded his boots but not his wrinkled shirt and pantaloons. Propping a pillow under his knee, he'd started to read a silly novel borrowed from the library as his eyes drifted closed. But three hours later they flew open. He wasn't sure what had awakened him, for the quiet of the house surged around him like a living thing. He could hear no signs of the activity in Garrod's bedchamber on the floor below. He sat up and pulled on his boots. After dashing some water on his face, he relit his chamberstick with a spill thrust into the lamp he'd left burning on the dressing table. He crossed the room and glanced out the window, observing that the rain had stopped. Beyond the flowerbeds directly beneath him, he could see, outlined in the moonlight, a stretch of greensward broken up by clumps of trees and, farther off, a small bridge that spanned a stream. He was about to turn away when a spark of light appeared, blinked out as it was swallowed up by the trees, and appeared again. His eye traced its sinuous progress. He grabbed his coat, stowed his pistols in his pocket, and left the room.

When Chase stepped onto the terrace, his candle blew out in a gust of wind. Navigating by moonlight, he walked past a summerhouse and turned down an offshoot of the main route. For a long way he managed to keep the bobbing light in view. Then, as the path ascended a small rise, he saw a dark form revealed against the gray-black sky. It could have been male or female, young or old, innocent or not, and before he could make up his mind on any of these points, it was gone. He supposed it might be one of the groundskeepers, though he couldn't imagine what his business might be at this hour. Cursing, Chase willed his knee to cooperate and increased his pace, his greatcoat flapping about his legs. His leg ached like the devil because of the dampness, but he ignored it. Finally, the path entered an arbor clothed in heavy vines. Lewis Durant was sitting on the low fence that separated the pleasure garden from the surrounding meadows.

"What are you doing here, Lewis?"

"Just at this moment I was waiting for you."

"Helping Miss Garrod play tricks with ghostly lights?"

"The opposite. I want to help her catch the person who does this."

Chase felt a foreboding. "Where is she? She's not the one with the lantern?"

"No, I tell you. I told her I'd stay awake and follow the light if it appeared. I heard you coming behind me. I knew it was you from the sound of your walk—and the cursing, of course." He grinned.

Annoyed that he hadn't been aware of Lewis' presence, Chase said, "I'm glad Miss Garrod is asleep in her bed, which is where you should be."

"Did you see the light?" said Lewis eagerly. "It's proof Marina isn't imagining things."

"I saw it. In the time we've wasted talking here, it's gone."

"Maybe not. Let's go find out." Lewis jumped down from the fence, ducked to avoid a low-hanging tree branch, and bounded up to Chase with all the energy of youth. They emerged from the arbor on the other side, but now the path in front of them was empty, silvered by moonlight.

Chase cursed again. "As I told you. Do you suppose this walk returns to the house? I've had enough of this May game for one night. I need to make sure Miss Garrod is safe."

"You are walking rather stiffly, sir. You're injured?"

"It's nothing," said Chase, his tone ungracious.

This was accepted without comment. They continued in silence, as the path, bordered by concealing hedges that formed the boundary to the grounds, looped past the hothouse and a series of sheds until the walkway did indeed return to its starting point.

They rounded a bend, and Lewis pointed at the terrace of the villa, where two figures grappled in the shadow of the enormous Chinese vases that lined the edge. "Someone's there. What are they doing? Dash it, is that Penelope and Marina?"

It was. Locked in an embrace with Marina Garrod, Penelope gave a cry of pain as two hands came up to shove her. The two women were of much the same height, though Marina's build was slighter. Still, the force of the shove made Penelope stumble back a few paces. She righted her balance, glanced up, and saw them approaching.

"Help me get Miss Garrod into the house," she called.

The girl took a few steps toward the lawn as though she meant to flee. Chase and Lewis broke into a run, Lewis gaining the terrace first. His arms went out to enfold Marina, and he lifted her off her feet, just in time to stop her from falling to the flags. Pressing the girl against his shoulder, he traced his finger over a smear of blood on her cheek. Marina stirred, but Lewis' grip was too strong. She subsided into his embrace.

"She's hurt," he said, sounding angry.

"What's happened, Penelope?" said Chase.

Penelope looked from him to Lewis, hesitating. "Never mind now. She is chilled to the bone."

Chase thought that Penelope, pale and exhausted, wasn't in much better condition than Marina. Her feet were bare, and she shivered. "You're right. Questions can wait," he said.

Lewis spoke over the girl's bent head. "Marina was asleep. That's why she struck out at you, Penelope. She'll be confused and frightened."

A moan escaped the girl's lips. She opened her eyes. Looking into them, Chase caught the moment when awareness flickered to life.

Lewis pulled her closer. "You're safe," he whispered. He touched her hair.

"I beg your forgiveness for disturbing you," Marina said in a soft monotone. They all stared at her. It was unclear to whom this remark had been addressed.

"It's quite all right," said Penelope, trying to smile.

"How did I get here?" she whispered.

"You've had a bad dream, Miss Garrod," said Lewis. Reluctantly, he allowed Chase to take the girl from his embrace and went to retrieve his sister's abandoned slippers, presenting them to her. He extended a hand to Penelope. "Let's go, old girl. It's going to rain again."

Chapter Twelve

Beatrice Honeycutt met them in the upstairs corridor. As if already in mourning, she was garbed in lusterless black and carried a prayer book in her hand. Directing one horrified glance at Marina's bare feet and diaphanous nightgown, she said, "I awakened your maid to see if she knew where'd you gone, but she was no use. We must see your father in a few minutes. Ned is there with Mr. Tallboys."

Marina said, "Should you and Mr. Tallboys be out of your beds? Are you well, Beatrice? I've not seen you since—"

Beatrice swept aside this concern, though in truth she looked harassed, a few strands of lank brown hair plastered against her round cheeks, her small, white teeth worrying her lip. "Where on earth have you been, Marina? Our aunt sent me to find you."

"I was sleepwalking. Don't fuss."

Beatrice sighed. "Get dressed. You'll want to do your part." She nodded in Chase's direction but pointedly ignored Penelope and Lewis. Penelope seemed embarrassed. Lewis stared at Marina's cousin with open hostility, and Chase was surprised by the intensity of his own dislike. Beatrice Honeycutt had rebuffed the girl's attempt at conciliation in no uncertain terms.

"My father?" asked Marina after an awkward pause. She was blinking in the stronger light and still looked bewildered. But the reality of Garrod's plight had steadied her.

"My dear, I'm sorry. The doctor says it won't be long."

Marina's eyes widened. Her mouth trembled, and her grief overflowed in tears.

Chase said, "Will you come into Miss Garrod's bedchamber with us, Miss Honeycutt? There is more you should know about tonight's incident."

Beatrice frowned. "You choose your time well, Mr. Chase."

"My apologies, ma'am. I understood you to say Mr. Garrod is not ready for you yet."

She inclined her head with ironic courtesy and accompanied them. When they entered the bedchamber, Marina's maid, who had been resting in a chair, her head slumping wearily, leaped to her feet. After helping Marina into the chair she had vacated and tucking a shawl around her mistress' shoulders, the maid said to Beatrice Honeycutt, "Oh, ma'am. I had gone to bed. I never heard a thing this time."

"This has happened before?" inquired Penelope.

The maid, uneasy, did not respond.

Chase pressed her. "Did your mistress take her medicine tonight? It was too strong. How much did you give her?"

"Just the usual, sir."

Beatrice Honeycutt intervened. "Go down to the kitchen, Todd, and fetch Miss Marina a hot drink. I don't want her to catch a chill. We don't need any more illness in this house." After the maid had sidled from the room, Beatrice said, "In justice, Mr. Chase, you can't blame Todd. The draught is intended to keep my cousin quiet. You might say with more truth that it's not strong enough."

This was said as though Marina were not present. A flush of anger mounted in the girl's face, but she controlled herself, merely eyeing her cousin rebelliously. Chase crossed the room to the nightstand and picked up the bottle to sniff its contents. He himself had taken opium over the years to alleviate his pain but had never liked the disorientation it caused. It may be that the family meant well by the girl, though Chase was by no means convinced of that, but in Marina's anxious state, the laudanum could have excited rather than pacified her. It certainly hadn't kept her in bed.

Lewis snatched up the towel draped over the washbasin. He wetted it and knelt by Marina to wipe away the streak of blood on her cheek. She allowed him to help her, her gaze warming under his. Beatrice watched this byplay without reaction.

Penelope whispered to Chase, "We must send Lewis to bed. He shouldn't be here. I'll tell him."

"Leave them, Penelope," he said.

Marina glanced down at her blood-caked fingernails and discreetly slid her hands under her shawl. "You are all very kind to be concerned about me, but I am better." She turned to Penelope. "Did I hurt you in my frenzy, ma'am? I am truly sorry."

"Not at all, Miss Garrod."

The housekeeper Mrs. Yates came into the room. She, too, was fully dressed, and she scurried across the carpet, her keys jingling at her waist. "Did you find her, Beatrice?" she said. Her eye fell on Marina, and she began to deliver a scold, seeming oblivious of her audience.

"Enough, ma'am," broke in Chase when the spate of words showed no signs of drying up. He explained what had happened, then said to both ladies, "To your knowledge, was anyone from the household out of doors tonight? I saw a light from my window—someone carrying a lantern across the grounds."

"A light?" echoed Mrs. Yates. "What can it matter? Everyone on the estate knows my brother is on his deathbed. No one sleeps peacefully."

"It matters because this person may have tried to draw your niece out into the dark. He or she may have known she was in the grip of an opiate, the effects of which can vary. I've heard it can cause intoxication and a susceptibility to visions. It would be child's play to frighten her once she had been roused in this way."

"For what reason?" demanded the housekeeper.

"I intend to find out." Chase restored the medicine bottle and approached Marina. Having decided he would not betray her scheme with Lewis, he tried to exude reassurance. And yet he believed that the inveterate secrecy in this household could do the girl no good and was determined to root it out. When he realized he loomed over her, he drew a chair close to hers and sat down. "Did you take your composing draught tonight, Miss Garrod?"

She'd had more time to gather her wits. "I tried to refuse," she said. "I thought I would be called to my father's bedside. But Todd said she had orders that I was to take it. I didn't want to get her in trouble."

This made sense. She'd been forced to leave the pursuit of any false will-o'-the-wisp to her new ally Lewis Durant. Chase scrutinized the circle of intent faces before he again addressed Marina, who still shivered even under her shawl. "And this potion caused your confusion?"

She lifted her chin. "It's true I felt unaccountably strange when I left my bed. But I believe that prolonged exposure to the night air has revived me."

"What awakened you, Miss Garrod?"

He had thought she wouldn't answer, but she said, "Gravel against my window like the last time."

"The last time? We'll pass over that for now. How could this gravel awaken you if you were so soundly asleep?"

She sent Lewis an appeal. "I…I often wander in the night when I am disturbed in my thoughts. Tonight I had vowed to stay awake. I felt there was something I needed to do, but I couldn't stay awake. I can't tell you what happened after that."

Penelope reached into her dressing-gown pocket and extended her hand. "These are yours, Miss Garrod. You dropped them as you ran."

Before Marina could move, Chase took the red and black beads and held them up in his own palm close to his face so that he could examine them. "Beads from your broken necklace," he commented.

One of Marina's hands emerged from under the shawl to take her property. "Yes, I had some left over when I made the bracelet."

When Penelope looked as though she meant to ask a question, Chase gave a small shake of his head. He could read her thought easily. Penelope was wondering why Marina Garrod carried the beads with her. There was no pocket in her night rail, so that meant she must have clutched them in her hand when she left her bedchamber. But somehow Chase didn't want that question asked of the girl.

Marina laughed mirthlessly. "How you all stare at me. Oh, don't worry. I am not the mad creature you must think me."

"Of course, you aren't," burst in Lewis, unable to hold back any longer. "Anyone might have a nightmare. You've had a great deal on your mind, Miss Garrod."

She acknowledged this with a ghost smile but didn't break the contact with Chase. He said, "Were you dreaming, Miss Garrod?"

She ran her slender fingers over her wrist. "I dreamed about a story I heard in my infancy. A Jamaican bogey, a demon that sucks the blood of children. You see, I'd been thinking about this story before I went to sleep, even though I don't suppose such spirits can cross the ocean. I heard pursuit behind me on the stairs and thought to distract the demon...compel it to pause long enough to retrieve my beads so that I could get away. All nonsense, but one doesn't think of that while in the throes of a nightmare."

"Pursuit?" said Penelope.

Again came the mirthless laugh, and Marina said lightly, "I suppose the demon was you, Mrs. Wolfe."

"There's nothing more we can do, Mr. Chase. He's stopped vomiting, but his pulse is elevated, and he has burning pains in his stomach. Convulsions and delirium weaken him rapidly," whispered the surgeon Aurelius Caldwell.

Gray morning light crept through the windowpanes, slanting over the mourners clustered around Hugo Garrod's bed. Ned Honeycutt stooped over his uncle, gripping an unresponsive hand and sobbing openly. Mrs. Yates patted Honeycutt's arm in a tender gesture. Beatrice Honeycutt edged closer to the bed, kissed her uncle's forehead in farewell, and stepped back. She glanced toward the foot of the bed, where Samuel Tallboys stood, prayer book in hand, as if she expected him to take some more decisive action. But he appeared lost in his ceremonies, prayers issuing from his mouth unceasingly. The door opened, and Marina Garrod entered the room. Caldwell looked at her with pity, but he and Chase allowed her to go forward alone.

None of the family acknowledged her until she ranged herself by Honeycutt. He shifted to make space for her. Marina took Hugo Garrod's hand and held it between her two small ones. "Father," she said, trying to recall him to the present.

At the sound of her voice, recognition briefly illuminated Garrod's waxen features. His lids inched up; the dulled blue gaze sharpened as he turned his head in her direction. "Marina," he answered fretfully, "good girl, you're a good girl." He drew a labored breath and added, "Ned? Ned, Ned, Ned."

"I'm here," choked out Honeycutt, blanching at these sepulchral tones.

"Settle it. Promise me. Settle the business."

He said, "I'll do it, Uncle." He began to pace the room with hurried, uneven steps.

"Stop it, Ned," said Mrs. Yates sharply. "Have some decorum. You've a duty to your uncle to stay calm."

"I'll catch the villain who did this," said Honeycutt, his eyes traveling over the people assembled in the room even over the surgeon, who had removed himself to the window. Honeycutt's scrutiny stopped at Chase. "A lot of good it did my uncle to hire one of the famous Bow Street Runners. I'll handle this business myself, you mark my words." He strode back to the bed, jostling Marina out of the way so that he could take his uncle's limp hand again.

"Ned!" cried Beatrice.

Honeycutt was a tall man, at least a foot taller than his young cousin. He looked down his nose at the girl and seemed all at once to realize his discourtesy. "Come here, Marina, he said in a gruff tone. He pulled her in front of him and laid a hand on her shoulder.

Everyone watched Hugo Garrod. His shaking and moaning eased; then, clearly having overheard his nephew's mention of Bow Street, the sick man murmured, "Chase! Where is that man? I pay him, don't I? Curse him!"

Aurelius Caldwell shrugged in response to Chase's lifted brows. "Speak to him if the family doesn't mind," said the surgeon. "It can't make a difference."

Approaching the head of the four-poster bed, Chase saw that death was near. The man's breath came in shallow gasps, and his eyes were so sunken in their sockets as to make it seem they had been gouged out. When his spasm had spent itself, Chase said to him in an undertone, "Do you have any idea who could have done this to you, sir? Tell me what I must do to find your murderer."

He repeated this question several times, getting no response, until finally Garrod said, "One of them, must be."

Honeycutt, Tallboys, and Beatrice erupted in protest, Tallboys saying, "This is a disgrace. Hugo should be thinking of his soul and readying himself for eternity. You have no place here, Chase."

"Let him stay," said Beatrice Honeycutt. "Let's hear what Uncle Hugo would say while there's still time."

Chase had no intention of wasting this opportunity. He wasn't sure whether Garrod knew who he was, but he tried again. "You hired me to protect your daughter. I'll find the person who did this to you, and I'll keep Miss Garrod safe."

"Set her free, didn't I? Damme, what a pretty woman. Don't catch but one in ten of the Obeah Men, blasted slippery rogues, let alone the…women. Beauty, too dear, for Earth too dear. Jealous, the vipers. They were all jealous of her."

Urgently, Chase said in Garrod's ear: "Do you speak of Joanna? Your daughter's mother?"

"The blacks were always afraid of her. Afraid she'd curse them or some such tomfoolery." The dying man's lips twitched in a parody of a smile. Feebly, he wagged a finger to forestall an interruption. "Swore she'd curse me if I didn't look after her daughter. It won't do. It won't do. It won't do. Must make sure…

my advice to you, sir, is to tie up the money tight, only way… to be sure." He fell silent.

Marina dabbed the spittle from his lips and fell to her knees, kissing her father's hand repeatedly, tears streaming down her face. The man on the bed was beyond all human contact now. A fugitive feeling passed over his brow, but whether it was called forth by his daughter's grief or had emerged from his own soul could not be determined. He went rigid all over, relaxed again. His shallow gasps went on for another minute or two and stopped.

Ned Honeycutt reached down to raise his cousin to her feet. "Come away, Marina," he said. "It's finished."

Part Two

"'Tis ignorance that makes a barren waste
Of all beyond itself…"
                          —John Keats, "To the Nile," 1818

"'*The transitions of fortune!*' repeated he, stamping his foot with vehemence on the ground, 'say, rather, the hellish machinations, the sordid avarice of perfidious fiends of malice!—Oh, Olivia, amiable, revered Olivia! how may you regret the day when you left your native island!—better to have been landed on a savage shore of barbarians, than to have found, as you have done, your bitterest enemies, in uncle, brother, husband! *those* names which in the *common* lot of human life, are associated with all that is affectionate and tender!'"
                  —Anonymous, *The Woman of Colour: A Tale*, 1808

Chapter Thirteen

On the morning after Garrod's death, the atmosphere in the hothouse was sweltering. As John Chase stood on the dais listening to the under-gardener's story, he wiped his face with his handkerchief and contemplated the withered blooms of the night-blooming cereus. In the harsh sunlight pouring through the glass ceiling, it was an ugly plant, parched and commonplace. Its rangy limbs and green-yellow stems lined with black spines spread in a zigzag pattern over the trellis.

"Show me where you found the beads," Chase said.

The under-gardener, an old man in corduroy breeches, gaiters, and a slouched hat, displayed the glumness shared by all of Garrod's servants today, but the smile lines around his eyes and mouth suggested he was ordinarily good-humored. This man, whose name was Higgins, led Chase out a side door and around the back of the building. Opening the wooden doors, Higgins preceded him down the stairs into a space about ten by ten feet. This must be the apparatus Garrod had shown to Penelope and Lewis, thought Chase, examining the furnace, boiler, and cistern with interest.

Higgins reached a work-roughened hand toward the coal bin to the right of the furnace, but when the gardener got down on his haunches to paw at the dust on the floor, Chase snapped, "Don't touch it." The man stared up at him, amazed.

"There may be additional evidence," Chase explained. He knew his temper got shorter by the hour and resolved to tamp it down. He'd always believed that bullying tactics were to be used only when absolutely necessary and for limited purposes, and he had no patience for certain of the other Runners who relied on them habitually. To Chase's mind, only a stupid person needed to act the brute.

Higgins' brow cleared at this milder tone. "I take your meaning, sir."

Chase's patient exploration of the stone floor—pacing from corner to corner, working his fingers around the sides of the boiler and cistern and methodically poking a stick through the coals—revealed nothing beyond a jumble of footprints and the fold of paper containing three red-black beads with a hole bored in each, one half-crushed bead of the same type, and about a teaspoon of loose powder, presumably derived from the crushed bead.

"You found the fold of paper next to the coal bin?"

The gardener looked down at his boots. "Aye, this morning I was tending to the plants, making sure everything was in prime condition, just what Mr. Garrod would want, poor fellow. Little dusty, says I, so I poked around in a few pots to see if the roots was wet. They rot, you know, if you water too much, so I sprinkle a dab here and there. While I was doing that, I was told to check the mechanism. Seems it hadn't been right, but not a thing the matter with it. That's when I found them beads."

"How often do the gardeners come down here?"

"Not so often in summer. Once a day to feed the stove, maybe. More when the boiler's in use. We've been keeping it fired up hot for all the guests. Mr. Garrod did like 'em to admire the steam." He pointed upward. "See that window there? We can check the water in the cistern from there."

"You recognize the beads?"

"I surely do. Same as the seeds from our Jamaican wild licorice, except that these have holes. *Abrus precatorius*. We plunge them seeds into the hotbed until they take. When they grow bigger, we keep 'em in the stove like the other tender plants. But as to how these ones got here, that I can't tell you."

"Hotbed?"

"Let me show you, sir," said Higgins.

Chase stored the paper and its contents in his waistcoat pocket and followed the gardener back into the hothouse. Higgins halted by a frame of tanner's bark in which seedlings grew under a glazed surface. Next he took Chase to a corner of the hothouse, where a more mature variety flourished. *Abrus precatorius* was a twining shrub that smelled of licorice and had branches rising about ten feet. Spiky purple-pink blooms studded the branches from which clusters of pods depended like so many green hands.

The gardener took a cutting tool from a pouch he wore at his waist and cut open one of the pods to reveal the now familiar red and black seeds. "See here—jequirity seeds. Pretty, ain't they, sir? The natives make them into necklaces. But they're dangerous."

"How do you know that, Higgins?"

"Why, Mr. Garrod told me, God rest his soul, and I soon saw for myself. The seeds take too long to sprout 'less you soak them in water. We did that, but Mr. Amos—he's head gardener here—he must've had a cut on his finger when he handled the beans. Finger swelled up, then his whole hand. It was a fortnight before he could use that hand again. You don't want to be messing with this plant."

"I've seen a bracelet made of these beads. It doesn't seem to harm the wearer."

"You mean Miss Marina's gewgaw, don't you, sir? Safe enough, unless she smashes it and eats the powder, I warrant."

"Where did she get it?"

"From her father, maybe."

Chase doubted Hugo Garrod would have given his daughter an ornament that linked her to her Jamaican heritage, and his spirits sank as he digested the gardener's information. He would have to report it to Mr. Tallboys in his capacity as magistrate.

"Did you see anyone lurking around the hothouse, either before or after the party, Higgins? Someone where he shouldn't have been?"

"No, sir, I didn't."

"Was Miss Garrod in the hothouse on the day of the party or yesterday?"

"Not that I saw."

"Who then?"

Higgins shook his head in perplexity. "Lots of people. The ladies checking the arrangements for the party. Mr. Garrod and his guests what are staying at the house. Mr. Amos. The maids from the village. The party guests. Could have been more. I was in and out myself."

"You saw no one interfering with the tea caddy? No one showing an interest in it?" This too Higgins denied. No help, thought Chase. If he were right that the tampering had occurred during the period when Garrod's key had gone missing, the mischief could have been accomplished quickly and easily by anyone with the key and a minute or two to act unobserved. And without a witness, bringing the crime home to the murderer would be difficult.

Chase fell silent, tapping his fingers on the edge of the tub. The beads were identical to those Penelope had collected while following Marina; they had come from the broken necklace. Who had hidden them—and when? Had this person used the boiler room as a secret place to prepare the poison? He knew what would be said. Who better to have carried out this plot than an emotionally disturbed young woman with access to the poisonous seeds? But it was the obviousness, even clumsiness, of this maneuver that made him doubt this possibility. Marina Garrod was highly intelligent. Unless there was some purpose he could not discern, or she played the kind of deep game her father had enjoyed, Chase couldn't imagine why she would leave behind evidence that was bound to be discovered when the boiler room was serviced. Finally, he said, "Could the powder from these seeds have poisoned Mr. Garrod and the others?"

"Stands to reason it could. The plant ain't so well-known to English folk. I imagine the person who left them seeds was the same as laid all those gentry-folk low." Higgins leaned forward, his watery eyes challenging Chase, and dropped his voice. "I heard tell the master's woman in Jamaica is someone who might know a thing or two about heathen poisons. We've all been wondering, see. We knew Miss Marina's mother had been a slave, but we didn't know much else, her father not liking to speak of the matter. Still, there were…rumors."

"What rumors?"

Higgins shrugged. "Ah, well. Like mother, like daughter, maybe? It was one of the reports that do get around. I can't rightly recall where I heard it."

"Malicious gossip. Keep your mouth shut on that subject."

"Oh, yes, sir. Anything to oblige." He paused before adding irrepressibly, "It's a strange thing, though. Our young lady seems mighty interested in learning about how things grow. Full of questions, that one. Drives Mr. Amos to distraction, he wishing he could tell her to take herself off, but of course he can't. And look what she done to the roses last night. A crime, that."

"You know about the sleepwalking?"

"I saw the damage with my own eyes. Mr. Amos was that angry about it, though the girl apologized. Said she wasn't herself and imagined she was supposed to be weeding the garden." Higgins sniffed to show his opinion of the excuse, then added, "There was the business with Daisy too. Don't forget about that."

"Daisy?"

"One of the kitchen maids, sir. You'd best ask her. I've no call nor wish to say an unkind word against my betters."

Chase stroked his chin and regarded the man. "You don't much like Miss Garrod, do you? You and the rest of the servants, eh? Tell me why."

This question appeared to mystify him. "Well," he said in his slow, measuring way, "I suppose I like her fine. But who is she when all's said and done? I expect she'll be our mistress now, unless that's to be Mr. Honeycutt."

It was obvious which outcome the gardener would prefer. After he had shuffled back to his work, watering can in hand, Chase sought out the kitchen maid called Daisy, a buxom young woman, about thirty years old. She wore a faded stuff gown and had a black armband tied around her upper arm, a token of respect for her master. She willingly left her work peeling potatoes to follow Chase into the kitchen yard. Arms folded, she waited, watchful eyes fixed on his face.

"I mind the day you speak of," she said. "Miss Marina and I had words when she come down to the kitchen for a bite of gingerbread, not but what we'd have fetched it to her in the drawing room."

"Repeat this conversation, if you would, miss."

"You think it important? I was that upset at the time, but it's a while back. I shouldn't like to get the young lady in trouble. That would be making a noise about less than nothing."

"You can trust me not to do that."

She stole a glance at him from under sandy eyelashes. "You would know best, Mr. Chase, and that's a fact," she said with faint sarcasm.

Daisy described an encounter that had begun with what was to her an innocent question or two about Marina's history. She'd merely wanted to show the girl the cordiality that Daisy felt had been denied her by the other servants, so she'd asked Marina about what it had been like to be born and live her early years on a plantation. Daisy had felt she was humoring a child, Marina seeming little more than that to her.

"What did she say to you?"

"I suppose I got what I deserved for speaking out of turn to a lady. Miss Garrod wanted me to know that the folk on that plantation had been afraid of her mother. Afraid she'd curse them, or some such rubbish. I laughed, Mr. Chase. It seemed so ridiculous to hear her talking like that in our respectable English kitchen. I think I said something of the sort, and then—" Daisy broke off, looking a little stricken, but went on after a moment without further prompting. "Why then, sir, she came right up close to me. I'll never forget what she said, all my days. *Don't be so sure it can't happen here.* That's what she said."

Chase stared at her, appalled. That sounded like a threat. Could he be wrong, after all? What if Marina Garrod's heart had turned bitter beyond endurance and a thirst for revenge had grown in her, a revenge that had been fed by her fragile mental state and her delusions? He remembered Hugo Garrod's description of these delusions on the day he'd been hired, but the implication had been that Marina feared some kind of menace turned on her, not the other way around.

With a heavy heart, he went into the house and up the grand staircase. In the corridor, he found Aurelius Caldwell, who had called to check on his two recovering patients and assure himself that all was in readiness for Hugo Garrod's autopsy.

"A question for you, Caldwell," Chase said. "If I meant to murder someone and wished to allay suspicion, might it be worth my while to imbibe some of the poison myself?"

"Risky, that."

"But what if I was careful to take very little, just enough to bring on a reaction that would probably not be fatal?"

He stroked his chin. "I catch your drift, Mr. Chase, and I'll tell you that a determined or desperate person might take such a chance. After all, one could control how much was consumed and exaggerate the effects afterward. It would be hard even for a medical man to tell for certain unless the shamming were obvious. Have you a reason to lean that way?"

Choosing not to answer this question, Chase produced the unused bottle of medicine the constables had found in the rubbish, which he'd stowed in his pocket this morning. "Any idea what this is?"

"Ah," said Caldwell, a spark of enthusiasm brightening his gaze, "if you'll allow me, I'll add it to my samples. We've a very good chemical gentleman who has a villa nearby. A friend of mine, in fact."

He examined the bottle. Made of cylindrical green glass, it held about four ounces of liquid. Though most of the printer's label had been removed, the remnants of a decorative panel in gold, as well as the image of an urn with a sprig of greenery protruding, were still intact. A few letters of the original handwritten identification could also be seen. The surgeon uncorked the bottle and poured some of the solution from the narrow mouth into his palm.

He dabbed at the liquid with the finger of his other hand and tasted it. "Some sort of restorative tonic," he pronounced. "Mainly ginger and Peruvian bark." He peered again at the fragment of label. "The label ends in 'vous.' I'll warrant it said: *Tonic for the Nervous*. No harm in that. Do you still wish me to have it tested?"

"Yes, I'll give you a sample and try to trace the purchase myself. It's not from a local druggist? You can see at the bottom part of an address for the printer who made the label."

"It's not from here. Our man doesn't use labels of this design."

Chase nodded. "You'll let me know what your chemical friend says about the other samples as soon as possible?"

"Of course. He can run the tests that will be needed in court."

"You said before that you suspect arsenic as the poisoning agent?"

"I do," replied Caldwell, intrigued. "Why, have you another theory?"

"Not one I'm prepared to credit," said Chase.

Samuel Tallboys waved Chase to a seat in Garrod's study. The clergyman, wearing clerical dress, took his seat in a wing chair and rested against the cushions with a sigh. He looked around in reminiscent sorrow. "I've spent many a happy hour at Laurentum, Mr. Chase. Before Mr. Garrod helped me obtain my living, I resided with him as chaplain, curator to his treasures, and private secretary. Hugo was always good to me. I can repay him now by ensuring that everything will be done just as he would have wished."

"How long have you also held a commission of the peace in Clapham?"

"I've been a J.P. for several years and vicar for several more before that. I can tell you we've had nothing like this in the district before. You will have encountered a fair amount of violent death in your work, sir. It is quite out of my experience."

Chase was curious. "Weren't you in Jamaica with Mr. Garrod? I always thought it was a place of utter barbarity. The heads of erring slaves stuck on fence posts, vicious floggings—"

Tallboys was surprised. "Eh? Perhaps you refer to the incidents of slaves turning on their masters. Now that you mention it, I recall a story about a servant girl who poisoned her master's brandy. 'Twas said she stood at his bedside and watched his death agonies without a shred of remorse."

That wasn't what Chase had meant, but he let the remark pass. "Before we proceed to business, have you fully recovered your health? You should call in one of your brother magistrates to take your place." Chase didn't add that as Garrod's executor and trustee, Tallboys would have many additional cares pressing upon him, not to mention that he was also a suspect in the murder inquiry.

Tallboys narrowed his eyes. "You must leave that to my judgment. The inquest will take place two o'clock tomorrow at the Windmill Inn. You'll be ready?"

"Yes, sir."

"Postmortem?"

"Tomorrow morning. After that, the coroner's jury will view the body, and it can be released for burial."

"Good. You've been in contact with the coroner? He's a young man, bit green. You'll want to keep an eye on him."

"Yes, sir," said Chase. "I'll ask my friend Edward Buckler to help conduct the questioning if you don't think that'll ruffle too many feathers. He's a barrister of the Inner Temple."

Tallboys considered. "That would depend."

"Sir?"

"On whether your friend expects to command his usual fee." Tallboys brandished a letter and fanned his red face with it. "This is from Hugo's lawyers. They remind me that the estate is not authorized to pay the expenses of a criminal investigation. As the parish is likely to be stuck with the bill, we shall have to economize." He gave a derisive humph. "One of the richest men in the country, worth a king's ransom, and here I am worrying about how to meet costs! Your chemical tests won't come cheap. There's the autopsy and the coroner and the rest. You tell Mr. Buckler that he can pose his questions with my blessing if he means to offer his services *gratis*."

Chase answered him with what patience he could muster. "The chemical tests are necessary to determine the poison. The doctor mentions arsenic as the likely possibility." He paused, wishing again that he could omit this part of his report, though that would be futile. The under-gardener Higgins would never keep quiet. It would be better for Chase to offer the official information. "Mr. Tallboys, let me tell you of a discovery made just this morning."

As Chase related the testimony of the under-gardener and the kitchen maid, Tallboys' expression grew severe, and his thin lips stretched into a grimace of frigid distaste. "It wanted only this. I've been uneasy in my mind, Chase, but couldn't bear to give weight to my fears. Now—"

"I'm not sure what you mean, sir," Chase replied carefully. "I can tell you that I do not regard this evidence as conclusive. It brings guilt home to no one."

"How can you doubt it was *Abrus precatorius* that killed Hugo and sickened the rest of us? Why else should these beads have been found hidden near where the crime occurred? No, as much as I would like to think otherwise for my late lamented friend's sake, I cannot ignore the implications. When I think of the scandal, and the difficulties in regard to the settling of the will, I own I can't see my way forward."

"Have you any idea how things are left? It's likely the will can provide an essential clue to the culprit. We must know who chiefly benefits."

"Hugo didn't tell me. Why should he? I'm not sure he knew what was best himself. What am I to do if the heiress to this fortune is proved to have murdered her own father? She could not then inherit."

"You are hasty, sir. We must await the results of the chemical tests."

"But the maid's story about the threat? That too is significant."

Chase kept his tone matter-of-fact. "The worst thing we can do is jump to conclusions. Give me time, Mr. Tallboys. The so-called threat uttered by Miss Garrod was vague. It means nothing."

The clergyman snorted. "I'll have to take your word for that, Chase. I wish I could be as sanguine. Still, it would be best for the family if the matter can be hushed up. I need hardly say you must be discreet."

"Of course."

Tallboys reached over and picked up one of the beads that Chase had placed on the table between them. Heaving himself to his feet, he went to the shelves, frowned at the spines for a few minutes, and finally pulled down a volume. He flipped to the index and then to the relevant page. "*Abrus precatorius*. Red bead vine," he murmured. "What can we learn of this plant? Used as prayer beads or rosaries or as jewelry for slaves. Its name derives from the Latin *precatorius* meaning prayer. Leaves and tops given with advantage in coughs and pleurisies. Cattle poisoning in India. Administered in powder, it will operate with great violence both as an emetic and cathartic. Anyone ingesting this substance would suffer purging, lassitude, and so on." He put aside the book and confronted Chase. "We have found our poison."

"It doesn't make sense. For some inexplicable reason the murderer leaves the beads to be found? Beads pointing to one person?"

"That person is not in her full senses."

There was nothing for it. Chase's hope of avoiding open conflict was dashed. "I don't believe it," he told Tallboys. "The key to Mr. Garrod's teapoy was missing on the day of the party. Someone in the household stole it to tamper with the sugar, and we don't know who that person was. You yourself were in the house at the relevant time." He leafed through his occurrence book, making the pages rustle as loudly as possible. "Can you tell me more about your visit?"

"This is offensive, sir, and stupid. Do you think I'd poison myself?"

"Such details are important in these inquiries. What time did you arrive?"

"About ten o'clock. I was shown into the morning room to meet Miss Honeycutt."

"She was there waiting for you?"

"She and Miss Garrod both. We took breakfast together while Miss Honeycutt and I discussed our plans for a new religious curriculum at a local school. I had business of my own to attend to in the parish, so I left by eleven o'clock. Anything else?"

"No."

"Look, Chase. A poisoner is the most vicious of murderers. One might expect a villain like this to thrive in Italy—but here? Do your duty. I can sympathize with your reluctance to cast blame in a certain quarter. I, more than anyone, am bound to feel a solicitude for my old friend's daughter. I am left her guardian. Her welfare must be my chief concern. But it can be no use to balk at plain facts."

"The key isn't the only issue. You witnessed Mr. Garrod's agitation on his deathbed. He was worried about his will."

Tallboys returned to his chair. Lacing his fingers under his chin, he regarded Chase coldly. "Hugo was a careful man. Mark my words. He'll tell us how he intended his estate to be allocated, down to the last farthing. I beg that you not repeat this story to anyone. My friend was possessed of an income of thirty thousand pounds per annum—did you know that?"

"A large estate. More than enough brass to inspire someone to put poison in the man's tea. To my mind, we have motives to go around. Let's say Mr. Garrod was angry with someone and decided to make a change to his will. Maybe this person killed him to put a stop to this plan."

Tallboys' expression darkened further. "Nonsense. I warn you, Chase. You have no proof of any such thing, and you will only add to my headaches by continuing in this vein. Do you want to tear this family apart?"

"Better that than let a killer go free."

Tallboys brushed aside this remark with an impatient gesture. "I don't doubt the newspapers will be baying at our heels. They expect Bow Street to deliver, and you must hope they don't make too much of the fact that you were actually on the property when the crime occurred. Not your fault, I suppose."

"You are kind to say so."

Ignoring this sarcasm, the clergyman rose and made his way across the room to a curio cabinet in the corner. "I'll show you something." He opened the glass door, pulled out a bottle, and carried it back.

"What's this?" said Chase when Tallboys had put an old wine bottle into his hand. Shifting it back and forth so that the liquid sloshed to one side, he saw that it held black feathers as well as some waving strands of what looked like hair, bones, and animal teeth on a string. As he shook the jar, three or four red and black beads came loose from the bed of hair. They were of the same type as Marina Garrod's.

"A keepsake. Hugo's had it for years," said Tallboys.

"What's the animal necklace made of?"

"Cat's teeth, nine of them for luck. The liquid is rainwater."

"It's an Obeah charm, isn't it?" said Chase.

"Hugo took this off a particularly nasty character on his estate. He found it concealed in the thatch of the man's cottage and preserved it out of scholarly interest."

"Miss Garrod told me you have indulged her recent interest in Obeah and Jamaican culture. Do you think that wise, Mr. Tallboys?"

"Not particularly. I couldn't think how to stem her questions. She is a most determined young woman." He shook his head, bemused. "You seem inclined to take Marina's part, sir. But do you truly believe any child could bury a past like hers? It was sure to mark her. In the end it was sure to mark her."

Chapter Fourteen

The cavalcade of coroner, jury, and constables, with a clutch of reporters trailing at the rear, approached Garrod's villa. The day was fine, a little sultry, with a sprinkling of rain that had speckled the pretty coat and Hessian boots of the coroner, a bright-eyed young man stepping bravely down the road. He strode up the carriage drive, swept by the line of waiting servants, and met Samuel Tallboys in front of Laurentum's pillared entrance porch. Tallboys dispersed the journalists with threats of a citation for trespassing and took his place next to the coroner at the head of the procession.

The jury's first stop was the hothouse, where the twelve local men stared at the exotic blooms with an awe they concealed behind stolid faces. Tallboys conducted them to the place where the poisoning had occurred. Afterwards they went upstairs to view the body. Earlier that morning, the knowledge that a trio of physicians, one a lecturer from St. Thomas' Hospital, had taken their saws and scalpels to the corpse had vibrated through the household, sounding a note of dark excitement. Forced to shoo away several curiosity seekers from the upstairs corridor, John Chase had finally remained on guard at the door. Now when the coroner entered the chamber of death, he took one look at the corpse's distended belly, his thin nostrils quivering, and buried his face in his nosegay. A peacock, thought Chase, but he kept his expression bland.

Next the men filed into Beatrice Honeycutt's bedchamber to find her propped against her pillows with her aunt Mrs. Yates and the surgeon Caldwell in attendance. Dressed in a pink silk dressing gown and a delicate lace cap with flaps that draped down her shoulders, Miss Honeycutt expressed herself exhausted from the combined effects of her recent sickness and her uncle's death. Gallantly, the coroner said she was not to rise from her bed, for he would not keep her long. Beatrice gave her hand first to him and then to Tallboys, who lingered over it a fraction too long. She held herself rigid, embarrassed by all these strange men looking at her. The jury waited in respectful silence, seeming sheepish and uneasy in this feminine domain.

"My dear, madam," said the coroner, "I was relieved beyond measure to hear of your deliverance. Words fail me on this occasion, but may I offer my condolences on the death of your uncle?"

Lips trembling, Beatrice turned her head away.

"My dear," said Samuel Tallboys, "we shouldn't ask this of you. It's far too much. Do forgive me for permitting it. I felt I had no choice but to give our cooperation. Perhaps...perhaps we can come back later?" Observing the man's anxiety, Chase wondered if there could be a romance afoot, though the pompous and unimaginative Tallboys struck him as an unlikely candidate for a lover. Hugo Garrod had said that Beatrice had made a better success of her London season than had her cousin, but apparently she had not achieved a match for herself. In which case Tallboys might appear a reasonable prospect, especially if he was to receive a bequest in the will.

"That's an excellent plan. Poor Beatrice is exhausted. Can your questions wait, sir?" Mrs. Yates said to the coroner. She too seemed overcome by the magnitude of the change in her life. She kept her shoulders bowed, her gaze lowered, her hands folded sedately over her apron. She might have been thinking about what would become of her if the household at Laurentum were to break up. Too old to seek another position, she would be counting on her brother for security in her final years. Or she might have been immersed in her grief for Hugo Garrod and her busy concern for her nieces and nephew.

The coroner bowed to the older lady. "I must express my sympathy to you as well, Mrs. Yates. Your brother was a true gentleman and a philanthropist who has a done a world of good for his country. He will be sorely missed."

"Thank you, sir." Mrs. Yates raised a mild gaze to his face, then returned it to the carpet.

"That won't be necessary," put in Beatrice in a stronger voice. Shifting to face them, she adjusted the sleeves of her gown and smiled on the clergyman. "If Mr. Tallboys can do his duty under such trying circumstances, I would be ashamed to do less. With the example of my dear aunt before me—she who is ever active in promoting the good of others—how can I not follow her line of conduct?"

This was received with a cry of pleasure and a clasp of the hand from Mrs. Yates and a reverential bow from the clergyman. Watching this little show, Chase found himself, not for the first time in his life, thinking about the hard work of being a lady, and it seemed to him that Penelope was in some ways better off in her current unorthodox situation. He understood that Marina Garrod's failure to adhere to the code required of her was at the root of her alienation from her family, though illegitimacy and race must also play roles.

Once it was established that Miss Honeycutt had drunk only a few sips of her tea, could not inform them about the key to the teapoy, and had noticed nothing out of the way until she herself took ill, the coroner began a more delicate probe. "Had there been anything to trouble the family prior to these tragic events, ma'am? I beg your pardon for intruding into your private affairs, but we must find the villain who did this."

"Of course, you must ask, sir, but my answer is no. My uncle was looking forward to his party. He was in good spirits. We all were. In truth, we'd been finding the days a little quiet and welcomed the diversion."

"You know of no threat? Nothing had disturbed him?"

She thought a moment. "We had a brief conversation that indicated a certain uneasiness. I can't say much more than that. I'm sorry to be of so little use."

"No, no, ma'am," the coroner said graciously. "When was this conversation?"

"The day before the party. I shouldn't think it could have anything to do with…what happened. A remark or two in passing." Her voice trailed off, and the surgeon Caldwell hastened to pour a small amount of a cordial in a glass for her.

The coroner waited while she took a sip; then he said, "Mr. Garrod had been worried? About what, may I ask? Business affairs or family?"

A hint of alarm showed on her features. The pause stretched to the breaking point. She finally said quietly, "He was worried about his daughter."

"Ah," said the coroner, and he flashed a gleam of triumph at Tallboys as if to suggest his own efforts would be crowned with more success than had yet been achieved. "The charming Miss Garrod. What reason did he give, ma'am?"

"He'd hoped her sojourn in Clapham would restore her to health. She found the bustle of town rather a trial, I'm afraid. Uncle Hugo had been concerned with keeping her safe—and well. That's why Mr. Chase was hired."

"Safe? From what? You alarm me exceedingly, ma'am."

She slumped against the pillows and closed her eyes. "I really don't know, sir."

Mrs. Yates said, "All that can have nothing to do with Hugo's death. Sir, I beg that you proceed cautiously with Miss Garrod. Her grief is profound. As Beatrice has mentioned, we do not wish to see her more disturbed."

"But what's this about malice?" The coroner's brows drew together in an assumption of authority Chase thought ludicrous in a man of less than thirty years.

He stepped forward. "Mr. Garrod employed me to inquire into some nasty tricks played on his daughter. I have yet to determine who is responsible, nor can I tell you what bearing, if any, this malice has on the murder."

"Why, none," cried Mrs. Yates. "Foolish games, that's all."

Obviously startled, the coroner said, "You must leave these matters to me, ma'am. We shall hear from Miss Garrod at the inquest."

Chase's foreboding intensified. How much had Tallboys, eager to avoid scandal, told the coroner about Marina Garrod? And was Beatrice Honeycutt artfully planting insinuations to force the fruit of suspicion against her cousin—with the aid of her aunt Anne Yates and perhaps her brother Ned Honeycutt? Though Chase himself had reluctantly handed over the seeds of wild licorice as evidence, he intended to say as little as possible on the subject. He hadn't thought much about why this should be so. He just knew the decision felt right.

"Chase," a voice hissed as he stood in the taproom at the Windmill, where the jurymen had stopped for refreshment. He lowered his tankard to the bar and turned to see Noah Packet at his elbow. Packet had oiled his dirty brown hair and trimmed his side-whiskers so that for once his angular face was perfectly clean.

"Come to pay your respects?" said Chase.

"How'd this happen? I nearly bust my breeches when I heard the news. You might've sent word."

"I've been busy."

"Not busy enough," said Packet bitterly. "Too late to cry over spilled milk, ain't it? What do you mean to do now?"

"I'm sorry to have disappointed you."

At this Packet sighed, letting his glance stray to the sawdust strewn floor. "Ain't often I find myself a prime rig. Mr. Garrod might've let me put my hand in his pocket for years. I'll be shivering in my boots come winter, thanks to you."

Chase shook his head. "There for a minute I thought you actually had a heart, Packet, but you're just sad your milk cow is dead."

"Well, I am. Ain't I been telling you as much? Not but what I thought right highly of Mr. Garrod."

"Did you catch your thieves at the docks?"

"One or two. Enough to earn my keep, at any rate." Packet indicated the jurymen, who had retired to several tables to drink and converse boisterously, the coroner big among them. "Fools. I'd better stay to make sure they do this right."

"You are going back to town." Chase took out the unidentified medicine bottle and handed it to him.

After he'd described the task, Packet snorted. "You don't ask much, do you? A bottle with no label, and you want me to find where it come from. Why? This the poison?"

"No, but it doesn't fit, and I want to know. Just do it. See if you can get the address of the chemist where this bottle was purchased. Try the printers of medical labels on Fetter Lane."

"Why there?"

"It's a guess. Look closer. A few letters of the address at the bottom are intact. Might be Fetter Lane, might not. I seem to recall some printers there."

Packet folded his arms over his stomach. "Who's to pay my fee, is what I want to know."

"Don't I always take care of you?" Chase extracted a few coins from his pocketbook, which he tossed over.

As Packet was following him out, they met one of the Bow Street officers, who took one look at Chase's companion and bristled with suspicion. "Friend of yours, sir? I saw this man skulking in the inn yard and was about to send him to the right-about. A patron complained she was the mark for a pickpocket."

Observing that Packet had swept off his hat and was about to address the officer, Chase took his elbow with one hand and opened the door with the other. "He was just leaving," he said.

Upstairs, John Chase contemplated the room where the inquest would be held: a long, narrow rectangle with broad overhead beams and paneled walls emitting the reek of many years' accumulation of stale tobacco smoke and beer. Notebooks poised, the journalists had gathered under the single, high window. At the front next to the coroner's table, the jurymen fanned themselves and squirmed in their seats. Opposite the jury sat the members of Hugo Garrod's family, with the exception of Beatrice, who had given her testimony at Laurentum. Chase's eyes sought and found Marina Garrod among them.

As he watched, she edged her chair a little farther away from the clergyman Samuel Tallboys, though she seemed to listen politely to his speeches. It was difficult to tell for sure because Marina was swathed in black from head to foot and wearing a veil to cover her face. She presented a small, touching figure that drew the regard of the crowd. There was a heavyset man a few feet away keeping his head cocked in her direction. A sharp-faced woman in an ugly gown loitering nearby. A boy with a shock of red hair making faces at his sister and pointing. And there were Mr. Garrod's servants ranged in prim rows—all focused on Marina Garrod. It seemed impossible that she would not feel the power of those eyes. Her handsome cousin Ned Honeycutt drew some of the attention too, especially when he made his way to Marina's side and stood guard over her chair.

Edward Buckler rose from his seat behind the servants to approach Chase. "Quite a crowd, isn't it? Are you ready?"

"Ready to get this done so that I can get back to work," said Chase.

"You don't expect our coroner to solve the murder single-handedly?" Buckler nodded toward the young man basking in his pomp. When Chase merely raised an eyebrow, Buckler went on. "Penelope and Lewis can go home today or tomorrow, don't you agree?"

Chase followed Buckler's glance to Penelope. She smiled, a militant sparkle in her eyes. Clearly she was ready to tell her story, but he also thought she looked brittle and that the smile seemed forced.

"The sooner the better."

"Good God, yes," Buckler said. He added, "The poisoner must have been someone close to Garrod. Which means you and Penelope are likely sharing houseroom with a killer."

"She'd better not fight me when it's time to go."

"I don't think she will. But Lewis—the boy has appointed himself Miss Garrod's champion. He sees her as some kind of romantic heroine, a young girl alone in the world. You won't easily convince him to abandon her."

"Reminds me of someone else I know. Chivalry must be a disease that's catching."

Buckler's smile was wistful. "Point taken."

Chase immediately dismissed the matter from his mind. He had no time to worry about whatever had gone wrong between Penelope and Buckler, and it wasn't his place anyway. The tangled strings of the heart's desire were beyond his unraveling, even when it came to his own heart. No, his business was to protect Joanna's daughter and solve this murder, thereby paying his debt to the woman who had saved his life. But he sensed malevolent forces around Marina, forces that masked harm with dagger smiles and hatred with venomous love. He wished he could be entirely confident of her innocence, but that wasn't his way. His way was to follow the trail of evidence to the end, let his personal feelings be what they would.

In an undertone, he said, "Miss Garrod must confide her secrets without delay. You tell Lewis that for me."

"I'm sure Penelope already has. Chase, we need to know what's in Garrod's will. I suspect—"

Chase stopped him. "Better sit down. The coroner is ready."

Buckler strolled away to take his place in the chair Penelope had saved for him, though Chase noticed that their greeting was stiff. Irritated, he returned his attention to the table at the front. Two men had approached to engage the coroner in conversation. They were Garrod's solicitors, who had been closeted with Ned Honeycutt and Samuel Tallboys earlier that morning to discuss the arrangements for the reading of the will. Now Honeycutt and Tallboys also joined the group.

"There's no provision for it," Chase heard one of the lawyers say. "How could Mr. Garrod have foreseen—? You must understand, sir, our hands are tied."

"What Mr. Dudley tells you is true enough," said Honeycutt. "Apparently, the will does not provide for the settling of a bill likely to exceed 150 pounds. The expenses would have to come out of the executors' pocket, and Mr. Tallboys, for one, is not able to meet them from his own purse. I'm afraid it's on the parish this time."

The coroner did not like this response. "But the family. Naturally you'll wish to…"

"My pockets are to let, sir," said Honeycutt. "We none of us have independent resources. It will take some time for the will to be given probate and my uncle's affairs wound up."

"It's too bad," agreed Tallboys pettishly. "How we are to pay for the postmortem and the chemical tests is more than I can tell you."

The solicitors offered regretful bows and moved away. Honeycutt and Tallboys resumed their seats. The coroner opened the proceedings, first calling upon the surgeon Aurelius Caldwell to relate the progress of the victim's final illness, then summoning the physician from St. Thomas' hospital to report on the autopsy.

After describing the inflamed digestive tract, excess blood in the lungs, and yellowish spots in the stomach lining, the physician concluded: "Hugo Garrod's death resulted from a general disturbance of the constitution produced by the introduction of irritating matter into the stomach."

"Poison, in fact?"

"There can be little doubt."

"You are satisfied it was not the ordinary species of English cholera that sickened the victims?"

"Quite. For one thing, there was blood in the stool, which is not usual in the case of English cholera."

The coroner indicated the beads and the powder from the crushed seed, which now sat in a small glass jar on the table. "Can you be more precise, sir? I am told that these seeds found near the spot where the victims took ill are a virulent poison. Could this powder have done the mischief?"

The doctor took his time in examining the specimen, taking off his spectacles to peer into the jar in a vague, nearsighted fashion. "What are they? I am unfamiliar with this substance."

The coroner consulted his notes. "*Abrus precatorius,* also called wild licorice or the rosary pea."

"It's possible, I suppose," said the physician doubtfully. "The agent, whatever it is, has scoured the intestines and the stomach, causing ulcers. As to what it was, we must await the test results and hope they are conclusive."

Chapter Fifteen

"Yes, sir," said Garrod's sister Mrs. Yates, "on Thursday last, I restocked the teapoy with tealeaves and sugar from the pantry stores and sent a maid to return the key to Mr. Garrod. I never touched the key after that, though I knew it went missing for a few hours on the last day."

"He brewed a pot from this tea the day before the attack?"

"And locked up the teapoy afterward. Then on that terrible night, Mrs. Wolfe drank her tea without sugar and did not fall ill. That's why we all think the poison was in the sugar."

"So, as far as you know, the tea was fine?"

"Yes, sir."

At this juncture one of the jurymen asked leave to pose a question, which was granted. "Could the sugar have been contaminated before it came into the house, or could it have been got at before it left the kitchen?" asked the man.

The cook, who had already testified, opened her mouth to protest, but the coroner waved her to silence. "We've already heard that the sugar was locked up," he said, answering the man's question with some impatience. "We've no reason to question the cook's testimony. Sugar from this same supply had been used in the kitchen for several weeks. No, the tampering must have occurred while the teapoy sat in the hothouse." He turned back to Mrs. Yates. "What time was it that Mr. Garrod missed the key?"

"Close to ten o'clock. It was found again by three." At the

coroner's prompting she detailed the members of the household who had access to Hugo Garrod's dressing room.

"Why, that could be anyone," said Mrs. Yates.

"But, to be more precise in regard to the family, Miss Garrod was in her father's bedchamber that morning?"

"Yes, sir," she said. "And the valet."

Hugo Garrrod's valet added little to this account except to offer that his master had been so fond of the "cunning" teapoy as to make it unlikely he would be careless with his key. The valet was certain the key had been in the writing desk in the dressing room when Garrod went to bed the night before. As to his own movements on the morning of the poisoning, the valet testified that he had left the bedchamber around the same time as his master and had gone down to the servants' dining hall for a cup of coffee and a roll. But he thought he was gone for only about a half-hour. After that he'd returned to his work upstairs.

To Penelope, who had taken the valet's place in the witness chair, the coroner said, "You're quite sure it was this key Mr. Garrod discovered on the dais, ma'am?"

She nodded. "I noticed it particularly because the ring is distinctive, and he was so pleased to find it again. He attached the teapoy key to his watch fob and put the ring in his pocket."

"Later when you helped serve the tea, did you notice the key?"

"Mr. Garrod used it to unlock the teapoy." Penelope paused, looking uncertain. Her gaze sought and found Chase's, and he gave her a nod of encouragement.

"Who was present on the dais, ma'am?"

She listed the names; then the coroner said, "Not Mr. Honeycutt?"

"No, he had gone to look for his cousin Miss Garrod."

"And where was she?"

Addressing him calmly, she replied, "In the orangery with my brother, Lewis Durant. She was conducting him on a tour, and Mr. Honeycutt went to remind her that her father wanted her."

"So neither Mr. Honeycutt nor Miss Garrod was present when the poisoning occurred? How fortunate for both of them," murmured the coroner.

Penelope described the scene in the hothouse: the displaying of the teapoy, the dispensing of sugar and cream, the handing round of the cups. The coroner seemed interested that she had been asked to serve but accepted her explanation, saying only that he thought it a pity she would not be able to write her sketch of Hugo Garrod, after all.

"As to that," she said, "my plans are uncertain."

He nodded and returned to the tea party. "You noticed nothing out of the way, ma'am?"

"Nothing. No, that is not strictly accurate. I observed every detail with an unusual clarity. Afterward I wondered why I was not more surprised by what happened." She shook her head in frustration. "It's difficult to explain it to you, sir."

The coroner leaned forward in some excitement. "You can't mean you had a premonition?"

"Hardly that, but I suppose I was nervous. I'd been feeling that from the first moment I entered Mr. Garrod's home. It was…is…an unhappy one," she returned.

"Why unhappy?" inquired the coroner, seizing on this remark. "One of our most prosperous and well regarded families?"

"Mr. Garrod is dead, most likely at the hand of someone in his household. Nothing else makes sense. That is all I meant."

"Have you any suspicions to share with us, ma'am? Speak out if you do."

"I do not," she answered in a resolute tone.

The coroner did not press her further. As the afternoon advanced, several servants, including the under-gardener who found the wild licorice beads and the kitchen maid who had the confrontation with Marina Garrod, gave their testimony. Both darted sidelong looks at the girl as they perched in the witness chair, but only the under-gardener seemed to relish telling his tale. Marina sat through it all, a slender and erect figure, not even reacting when the jurymen began to whisper amongst themselves and look her way.

Though the kitchen maid emphasized that she herself had not viewed Marina's remark in the light of a serious threat, the coroner seemed to think otherwise. "You were right to tell us," he told the girl when she had difficulty stemming her tears. "The truth cannot harm an innocent person."

When it was Chase's turn, he described how he'd secured the suspect foodstuffs and inspected the lock on the teapoy.

In response to the coroner's request that he detail the procedures when a case of poisoning is suspected, Chase explained: "We inquire as to whether anyone prevented a doctor being called, was unwilling to leave the victim alone with other people, or hastened the funeral. None of which occurred in this case. We also determine whether the victim voiced any accusations on his deathbed or whether anyone had quarreled with him. Finally, we investigate whether anyone tampered with the evidence—to dispose of food or drink or of the poison itself."

"We know something of this nature occurred because the under-gardener swore to finding Miss Garrod's wild licorice beads," said the coroner.

"We know nothing of the kind. It's true the young lady wears a bracelet made of these beads. But the beads came from a necklace that had been broken. If *Abrus precatorius* was the poison, someone could have collected a sample, either from the necklace or the plant itself, which is grown in the hothouse, though in that event he would have needed to bore a hole in the seeds to make it seem they had come from the ornament. At all events, until we have the results of the chemical tests, there's no way to know whether the beads are of significance."

Seeing he was not believed, Chase took out his pocketbook and read out the description of Ned Honeycutt's argument with his uncle. "So, you see," he told the coroner, "we have other possibilities to explore. For another avenue of inquiry…" Here he reported Garrod's request for legal counsel and cryptic deathbed comments, concluding flatly with, "I have thought from the first that money was the motive for this crime."

"We should consider who is named heir? That's not much help unless we learn the terms of the will. I'm sure you would not wish to cast suspicion without proof." But as he spoke, the coroner persisted in eyeing Marina Garrod.

His train of thought was obvious when he next asked Chase to explain his presence in Clapham, listening with interest as Chase described the rubbish in Marina's reticule and the Obeah charm placed above Garrod's door. "How curious," the coroner said. "Do we have two such pranksters at Laurentum? The gardener Higgins has already testified that Miss Garrod apologized for destroying some blooms in the night. What can you tell me of this incident?"

"The destruction of the flowers was no prank, sir. Miss Garrod's maid had given her too strong a dose of laudanum. She wandered in her sleep and was unaware of her actions."

"Unaware?" the coroner echoed. Now his apprehension was plain. He wouldn't want to disoblige a wealthy and connected family by accusing its presumed heiress without solid reason, and yet he was worried. He would have heard the rumors about Miss Garrod's oddities—her behavior at parties, her determined isolation, her quicksilver moods. "What did Mr. Garrod tell you about his fears for his daughter?" he went on after a frowning silence.

This was the moment Chase had wished to avoid. At all costs he did not want to repeat the exact language Hugo Garrod had used in describing Marina's "delusion." But he was compelled to say at least: "Mr. Garrod did mention that the trickery had upset his daughter a good deal."

Curtly, the coroner told Chase to step down.

Then it was Ned Honeycutt's turn, and John Chase discovered he had underestimated Garrod's nephew. Honeycutt's explanation was simple: he'd long been a disappointment to his uncle, and he regretted his actions.

"One wishes to turn back the clock," Honeycutt told the jury with disarming frankness. "But that's impossible."

"You show yourself a man of proper sentiment," said the coroner. "But I must ask you, sir, had there been bad feeling between you and your uncle?"

Honeycutt studied him a moment before he spoke. "Ah, you've heard about my wretched debts. My uncle recently discovered I had borrowed a sum of money on my expectations and swore he would no longer pay my allowance until I proved myself penitent. Of course, he wasn't pleased with me. I am ashamed of myself." The jurymen watched him, some shaking their heads in disapproval, others rapt in this narrative of sin and redemption.

The coroner said sternly, "There's no denying it was very wrong of you and bound to look bad in the eyes of the world. I must say your timing was atrocious." He permitted himself a small smile. A jury member coughed.

"It wasn't *my* timing" was Honeycutt's reply. "I've no doubt I have enemies, for how else did word of my debts come to my uncle's ears?" He raised one hand and said in ringing tones, "I tell you straight out that I loved my uncle and would never harm him. Never. I'll challenge any man who dares say otherwise."

It seemed to Chase that the response to this was favorable. A sigh of sympathy went around the spectators. When the sensation had subsided, the coroner said, "Can you clarify the uncertainty surrounding your uncle's will? What did your uncle say on the subject? Had he ever threatened to disinherit you, for instance?"

He laughed. "Any number of times, but, no, I doubt it would ever actually have come to that."

"But your cousin, Miss Garrod?"

"Miss Garrod and I are not in competition for our inheritance. Any division of interests will not endure."

The coroner looked wise. "Ah, you expect to wed the lady?"

"It was my uncle's dearest wish. Today we've heard some thoughtless gossip about my cousin, and it's true her health has been...delicate. Believe me when I say her condition is nothing more than can be dealt with in the bosom of her family." He gazed at Marina and allowed his voice to soften. "You must allow that I know her better than anyone here. Who better to vouch for her than her affianced husband, the man anxious to relieve her from any unpleasant associations? I made a sacred promise on my uncle's deathbed, and I intend to honor it."

As Edward Buckler listened to Ned Honeycutt's testimony, he saw that the jurymen liked Garrod's nephew and were swayed by the display of tenderness for his young cousin. Still, enough had been hinted in Marina Garrod's disfavor that the court was bound to inquire further, especially in the absence of viable suspects.

It wasn't difficult for Buckler to appreciate the coroner's dilemma. The coroner was anxious to manage this high-profile case without mistakes. On the one hand, he approved of Honeycutt and thought that if something were indeed wrong with the girl, the private solution of a quiet marriage would be best for all concerned. On the other hand, a prominent resident had been poisoned, and it was the coroner's job to bring the crime home to someone if he could. Then, too, he could not have failed to observe the youth and beauty of Hugo Garrod's daughter as she tripped forward, lifted her veil, and turned a guileless smile upon him. So lovely, so fragile a girl could not be guilty of a heinous crime. And yet the coroner was bound to inquire. Edward Buckler knew that everything must depend upon the way Marina Garrod conducted herself on the stand.

She took the oath, arranged the folds of her dress, and awaited the first question.

"My condolences, Miss Garrod, on your tragic loss," said the coroner. He blinked as he took in the full effect of her large, liquid eyes and piquant face.

"Thank you, sir."

"You understand we would not trouble you at this time of grief if it were not absolutely necessary, ma'am?"

Marina clasped her hands in front of her. "But I want you to find the person who did this to my father. Ask me anything you wish."

The coroner sat back in his chair and studied her. At length, he said, "It's very good of you, Miss Garrod. Well, tell me about the conversation you had with the kitchen maid. You can understand why this might be interpreted as a threat, and certainly Daisy thought you were predicting that evil would come upon the house—as it now has."

"No, sir."

"Do you claim Daisy lied?"

"Merely that she misunderstood me. I found her questions impertinent, so I said what I did to quiet her." She raised those fathomless eyes to his. "I didn't like her vulgar curiosity about my mother."

A blush covered the coroner's cheeks, making it obvious he had heard something of Marina's history but had not expected the subject to be raised. Hesitantly, he said, "Your mother, Miss Garrod?"

"She was a slave on my father's plantation in Jamaica, sir. I thought everyone knew that." A few titters were heard in the room; then everyone got very quiet.

"I…I had heard something of that story, I do confess, ma'am. You cause me to remind the court that we also heard a hint from the gardener Higgins that your mother was some kind of native doctress, well versed in plant poisons. Forgive my rudeness." His voice quivered as he spoke.

"She used plants as remedies, not poisons. You should have asked Mr. Chase about that. He'll tell you himself that my mother once saved him when he was dying of the yellow fever."

Chase came forward. "Miss Garrod speaks the truth about her mother. But this has nothing to do with Mr. Garrod's death. May I suggest we move on, sir?"

"In good time," said the coroner, dismissing this interruption with a glance in Chase's direction. He collected himself for a renewed attack. "So you deny, Miss Garrod, that the seeds— identical to those worn around your wrist and that were found in the boiler room near where the victims took ill—had anything to do with your father's murder?"

"I didn't say that," she replied, demure.

This time the noise was deafening, and the bailiff had to raise his voice to quell the disorder. Chase uttered a smothered exclamation and stood in front of Marina's chair, willing her to look at him. But she resisted him.

Behind the coroner's assumed gravity, excitement blazed. "Explain yourself, Miss Garrod," he said when he could make himself heard.

"The *Abrus precatorius* seeds were deliberately placed there. The person who buried them hoped suspicion would fall on me. This person did it to torment me. It is this same person who murdered my father."

"An extraordinary assertion. Have you any proof, ma'am?"

She wouldn't look at him either, as though she feared to be silenced. "No proof, sir. But it was the same with the Obeah charm left above my father's door and the rubbish left in my reticule. There was another time that my cousin Ned didn't mention to you when someone put what I assumed was meant to be grave dirt in his bed."

"Grave dirt?" he said, appalled. "What is this superstition you mention?"

"Obeah? A spiritual practice from Africa carried out among the slaves, often by old men and women who came from that continent. More and more, it has been eradicated by the Christian missionaries."

"The intent of this practice?"

"It depends. Sometimes to offer a protective charm or a fortune-telling. An Obeah man or woman may also offer herbal remedies to cure disease."

"You were born on the island?"

"Yes, I was."

Again he stumbled a little over his words. "I'm sure you don't...subscribe to such notions."

"Of course I don't," she replied scornfully. "They say Obeah imposes on the credulous and encourages schemes of revenge and communion with spirits. They say it leads to wicked curses that cause harm and death. Many are afraid of it still—but its power depends on the belief in its validity."

Surprised at the frankness of this answer, the coroner asked the next question quickly. "What do you think of it? Is it good or evil?"

"Neither, sir. Only a human can be good or evil."

Chase, still hovering nearby, burst out: "Sir, this line of questioning is absurd. Miss Garrod is a gently bred Englishwoman who has been strictly reared in the Christian faith. She is very young and does not realize that she should guard her tongue. Allow me to speak to her in private."

Waving a disdainful hand, the coroner said, "So that you can tutor her, Mr. Chase? I think not. You must trust me to handle this witness."

As he listened to this exchange, Buckler had been thinking that Marina Garrod knew exactly what she was doing, though he understood why Chase was worried. His friend wore a look of unusual agitation, seeming too restless to remain in his place by the coroner's table. Buckler himself felt a heavy foreboding. Marina had decided to challenge her accusers, but this was a risky ploy in that it could easily feed the speculation about her lunacy. Lunacy was a subject to which Buckler had devoted a great deal of thought—too much thought. It was said that diseases of the mind had increased rapidly in recent years and that this affliction was increasingly common among the young. Buckler had fought a long battle with his own melancholia, fearing it might tip over some unseen ledge into something more alarming. And he knew how easily such ideas about a person could gain currency and become settled fact.

The coroner drummed his fingers on the table. "I must admit this testimony troubles me, since, as we've all heard, the seeds of an exotic plant are likely the agent that has taken the life of one person and nearly that of two others. Mr. Chase is correct in one thing. You must be careful what you say, Miss Garrod."

Chase said, "You've no right to browbeat the young lady, sir. Let her step down. She has just lost her father—"

"We have a poisoner among us," said the coroner, cutting him off. "Of all deaths, murder by poison is the most detestable and least preventable. How do we know but that the poisoner may strike again? It is my duty to get to the bottom of this matter."

Several jurymen gave wise nods at this juncture, but Chase folded his arms and assumed a belligerent stance. Abruptly, he glanced over his shoulder in Buckler's direction. And Buckler realized with a jolt that Penelope was looking at him too, her expression very troubled. He put his hand over hers for a moment and rose to his feet to approach the coroner's table.

"I wonder if I may be of service in drawing out this witness, sir?" he said, bowing. "I am Edward Buckler, a barrister of the Inner Temple."

Chapter Sixteen

The coroner was inclined to resent this interference but unsure how to reject it. He said, "You are too good, sir. But I believe we can dispense—"

"Let him do it," interrupted Chase. "Mr. Buckler is well-versed in the art of examination. You could do much worse in this fix."

Buckler smiled. "A moving tribute, John," he murmured. In truth, he wondered if he did right to thrust himself into these proceedings, but, obedient to his lady's will, he had not thought to refuse. Over his shoulder he saw that Penelope was giving him a look of encouragement. Foolish woman, he thought fondly, glad to take action and lay aside the stark depression he'd been feeling ever since she'd told him their relationship must come to an end. He supposed it was worth it to interfere if he could be of use to Chase. Besides, Marina Garrod intrigued him. What was she about here? As usual in these situations, he could hear the voice of his lawyer friend Ezekiel Thorogood advising him to charge to the rescue of some unfortunate: *On your feet, Buckler. Any action is better than nothing.*

Trying to be tactful, he said, "I am more than happy to put myself at your disposal, sir."

As the coroner started to shake his head, Samuel Tallboys, both vicar and magistrate in this parish, called from his seat, "A capital idea. Mr. Buckler may be able to help us shed some light here. Why not make use of his considerable experience?"

"You know this man?" asked the coroner.

"He is a well-known Old Bailey lawyer, whose name is often in the papers. Mr. Chase had already mentioned him to me as a possible resource. Do remember that Miss Garrod is a minor under my wing. I am responsible for her, and I say let Mr. Buckler question her."

"He'll demand a fee for his services. You hold the purse strings, Mr. Tallboys. You know we can't afford it." Though he protested, the coroner's tone toward the much older man remained deferential.

Buckler put in quickly, "I would be happy to do this for you at no charge, to see justice done."

Left with no more to say, the coroner sat back, looking sulky. Buckler turned to Marina. "First, I must tell you that you are not charged with any crime. I wish to allow you to tell your story more fully. Will you answer my questions?"

"Willingly," she said, her voice steady.

"Good. Let's begin. My friend Mr. Chase was hired to discover who has been making you the mark of a secret malice. Is that correct?"

"Yes, sir. My father was worried about me."

"What were these tricks? Describe them, if you please."

"Some of my possessions would appear and reappear to make it seem I had been absent-minded. My shawl was slashed with a knife. There was the dirt put in Ned's bed to make it look I had played a vindictive game with him—and the same rubbish put in my reticule to embarrass me. The worst of all was the light that would be seen at night in the garden. Someone would throw a handful of gravel at my window to awaken me. Sometimes I would go outside to try to catch the trickster. But I never could."

"That sounds most distressing, Miss Garrod," said Buckler.

"It was." There were tears in her eyes, and she raised a handkerchief to her face and staunched them angrily.

"How did this treatment affect you, ma'am?"

"I was never comfortable in society, sir. The rooms always seemed too bright and too loud for me. Too many richly dressed strangers who knew nothing about me. But this made it all so much worse. I'm afraid I disappointed my father with my awkwardness, but, indeed, I could not help it."

"I am as certain that your father loved you dearly as I am of my own belief in your account, Miss Garrod. I hope you may take comfort in that." This was not said just for effect, he realized. He did believe in the girl and wanted to help her for her own sake. He waited until he thought her ready to resume. The spectators weren't sure what to make of Marina Garrod. She made a convincing witness, but there was something about the way she opposed the world that made them uneasy. From his long experience in reading the mood of a courtroom, Buckler could feel their doubts surging around him. The whispers grew in volume.

He signaled for quiet and turned back to the witness. "What do you think was the motive for these tricks?"

"To lower me in my father's eyes. To make it plain to him that I could never belong here. And it worked."

"You think this person would go so far as to poison your father? You can see why that would seem improbable to an unbiased observer. It must seem an exaggerated fancy."

"I don't know why! There must be a reason."

"Miss Garrod," he said gently, "it will be said that you are not to be credited because you have become disordered in your mind. It is known you take a powerful opiate to sleep. And you tell us that you have sometimes left the safety of your bedchamber to wander in the night, performing acts you only imperfectly recall."

"Yes."

"For instance, you destroyed some of your father's flowers in the presence of Mrs. Wolfe?"

Her head drooped, as though her fatigue were suddenly intense. "I did that, yes. I was dreaming of uprooting weeds from the garden. It's true I was not myself that night."

"So you can see why this behavior might be questioned, especially in view of the recent tragedy at Laurentum? Why didn't you tell anyone about your persecution and ask for help?"

"Why?" she cried. "Because I don't trust any of them."

Not a sound could be heard in the court as Marina made this pronouncement. Even the journalists had lifted their pens from their notebooks to stare at the witness in fascination. Feeling a sudden reluctance to continue, Buckler glanced at Chase, who gave a sharp nod. *Carry on*, it said.

"Your family?" said Buckler. "The family that has nurtured you and showered you with the gifts of fortune—and love?"

"They don't love me. They only pretend and scheme for their own advantage."

That was enough, Buckler judged. He moved on. "Let's have it out, Miss Garrod. It will be better for you to answer these questions now rather than later. Did you take the loose beads from your necklace and crush them to make a powder?"

"I did not."

"Have you any notion how the wild licorice beans came to be in the boiler room?"

"None."

"You are on your Bible oath, ma'am," he reminded her. "Did you tamper with the sugar or with any other foodstuff in the household?"

Marina's lips tightened, and she gazed back at him somberly. "A wicked person did that. No, I was not the one."

"Why did you leave your bed the other night?"

"I saw the light again. Mr. Durant and Mr. Chase saw it, too."

Buckler could feel the attention swinging toward Chase, but his friend stayed by the coroner's table, his expression impassive, though his jaw was rigid. Buckler also saw that Lewis had laid one hand on his sister's arm as she leaned forward, intent on the questioning. Most of the spectators had probably never been out of England, and it struck Buckler how strange this encounter must seem to them. They would be shocked, too, by the young girl's charges against her family. Most would deem her ungrateful and shockingly indecorous to speak these words in public.

"Miss Garrod, have any measures been taken to keep you from your friends or restrict your movements? Has your liberty been restrained in any way?"

"Never, sir."

"Knives are not withheld from you, for example? No one has expressed a reluctance to leave you alone? You are not considered a threat to yourself or others?"

"Never."

"In fact, you spent the last few months mixing in the best society and pursuing all the normal activities of a debutante?"

She smiled at him. "Yes, sir."

Buckler bowed to the coroner "I believe that is all for the moment, sir, unless you have other questions to pose?"

He seemed uncertain. "Thank you, Mr. Buckler," he said at last. "You have given us much to think on. The hour grows late. We will adjourn these proceedings pending the results of the chemical tests."

"An appropriate decision, sir," said Buckler.

"I own I'm ready for some refreshment," said the coroner, stretching and glancing toward his companions. The jury brightened, the spectators stirred in their hard chairs, and conversations began to break out. One or two people got to their feet and began to edge toward the exit. Others remained to watch the final moments of the play.

Buckler put out a hand to help Marina to her feet. Chase, Penelope, and Lewis joined them, forming a tight circle around the girl.

"Let's go," said Chase urgently.

Tallboys was there too. "Marina, how could you say such things? My dear girl, I am beyond words. Come let us go home, where we can speak privately." He pushed rudely by Lewis, sweeping past the journalists who, scenting blood, had started to converge. "At once, Marina," he snapped.

Chase said, "Allow me to escort Miss Garrod. I am better able to deal with the riffraff than you, Mr. Tallboys."

A few feet away, Honeycutt looked as if he was about to come to blows with the reporters. Chase strode over, grasped Honeycutt's arm, and drew him away. "Do you want to figure in the press as the man who started a fight at your uncle's inquest? Don't be an ass."

"Mr. Chase is right, Ned," said Mrs. Yates. She wrapped an arm around Marina, but the girl shook her off. An arrested expression showed on the old woman's face, and she shrank back, her eyes wide. At this, Marina began to sob with deep, hopeless gasps that seemed torn from her body.

Lewis said, "Don't be distressed, Miss Garrod. A cup of tea in your own room at home will revive you." Then he became tongue-tied, having realized the implications of this artless sentence.

Her shoulders heaving, Marina choked out, "I understood the kindness meant in your remark, Mr. Durant."

Chase used his walking stick to clear a path, and they made their way out of the courtroom. With high-handed dispatch, he got Marina and Lewis into the carriage with Buckler and Penelope, jumped on the box, and instructed the coachman to drive on. A scowling Ned Honeycutt was left to accompany his aunt and Mr. Tallboys back to Laurentum.

◇◇◇

As evening fell, Buckler and Penelope walked through a small wilderness of beech trees and followed the path, which led by a moderate ascent to the summerhouse. It was a stone, octagonal structure with a bell-shaped roof and cupola from which a statue of Mercury pierced the cool, blue sky. After pausing to admire the statue, they went up the stairs and stepped through a door set between Ionic columns. Inside they found walls decorated with paintings of the seasons and a row of windows that framed a serene view of the surrounding fields. In the foreground they glimpsed the corner of the farmyard and piggery; in the distance the city steeples blurred to extinction in the waning day.

Having opened a window to admit the air, Buckler turned from a contemplation of the meadows to study his love. She looked tired after several sleepless nights, and this touched him and filled him with misgiving. He knew his duty: he must persuade her to leave Laurentum that very night. Even though the inquest was not complete, she had already given her testimony and was unlikely to be recalled. She would not attend the funeral, which was to take place on the following day, though

Buckler himself was to remain in Clapham. Surprisingly, Ned Honeycutt had taken him aside on their return to the villa and had requested he make himself available in case the coroner should again summon Marina.

"You've shown you'll stand by her," Honeycutt had said. "Of course, we must give you a bed here in the meantime."

"I am comfortable at the pub," Buckler had objected.

"That won't do. You'll be pestered. I believe the journalists have taken over the place." So Buckler had allowed a servant to be sent to collect his shaving gear and clean shirt.

Now Penelope said abruptly, "Did you observe John's face when Marina Garrod was testifying? He seemed so grieved."

"Natural, isn't it? The girl has fought him at every turn."

"I suppose you're right." She added on a tentative note, "The evidence against Miss Garrod is merely circumstantial and not very persuasive at that. Do you agree?"

"That's common in poisoning cases," he answered, carefully nonchalant, for he did not want to encourage Penelope's investigative instincts on this occasion.

She sat down on one of the chairs covered in red silk cushions. Untying the strings of her bonnet, she removed it and set it aside on the table, a beautiful piece inlaid with several different kinds of tropical woods. As she ran her hand over its polished surface, Buckler watched the thoughts chasing across her mobile features. Her pallor and the dark circles under her eyes were pronounced, and he felt the urgent need to keep her safe. Recollections of that horrific tea party had been keeping him awake too.

Her hand stilled. "Don't you think, Edward, that it's all rather convenient?"

"You mean the campaign of suspicion against Miss Garrod?"

"All the stories intended to discredit her. The effort to make her look unbalanced. She's little more than a child, certainly not a monster."

He went to sit with her. "She was very adult today, self-possessed and entirely rational. But, Penelope, the deranged often seem sane. It is sometimes only on one topic that a lunatic reveals his mania. Reasoning well from false premises—that's the essence of delusion. I have met such people. Once I was asked to defend a patient who had been confined to a private madhouse. It was one of the few times Thorogood was fooled into taking an unworthy case. The madman was that convincing. We lost on our writ of *habeas corpus*. The doctors produced witness after witness to prove his insanity. The man had threatened to stab his own wife multiple times."

"You don't believe that of Marina."

"No," he admitted, "but it is wise to be cautious. Don't worry. Chase will uncover the truth."

She seemed unimpressed with this response. "*We* must help him. You're right. I would be better off at home, but how can I turn my back on John? You do remember all he did for me—for Lewis?"

Buckler concealed his frustration. Evenly, he said, "There is no *we* in this inquiry, Penelope. A murderer is at large. All the more reason for you and Lewis to remove from this house tonight. Chase expects it of you. I assured him you wouldn't make difficulties."

"And I won't," she replied, her face shuttering. "Tomorrow after the funeral will be soon enough. I understand you. The culprit is one of them. One of the family."

"Whom do you suspect?"

"I don't know. Mr. Honeycutt seems eager to leap to his cousin's defense. Do you trust him?"

"No."

"His sister? What a piece of work she is. Perhaps you as an unsuspecting gentleman cannot discern the spite behind her treatment of Marina, but I was conscious of it from the first. She both envies and hates the girl, Edward. That Mr. Tallboys is left Marina's guardian, I understand, but he doesn't approve of her either. And did you see how Mrs. Yates retreated from her in the courtroom? Not much love there, as Marina herself told everyone. Oh, I admired her in that moment. She is so young and friendless, but she spoke out on her own behalf."

"Don't you see that Lewis has become too involved with Miss Garrod? Aside from any danger we might have to fear, he'll only be hurt. Take him home tonight, Penelope. If you ask him, he'll go."

Her gaze drifted to the open window. "He won't. He's every bit as determined to stay as you are that he should go." She paused, turning inward. "Don't you think I've been worrying and planning how to make a place for Lewis in the world? I curse my father sometimes for his sublime indifference, his selfishness. He leaves his infant son to fend for himself, never reveals his existence to a soul, and makes no attempt to contact him." She jumped to her feet and took several agitated steps across the floor.

"Your father was wrong." Buckler followed her and grasped her by the shoulders. "None of that matters right now, Penelope."

It was as though she hadn't heard him. "Then there is Jeremy. I don't know where he is or if he might ever decide to return to us. Nor do I want him. I don't think I could ever live in the same house with him again. I won't have Sarah disappointed." Finally, she looked fully at him, her eyes hard and bright. "I haven't told you about my father's letter. He is anxious that Sarah and I remove to Sicily. Well, I won't go."

"Penelope—"

"No, Edward. You want to help me, and I respect your opinion. But I must do what I feel is right. This is not the first time you have tried to direct my conduct, and it won't wash. If we were wed—"

His control broke, and he pulled her closer. He was kissing her, and the blood was roaring in his ears. She melted under his hands until at length she raised her head to look at him, a glint of humor in her eyes. "That's all very well, sir, but can alter nothing."

He laughed and released her. "Even though I love you, Penelope?"

"You don't fight fair, Edward," she told him as she smoothed her hair and tried to quiet her quickened breathing. "You deprive me of my weapons."

"I fight for you, always." He paused, knowing what he was about to say would cut her deep, yet he must say it: "Sarah needs you. You can't take the risk."

Her face went white, first with distress, then with anger. Before she could answer him, the door to the summerhouse opened.

Chapter Seventeen

Lewis and Marina stepped over the threshold. Lewis observed his sister's startled expression and stiffened in response. Damn it—it needed only that, thought Buckler, exasperated. A time or two recently he'd fancied Lewis had begun to question his relationship with Penelope, though he hadn't, so far, asserted any brotherly rights. As the boy came forward, looking down his nose at them from his greater height, his newfound maturity was evident. Penelope was right about the determination; there was a pugnacious tilt to his chin.

Lewis said to his sister, "There you are. We've been looking for you. Mrs. Yates said you'd come in this direction."

Hiding her embarrassment, Penelope answered him casually. "We were taking the evening air and happened upon this lovely summerhouse. Miss Garrod, is it wise for you to be out without your guard? Mr. Chase was most insistent that you be protected."

Marina Garrod stood close to Lewis. She was garbed in a fresh black gown and a pair of delicate sandals, her hair confined in a dark braid that snaked down her back and twitched as she moved. She pointed at the door, where one of the constables trailed on her heels. "Don't worry, Mrs. Wolfe. He's there. I would escape him if I could."

"Orders, miss," said the man.

"Take yourself off," cried Marina. "I have something to say to Mr. Buckler and Mrs. Wolfe in private." She made an imperious gesture. "I can scarcely stir without that man."

Buckler addressed the constable. "Why don't you withdraw to those trees over there? We'll leave the door ajar so that you can keep Miss Garrod in sight. Will that suit?"

"Yes, sir," said the man, withdrawing.

"Won't you sit down, ma'am?" said Buckler to Marina.

After she had consented, somewhat grudgingly, to take a seat, they waited until the constable was out of earshot. Then Buckler said, "Where is Mr. Chase? He should hear this too."

"He's coming," said Lewis. "We just saw him on the terrace."

Marina spoke. "Before he arrives, I must thank you for your assistance at the inquest today, Mr. Buckler."

"I'm not at all certain I did you any lasting good."

She studied him, and Buckler was sure Penelope was wrong to consider her little more than a child; Marina Garrod had a presence rare in someone her age. He couldn't account for it, but perhaps she'd been refined, made stronger and brighter, by her unhappy life. "No, you did me good," she said at last, "and I hope you can do something more for me. I want you and Mr. Chase to advise me." As if on cue, they heard Chase's voice calling a remark to the constables and his footsteps crossing the gravel.

"We are at your service, Miss Garrod," said Buckler.

"I know you are."

"Glad you've realized that," said Chase who had entered at that moment. He frowned at Marina, nodded at Buckler, ignored Lewis, and cast a searching stare at Penelope. He stood at the other end of the table, a little apart from the group. This was Chase at his most forbidding: he was as tall as Lewis and twice as sure of himself. He was also laconic and resolute and fuming with irritation. His recent improvement in dress had vanished to be replaced by a half-buttoned waistcoat and dusty boots.

Marina didn't flinch. "My one wish is that my father's murderer be discovered. I can have neither peace nor safety until then."

"So you want my help?" said Chase.

"Exactly, sir." She smiled at him and went on in a strangely blithe tone. "I already told you I had a longing to learn more of my mother. No one would say a word to me on the subject. My father would tell me I was to consider myself an English girl and must forget all about her. I couldn't do that."

"I imagine that would be difficult," said Buckler, feeling awkward. He saw that Lewis leaned over the back of her chair and suddenly understood the bond that had formed between them. Both were love children. Both had been motherless with mothers who could not be mentioned in polite company. Both had strained relationships with the family left to them, though Lewis had been lucky in his sister at least.

Marina spoke. "You understand me, don't you, Mr. Chase? You've met her—you've met Joanna. For years I kept quiet and did as I was told. I learned my lessons and studied to please my family. I knew none of them liked me, not really. But I wasn't afraid of them. No one bothered me until my father started planning my grand London season and talking day and night of my marriage. That's when it started."

"The malice," said Penelope. "It was intended to ruin your chances at fulfilling your father's dearest wish. The feathers and the rest of the superstitions were to make you seem irrational and foreign, as if you didn't belong and couldn't play your part as your father's heiress. The trickster aimed to revive the stories about your mother being an Obeah woman."

"More than that, Mrs. Wolfe," said Marina. "I was to figure as mad enough to believe I could follow in her footsteps. English Obeah to get revenge on those I fancied had been unkind to me."

"Why then did you play into their hands by expressing an interest in botany and Jamaican culture?" said Chase.

"I knew you'd ask me that." She sought reassurance from Lewis, who had sat down at her side. Not seeming to like Chase's confrontational tone, he clasped Marina's hand.

"Well?"

"I hated them, Mr. Chase. It was the only way I could punish them—by flaunting my past. I found that necklace on my pillow one evening. It was intended to frighten me, but I wore it and refused to remove it. I watched them all. I would ask my questions and see how they reacted."

Chase seemed unsurprised by this answer. Suddenly he grinned down at her, pulled up a chair opposite hers, and said, "Good girl." As Marina flushed with pleasure, he added, "Which of them is your enemy, Miss Garrod? You must have some idea. Or is it all of them? A conspiracy to defraud you of your inheritance?"

"I don't know who it is. It often seemed my father didn't trust them either. It's been worse lately. They stop talking whenever I enter a room."

"They all have motive," said Buckler, "depending on the terms of the will. Did Mr. Garrod ever mention to you how he intended to leave matters?"

She shook her head. "He wouldn't have discussed that with me, but I know he changed his mind frequently. He used to summon Ned to his study to hint at the current plan. By the next week, it was on to something else. Ned used to get so wild with him, but my father said he deserved this treatment because he kept exceeding his allowance. I must go back before they miss me."

Buckler heard the rustle of her gown as she moved toward the door, but then she turned back, as if some fresh worry had struck her. "You heard I was born into slavery? Is…is the position of a manumitted person in any jeopardy should she be accused of a crime?"

He was puzzled. "You mean the manumission itself?"

"I just wondered if I could ever be deported back to Jamaica."

"How should that be, Miss Garrod? You're a free woman with the papers to prove it. At all events, Lord Mansfield's decision in the Somersett case made it clear that slavery cannot exist in England. Even if you did not have these papers, having set foot on English soil, you can't be forced back into bondage."

"I thought so," she said gravely. "Still it was as well to be certain."

Buckler hesitated, then said, "I hope you'll forgive my frankness, ma'am, but there's a law that limits the amount individuals of mixed race can inherit to two thousand pounds in Jamaican currency. I understand this law is likely to soon be overturned." He was human enough to enjoy Chase's raised eyebrows but explained, "I've been browsing in Mr. Garrod's library."

"I've heard my father speak of this law," said Marina. "He's had many consultations with his lawyers on the subject. But he said I'd received something called a privilege grant that made everything all right. As if I'd been worried about it!"

Everyone looked at her blankly except Buckler, who said, "Miss Garrod's circumstances are not unusual among the Jamaican planters. The privilege grant bestows most of the rights of an English citizen. One can also obtain an exemption from the inheritance statute. The inheritance exemption is rare and difficult to obtain."

"No doubt Mr. Garrod managed it," said Chase dryly. "Illegitimacy is no bar?"

"None." Buckler glanced at Lewis.

Marina said, "My father was always so worried about challenges to his will. He used to say that the John Crow vultures would pick his carcass clean as soon as he died. He wanted to be sure I would not be taken advantage of."

Buckler wished more than anything to reassure her, but he owed her the truth. "You haven't yet reached your majority, ma'am. You are entirely subject to the will of your guardians."

"That I was aware of." She flipped her braid over her shoulder with quick impatience. "Aside from that, I am entitled to the rights of an English citizen? The right of property and inheritance? The right to a defense when accused? The right to liberty once exonerated?"

Buckler bowed. "I devoutly hope so. Else we would all find England a barbarous land indeed."

Silence fell among them, as she looked into Buckler's face, her lips trembling a little as she tried to repress her emotion. A noise made them look toward the door to find the constable peering in. Before Marina could berate him, Buckler said, "Lewis, Chase and I will convey your sister back to the house. Why don't you take Miss Garrod?"

"Yes, sir." His eyes went to his sister. "Are you coming soon?" She nodded. "I need to speak to you anyway. Edward and I have been talking about our removal after the funeral tomorrow. We have overstayed our welcome."

"No," said Lewis and Marina in unison.

"Lewis," said Penelope, "I feel as you do, but it's best…I had no thought to be away from Sarah for more than a few days."

"You must go home, Penelope. But I cannot, not yet. I won't do it. I'll take a room at the pub if necessary."

Marina Garrod looked at the floor. "I understand that you miss your little girl, Mrs. Wolfe, but may I ask you to leave Mr. Durant with me for a few days more? His company is of great value to me at present."

Lewis said, "Don't be a little fool, Marina. Of course, I'm staying. Penelope, you go, and I'll return to London in a few days."

"I'm not leaving you," Penelope protested.

Buckler made an inarticulate sound, and Chase said, "This is all very pretty, but I have a murderer to catch. Miss Garrod, will you trust me to protect you?" He held out his hands to her, a hint of vulnerability showing in his face.

Marina raised her eyes to meet the keen gaze and gave his hands a firm squeeze. "Yes, I will, Mr. Chase."

Chapter Eighteen

Mrs. Yates sat with her worsted work in her lap. Her needle rested; her ears caught every word of the conversation. Her head was slightly cocked, her gaze firm and aloof, as it pivoted from one speaker to the next. She put in a word or two, only when there was need. Beatrice Honeycutt had arranged herself in a black lacquer and gilt armchair, its gold cushion gleaming dully against her stiff, black gown. She draped one arm along the back of her chair and leaned toward her brother, who lounged on a sofa, his eyes like bits of blue fire between half-closed lids. Beatrice's face was smooth, unreadable, but varied expressions flickered across the translucent skin of Ned Honeycutt, glowing warm, blazing hot, chilling pale, his voice rising and falling. Ned spoke of nothings: a party he and his sister had both attended, a morsel of scandal, the prospect of boredom during the period of mourning, hopes for his future. Beatrice answered him with a laugh, an exclamation of derision, a weary frown, a shake of the head, on cue. The door opened. The clergyman, sedate and slow, crossed the room to join them. Mr. Tallboys sat and spread the skirts of his coat on the sofa. He planted his feet in front of him and settled his broad back pleasurably, his greeting loud and authoritative.

The room darkened; the shadows lengthened and pointed across the wine-dark carpet to creep into the farther corners. It was Mrs. Yates' job to attend to the candles, but she sat on, perhaps forgetful. It was so dark now that Penelope Wolfe could no longer see her book. She had been watching them in a sort of daydreaming way. She didn't think they could have forgotten her perched in the window seat, for Beatrice and Mrs. Yates both looked over at her from time to time, and Penelope sometimes caught a hostile flash from behind the housekeeper's spectacles. Penelope thought about seeking out Buckler and Chase, who had escaped to the library or Lewis who had gone to his room, but for some reason she shrank from showing herself and making her excuses.

"Do light the candles, aunt," said Beatrice at last. Mrs. Yates put her sewing aside and fetched the tinderbox from the mantel. She circled the room, lighting a branch on each console table, another on the small table between Honeycutt and Beatrice, and one more near Penelope.

"Where's Marina?" said Honeycutt to his sister in an indifferent tone.

"Gone up to bed early."

"My God, did you hear her today? No, I forgot. You weren't there, but Aunt Anne must have told you. Are you feeling better, Bea?"

Beatrice's mouth hardened. "A day of rest and reflection has restored me. Yes, I heard about Marina. Were you surprised? I wasn't."

"I tried to mend matters, but she ruined my efforts. There's bound to be even more talk now. Just what we needed."

"You did very well, Ned," put in Mrs. Yates, pausing with a heavy silver candlestick in her hand. "Marina owes you her gratitude, though she won't own to that. She quite frightens me. When I think—"

"Hush," said Beatrice.

"She won't find it easy to get around me, Mrs. Yates," said Mr. Tallboys, lacing his fingers over his stomach. "We shall see what's what once the funeral is behind us and the will read. One could wish Hugo would have directed the girl's education better, but I won't speak ill of him. I owe him my gratitude for the rest of my days." He smiled at the housekeeper. "I've just been in to say prayers over him. The undertaker has done a commendable job with the hangings and the coffin ornaments, ma'am. I felt such a sense of peace sitting there. Your arrangements are most tasteful."

"Thank you, sir. I wanted all to be as it should," said Mrs. Yates.

"May I take this opportunity to say a word? Hugo's death can make no difference in your domestic arrangements. Everything will go on as before if I have any say in the matter, depending on his instructions, which must be sacred to me. I thought you'd like to know that."

"You are kindness indeed, Mr. Tallboys."

Ned Honeycutt came to stand over Penelope. "Will you and your brother be leaving us, ma'am? I wish we could have made your acquaintance under better circumstances. My uncle regarded your talents highly."

It was a less than subtle hint, and there was no other response than to say they would depart in the morning and voice her conventional thanks.

Mrs. Yates said, "You'll be anxious to see your daughter. She will have missed your care. I've long wanted to ask you, ma'am, about a pamphlet that Mr. Garrod insisted was of your authorship. 'The Proper Rearing of Children.' It was you, wasn't it?"

Penelope was surprised. She had published this pamphlet under a *nom-de-plume*, her usual practice. Her husband had asked so little of her in regard to wifely obedience that she had felt she should comply with his wishes in this one area. In any event, this had seemed a wise business decision, for what lady would take parenting advice from a woman whose family had become notorious? The pamphlet Mrs. Yates referred to had been quickly produced and sold. "How did you know?"

Now flanking her nephew, Mrs. Yates said, "My brother recognized your description of your education abroad, and you mentioned rearing a young daughter. I must tell you, Mrs. Wolfe, I take issue with your claims."

"Indeed?"

"You argue that a parent must not quell a child's natural inclination or risk destroying all that is pure and good in him. And yet it is a mother's duty to govern her offspring."

"Cannot a mother govern through love and respect?"

"Of course. But she must shun corruption, or the world will call her dangerously naïve. I know what of I speak, Mrs. Wolfe. That is why so many of the Creoles send their children to school in England."

Mr. Tallboys looked up, saying heartily, "Quite right, Mrs. Yates, though Miss Honeycutt must be a shining exception to this rule since she spent her formative years in Jamaica. In general, however, your point is indisputable. I myself deplore the license of modern youth, which is so often due to a lack of proper vigilance and control on the part of their elders."

"I do not see that bad influences or simply bad luck are easily avoided anywhere," said Penelope.

"Do you apply this philosophy to your own daughter, ma'am?" asked Beatrice.

"Too much indulgence is unwise, but I've always thought that children are born with a spark of the divine that society is too eager to stamp out. It is arrogant to think we have the power to create human nature."

There seemed little more to say on this subject, but the ladies of the house were not finished with her. "Your husband endorses your ideas, Mrs. Wolfe?" pursued Beatrice, her eyebrows a little elevated.

"Indeed he does, Miss Honeycutt. He allows Sarah to grow freely." Since Jeremy had never done anything more than sweep in and play games with his daughter when the mood struck him and when he happened to be around in the first place, this was disingenuous. But they were not to know that.

"A shame that Mr. Wolfe is missing so many of these joys. Children do grow fast," Beatrice observed. "Do you expect his return soon?"

"I'm afraid I don't know," Penelope said, keeping her tone even.

After a short silence, Mrs. Yates said: "A pity. Will Mr. Buckler accompany you back to London, ma'am?"

"Mr. Honeycutt has asked him to stay on for a day or two."

The housekeeper's cold eyes were on Penelope. "Such a handsome man. He is a good friend of yours, is he not? Have you known him long?"

Penelope had had enough. She rose to her feet. "A very good friend. I've known him and Mr. Chase for nearly two years." She waited a moment before she said, seemingly at random, "How fortunate we are that this tragedy was not so much worse. Mr. Buckler nearly drank the tea with the poison but was, by God's grace, prevented in time. Miss Honeycutt and Mr. Tallboys"— here she curtsied insolently in their direction—"were endangered but survived, though, come to think of it, Mr. Tallboys might have avoided his danger altogether had he not changed his mind about which variety of sugar to take at the last minute. And you, ma'am"—she looked full into the older woman's face—"set aside your own tea to attend to your duties, which probably saved your life. Curious that our fate may depend on such trifles." With this, Penelope got herself out of the room.

John Chase stared up at the blue damask valance above his bed. Uncomfortable with the feeling of confinement, he'd pushed back the hangings as far as they would go and cracked his window to admit air. It was no good. Every time he dropped off, he found himself surrounded on all sides by water, as though he'd put to sea. A glinting sheet of ocean would burst upon his sight, and he would jerk awake, the thoughts starting to jostle around in his brain again like waves slapping the hull of a ship.

He couldn't think of a single task left undone. The constables would return in the morning to help him keep watch on the heiress. Hugo Garrod's study and library had been locked up tightly at the lawyers' direction. The letter from Bow Street, which Chase had answered before bed, lay on the hall table, ready to be posted. *For God's sake, get this one right,* he'd been urged. A primary concern, the chief magistrate said, was that

Garrod's extensive business affairs must not be thrust into chaos. Representatives from the merchant house of Garrod, Bentley, and Stern, had waited upon Bow Street. They wanted the matter resolved, with or without the cooperation of the local authorities.

Reading this missive, Chase had been relieved to find no mention of Marina Garrod. What would happen once her testimony had been reported in the papers? Would the whispers about her die away or continue to spread unchecked? He had conquered his own doubts and was determined to do his best for the girl. Penelope and Lewis believed in her innocence; Buckler did too, though it was his way to hold back and question, no doubt because of his cynical, melancholic nature. But Marina's story had impressed them all with its truth, and Chase wished he could get her out of this house until the murderer was caught.

He shifted his knee to find a more comfortable position, closing his eyes. He knew he must sleep, but instead he rehearsed his next steps. First, a message to Noah Packet to find out if he'd had any luck in tracing the medicine bottle. Why strip off the label unless there was something to hide, Chase thought, not for the first time. Second, another round of interviews with the family, though the ceremonies of death were an obstacle since the bereaved could and did avoid him without excuse. Finally, a talk with Lewis. Blast the boy—he must leave with his sister tomorrow. Chase would not hesitate to thrust him in the coach himself, even over Penelope's objections. And yet he was glad Buckler would not accompany them. It would be good to have the support of one of his friends in Clapham. Besides, he felt an unworthy satisfaction in separating Buckler and Penelope. Chase didn't think he was jealous exactly, but it did seem that matters should not be allowed to go too far. He didn't want Penelope's peace cut up any more than it already was. With Jeremy Wolfe a ghostly fact of life for both his friends, there was no obvious solution to the tangle.

Exasperated, he punched his pillow into shape and stilled his breathing. This time, instead of the rocking sensation jarring him awake, he relaxed into it and felt a sudden joy as the deck of a ship heaved beneath his feet. He rarely thought about his navy days—such thoughts were too sore, to be put doggedly aside. Now he raised a hand to his brow to shield his eyes from the glare and strode smoothly to the helm, conscious that he felt no pain, only ease and rightness. His son Jonathan, the boy he'd never met, was at his side, and Chase was teaching him how to make his calculations and steer the little craft. In the dream, Jonathan called a remark, and Chase threw one arm about his son's shoulder and set the other on the tiller.

After that he must have slept for an hour or two until a scream tore through the silence.

Doors banged open. Voices called out. John Chase lit a candle and hobbled down the corridor. He launched himself down the stairs at an unsafe pace, using the banister for balance. On the first floor landing, all was dark except for the prick of another candle, which cast a circle of illumination on the people clustered around Marina Garrod's open door. Chase saw Lewis, Penelope, Buckler, Beatrice Honeycutt, and a few servants looking on.

"John!" called Penelope.

"What's happened?"

"I don't know. Mr. Honeycutt just went in to see."

When Chase pushed into the room, he found Ned Honeycutt looming over his cousin. Marina sat bolt upright in the center of the bed. She appeared drained of identity in the dimness, her features blurred by terror and the remains of sleep. Before Chase could intervene, Honeycutt had dealt her a slap across the face. She cradled her cheek and stared at him, too shocked to cry.

Rage exploded in Chase. He grabbed Honeycutt by the scruff of his nightshirt, spinning him on his heels. His fist smashed into the other man's jaw, and blood from his lip spurted over Chase's hand. Chase drew back to hit him a second time but stopped. He let go, stepping back. At that moment, Lewis rushed into the room. He gave a cry and threw himself on Honeycutt to rain down more blows.

Edward Buckler was there too. "Enough," he roared, dragging Lewis away. Lewis eyed him, unrepentant, then looked toward his sister. She was kneeling on the floor at the foot of the bed, where the housekeeper Anne Yates huddled in an untidy heap of sprawled limbs. Wispy gray hair escaped her cap, which was askew, and she trembled violently as she struggled to one elbow. Honeycutt brushed aside Buckler's restraining arm. He snatched up the candle Chase had left on the nightstand. Dropping to his knees, he held it close to his aunt so that the flame was reflected in her spectacles, glancing off her yellowed teeth and the red cavern of her open mouth.

Beatrice rushed to their assistance. "Aunt, are you injured? Help me with her, Ned." The sound of Beatrice's voice seemed to penetrate the housekeeper's stupor. She folded her lips and shuddered. "Thank God, you came," she said brokenly.

"Can you speak to us?" said Beatrice.

"She flew out at me. She crept down to the drawing room and took the stitchery scissors from my workbox. Wicked, wicked creature."

Chase approached the bed. One hand emerged from the folds of Marina's nightgown, and a gleam caught the candlelight. "What's that?" he said.

"Be careful," said Penelope. "It looks sharp. She'll cut herself."

"What have you done, Marina?" Honeycutt whispered. He reached out a tentative hand toward her. But Lewis glared at him with such ferocity that he retreated.

"Lewis," warned Buckler.

Chase plucked the scissors from Marina's grip. About four inches long, they had gilded silver mounts with mother-of-pearl handles. The blades were steel with sharp points. He handed the scissors to Penelope and lifted Mrs. Yates in his arms, staggering a little at her unexpected weight.

"Ned!" cried Beatrice. "Come help us."

With a muttered curse, Honeycutt strode over to take his aunt from Chase. He bore her to an armchair by the mantelpiece, where he deposited her gently. "It's all right, auntie. There's nothing to frighten you anymore." He hesitated. "Where's that fool maid of Marina's?"

Marina's maid Todd detached herself from the other servants, who stood gaping from the doorway. "Sir?" she said breathlessly. "Fetch the smelling salts," he snapped. Beatrice went to dab her brother's bloody lip with her handkerchief as Honeycutt fingered his jaw. He said to Chase, "I don't complain about your hotheaded conduct, for I know you only meant to do your job. You misinterpreted my actions; that's all. I thought Miss Garrod hysterical."

"Only a blackguard strikes a woman," flashed Lewis.

"You will leave this house at dawn, Durant," said Honeycutt between his teeth.

"Don't be rude, Ned," murmured Beatrice. "Though under the circumstances—"

Suddenly Samuel Tallboys appeared in the doorway, a majestic figure in a richly braided scarlet dressing gown. Without his wig, his skull with its short fuzz of hair resembled a sheep shorn of its coat, and his face radiated disapproval as he lumbered across the floor to Beatrice's side. "My dear Miss Honeycutt and Mrs. Yates. What in heaven's name has occurred?"

"Oh, sir," Beatrice said, "my aunt has been attacked. She might have been killed." She indicated the scissors in Penelope's hand.

"With the sewing scissors?" said Penelope.

Buckler came to stand at her side. "More to the point, no one appears to be injured."

Tallboys looked aghast. He raised a hand to scratch his head absent-mindedly. "Oh, this is terrible indeed. But who did this?"

"I startled Marina, Mr. Tallboys," said Mrs. Yates. "It was entirely my own doing."

Tallboys wheeled an ominous gaze on the girl. "Explain yourself, miss."

Chase had gone to light the lamp on the bureau. "Tallboys, dismiss the servants," he said over his shoulder. "You won't want an audience." In the increased illumination, he saw the disappointment on the avid faces at the door, but the group withdrew at a terse command from the clergyman.

When they were gone, Chase said to Mrs. Yates, "Are you recovered enough to explain? Why were you in Miss Garrod's room at this hour?"

"I…I was worried about her. I feared she might leave her bed again, so I put my head in. I was relieved to see she was asleep, but when I came closer, she leapt up and menaced me with the scissors."

"That's a lie," said Marina. "I don't know where those scissors came from. She slipped them into my hand as I slept." All eyes turned to the girl. She had her arms clasped around her knees and her head bowed, her long hair flowing down her back. Her voice was vigorous, and she seemed to have shaken off some of her initial confusion.

Mrs. Yates said, "How I wish that were true. To think this could happen in our family. Hugo would be so grieved." She sniffed dolefully.

"No one touched you with the scissors?" demanded Chase.

"No, but I tripped over the counterpane and fell. My nerves are shattered, and I am bruised. But I shall do very well with rest."

"Where can Todd be?" said Beatrice. "We must get my aunt to bed and attend to Marina." She sat on the edge of the bed, but Marina pulled away. Shrugging, Beatrice looked around the room as if seeking support. No one moved. Penelope laid a restraining hand on her brother's arm when he tried again to go to the girl.

"Here, ma'am," said the lady's maid, reentering from the dressing room. She waved the smelling salts under Mrs. Yates' nose, then offered them to her mistress, who flinched back.

"Why, what's wrong with you, miss?" said Todd, sounding indignant.

"Stay away from me," said Marina.

"That's no way to talk, Miss Garrod," said Tallboys.

Beatrice Honeycutt joined the maid. "Marina, let us help you. Tell us what happened. Why did you have our aunt's scissors in your possession?"

"But I didn't."

"For shame, Marina," said Mrs. Yates.

"Give her some room." Chase positioned himself so that he stood between the girl and everyone else.

Honeycutt shook his head. "Don't expect to get any sense from her, at least not tonight. We must leave her to the care of her maid. As my aunt says, I'm sure Miss Garrod was merely frightened when her sleep was disturbed. No surprise, I suppose, after the events of the last few days. We are all on edge."

Marina seized on this excuse. "Yes…yes, that is what happened. I apologize for rousing the house. I beg that you leave me now."

"That's right, Miss Marina," the maid scolded. "Let's have no more of this nonsense. You do as you're told, and you'll be fine. I'll heat some milk for you, and that'll settle you." Todd waved her smelling salts under the girl's nose.

Chase's eyes traveled to the nightstand upon which sat an almost empty glass. He picked it up and sniffed. Then he swiped a finger across the bottom to taste the residue. "Your composing draught, Miss Garrod? The same you took the last time?"

"Yes, Mr. Chase."

"You were deeply asleep? No wandering from your bed this time?"

"No, sir."

Honeycutt interrupted. "Can your questions wait for morning? Nothing can be accomplished tonight. We are exhausted and distressed. I am only thankful my aunt has not been seriously injured."

"Mr. Durant?" said Marina.

"I will see you tomorrow, Miss Garrod," Lewis said.

"You won't go before we can say goodbye?"

"I won't, I promise. Isn't that right, Penelope?"

She nodded. "Yes, we promise." She went to the washstand and poured Marina a glass of water.

Marina took the glass with shaking hands and drank deeply. "I'm sure…" She broke off, cleared her throat, and tried again. "I was dreaming," she said in a small, stony voice. "I awoke to my aunt's scream. I never took those scissors. I don't know why I had them."

As she spoke, she kept her eyes on Lewis, as if she feared she would drown. Chase felt a spark of pity ignite and roar to a flame. He'd been trying so hard to do his duty by this child that he had forgotten how young she was. He must do better, he told himself. What had really happened here tonight? He knew Marina felt threatened, but would she attack a member of her family, possibly in self-defense? An old woman seemed an unlikely assailant. Had they planned some kind of attack, or was this another trick to discredit her? Penelope regarded him somberly, and Chase knew she had seen the implications too. Anyone entering the room would have found Marina Garrod in a drugged sleep. Whoever it was would have realized she could not defend herself or, perhaps more to the point, give a coherent account.

"She's tired, John," said Penelope, leaning over to straighten the bedclothes.

Chase nodded. "We'll leave you, Miss Garrod. You may sleep without worry. I'll be outside in the corridor for the remainder of the night."

Chapter Nineteen

John Chase occupied the hours until dawn by establishing himself in a chair outside Marina's door, ordering a pot of coffee from a sleepy footman, and reviewing his occurrence book. When he had gone through the entire book twice, he turned to a fresh page. His pencil moving rapidly, he jotted notes:

Garrod gives daughter a season: malicious tricks begin. To disgrace and unnerve her? Drug her to make her seem crazy? Prevent her marriage to someone outside the family? Encourage Garrod to disinherit her? A conspiracy? Sewing scissors "attack": Does Mrs. Yates help someone or act alone?

Garrod keeps family guessing—was he about to change the will again? Thought Marina unstable? Nephew Ned Honeycutt has debts, argues with uncle. WHO IS THE HEIR? Marina? Beatrice? Ned? Ned and Beatrice? Ned and Marina? Mrs. Yates? Tallboys to hold purse-strings?

Garrod hires a Bow Street Runner, then is poisoned (Why? To preserve current will? Killer worried about what Runner might uncover?)

The key: Did Garrod drop it in the hothouse? Valet contradicts. An attempt to mislead the inquiry? Killer had no opportunity to return key to proper place?

Nothing wrong with sugar on prior evening when Garrod made tea; key safe in dressing room for night

Morning of Poisoning:
9:00 – Servants finished cleaning ground-floor rooms in time for breakfast; breakfast table laid in morning room. Note: morning room attaches to drawing room, where teapoy was placed

9:30 - Garrod leaves bedchamber for breakfast; valet goes downstairs; key in writing desk, which is left unlocked on this day (lucky for murderer)

10:00 – Valet back in bedchamber; key discovered missing; Tallboys: breakfast with Marina and Beatrice; chambermaids at work in first- and second-floor bedrooms

10:15: Garrod with messenger from the City in the study

11:00 – Teapoy moved from drawing room. A. precatorius beads in boiler room suggest tampering occurred in hothouse—did it?

3:00 – Key found in Penelope's presence

Where were family members between 9:30-10:00 in the morning (probable time of key theft)

Marina: sees father about 8:00; in her bedchamber until 10:00 (later that night: not in hothouse to drink tea)

Beatrice: breakfast with Marina and Tallboys around 10:00. In her bedroom at 9:30? Did she come downstairs earlier? (was in hothouse: got sick from tea, but how ill was she?)

Tallboys: could have arrived early to slip upstairs, steal key, and poison sugar (present in hothouse: very sick)

Honeycutt: says he was asleep until 11:00 (not in hot-house to drink tea, in orangery quarreling with Lewis)

Mrs. Yates: household duties downstairs, asked Garrod for the key about 10:00 (was in hothouse: didn't drink her tea)

Is the trickster the murderer—or are there two different people?

Tricks: The necklace/bracelet of A. precatorius *beads given to Marina*

John Crow feather, dirt, eggshells in reticule

Light in garden (seen by others besides Marina)

Obeah charm with another feather found above Garrod's door (Why? A curse on Marina? A curse on Garrod? Implicate Marina?)

A curse…means what? Cursed by pride? Envy of Marina's position? Marina…a cuckoo in the wrong nest

A deadly trick: Poison in the sugar: Abrus precatorius?

Under-gardener finds A. precatorius *beads in boiler room. When put there and why?*

Here Chase stopped, his heart pounding as he skimmed the pages to find the record of his conversation with the under-gardener Higgins. Chase had remembered Penelope's comment before dinner on the night of the poisoning. She'd told him that Garrod showed her his steam-heating apparatus, bragging of its marvels and perfections. No mention of any malfunction. This was on Tuesday, the day of the poisoning. Higgins had mentioned that someone told him to inspect the boiler on Thursday but he had detected nothing wrong with it.

Suddenly Chase knew why. Someone had wanted those beads discovered and was too impatient to wait for one of the staff to go down to the cellar on a routine visit. The inquest was to be held the next day on Friday, and the gardener's testimony would be too important. This was because he needed to tell his story about finding the exotic poison that pointed to Marina Garrod as a murderous lunatic.

Hours passed while Chase sat there thinking. His limbs were stiff, his shoulders tight with tension and his knee throbbing. From below, he heard the first stirrings of the household, as footsteps crossed the marble entrance hall. Then he heard hushed voices and muffled thumps. In the basement kitchen the maid of all work would be lighting the kitchen fire and putting the kettle on to boil. Soon she would be dusting and sweeping the ground floor rooms and laying the table for breakfast. Creakily, Chase rose to his feet and tucked his occurrence book back in his pocket.

Two hours later Anne Yates received him in the housekeeper's room. She was dressed in a dark bombazine gown and wore a black profile cameo on her massive bosom. She stood before Chase, a rounded figure with no hint of softness. Greeting him warily, she did not offer him a seat. "I can spare you but a moment, sir. I am needed elsewhere this morning."

"You're no worse after your fright last night, ma'am?"

"Thank you, I am well. A night's rest has restored me."

"I am glad to hear it." Chase waited.

"Did you wish to ask me something?" she said at last. She laced her plump hands in front of her with exaggerated patience but regarded the open door, as if eager to escape him. The housekeeper's claim of being occupied on this morning seemed plausible. From the kitchen, pots and pans banged, and voices sounded up and down the corridor. Not that Chase cared one way or the other, but Mrs. Yates would be overseeing the preparations for Hugo Garrod's funeral in addition to her usual duties. On his way down the stairs, Chase had seen several manservants in black gloves, carrying hats decorated with a band of flowing black material. The pallbearers, he'd assumed. The butler had told him that Honeycutt and most of the servants would attend the funeral in a few hours but not the ladies of the house, whom Tallboys had urged to remain in seclusion. There was to be no cold collation offered to the mourners on this occasion, a regrettable lapse in decorum, the butler had said, as was the rather hurried aspect of the obsequies.

"I won't take up much of your time," Chase said to Mrs. Yates. "I hope you can answer a few questions I have about the day of Mr. Garrod's party."

"I've told you all I know. Surely we covered that ground at the inquest."

"Not so. You see, ma'am, I've been a fool."

"I don't understand you. I'm sure you've done the best you could. It's difficult—you were put in an impossible situation."

"Impossible because I was hired to guard a girl who has lost her wits? I don't suppose she really understands her actions. We must forgive her, don't you agree? She requires special care?"

A hectic light showed in her eyes before it was doused. The color drained from her cheeks. She looked old and unsure and anxious. Chase watched her struggle to frame a reply and felt not the smallest compunction for pushing her. She said, "Marina is my niece, sir. You will not speak ill of her to me."

"No?" he said softly. "May I assume you're willing to excuse attempted murder? After all, those scissors were sharp enough to have done the job."

"Yes, yes, I would forgive her anything." She sat down hard in her armchair, the crimped material of her gown rustling. The grooves around her mouth deepened as she set her lips, her thoughts obviously unpleasant.

He watched her straighten her posture and compose her features; then he said, "Well, since you're busy this morning, let's turn to business, Mrs. Yates. You see, I've spent too much time thinking about the hothouse. An understandable error, perhaps, but still thickheaded on my part. The teapoy sat there, more or less unattended for much of the day, including the period when everyone was at dinner and when the staff had finished with their work. Moreover, the missing key and the poisonous beads were also found nearby."

"Because that's where the poisoning occurred," she replied in a dull, lifeless tone. She looked at her hands, which were clasped in her lap, and pressed them together so that the black-green veins protruded.

"True but not necessarily where the poison was put into the sugar. I believe that may have happened earlier in the day in the drawing room, specifically between half past nine and ten o'clock. So I'll ask you to account for your own movements and the movements of anyone you may have seen downstairs at this time. Start with Miss Garrod. Where was she?"

"I don't know," she said, almost whispering. "Upstairs, I think. I didn't see her until after breakfast."

"Were you anywhere near the drawing room at that hour? I see from my notes that you yourself take breakfast only after the family has eaten when there's a lull in your work, but you would have gone into the morning room to check the hot water or make sure nothing else was needed? You were there at ten o'clock to ask Mr. Garrod for the key to his teapoy. Isn't that right?"

When she didn't answer, Chase said, "I believe you are quite fond of your nieces and nephew? Active on their behalf?"

"I'm not sure what you mean, sir, but I have done nothing wrong, absolutely nothing."

"You haven't answered my question, ma'am. Were you or weren't you near the drawing room between half past nine and ten? And did you encounter anyone else? Mr. Tallboys eager for his appointment with Miss Honeycutt? A member of your family who came downstairs earlier than usual?"

She stared at him with dawning horror.

After his conversation with Mrs. Yates, Chase went in search of the under-gardener Higgins. But after following the circular walk for an hour, peering into the turn-offs from the main route to find fountains playing to no one and luxuriant flowers flaunting their beauty in innocent seclusion, he gave up and moved back toward the house. His temper was foul. The pleasant summer morning, cool and cloudy, offered a relief from the oppressive heat, though this could not compensate for the feeling that he was running out of time. He needed results—and fast. He had shaken Mrs. Yates but not broken her. Now she would have time to refurbish her narrative and strengthen her defenses, and Chase would be no closer to proving the truth of the suspicions now assuming solid form.

Then, as if in answer to his summons, he heard a voice: "Chase!"

He was in a small wilderness in a corner of the garden that he hadn't visited before. He stopped and looked around. Noah Packet stood in dappled sunlight, an uneasy expression on his face, his mouth pulled down, his eyes furtive.

"I was hoping you'd turn up," said Chase. "Got something for me?"

"I knocked at the kitchen door. They told me you'd walked out. Been looking for you." Packet cast a glance around, as if afraid the trees might be listening. As a general rule, Chase was not a man who appreciated the beauties of nature, but Packet, creature of grimy city streets and smoky taverns, looked as much a fish out of water as anyone he had ever seen.

"You found me," Chase said.

Packet drew the medicine vial from the inside pocket of his coat. As he held it out, the green glass sparkled in a ray of light. The thief's eyes shot briefly to Chase's face, then fell away. "You'll be glad to have this back."

Chase took it. "You've learned where it came from?"

Packet recited a name and address, then said, "The chemist would have nothing to say to me. Maybe you can persuade him."

"I'll do that." Chase extracted several coins from his purse and gave them to Packet. "Be off before someone decides you're up to no good."

"You mean up to no good like you?" Packet thrust the coins into yet another inside pocket and set off, whistling tunelessly, in the direction of the Wandsworth Road.

◇◇◇

The next step was to inquire how Marina Garrod had passed the night, but when Chase approached her bedchamber, Lewis stood outside the door with two new guards, one of them sitting in Chase's chair. As Lewis argued with them, a dark-haired, burly guard, who had an angry boil on his chin, patted the truncheon at his side. The man in the chair—slim, fair-haired, and vacant—stared at the wall.

"I just want to speak to her," Lewis was saying. "Can you at least deliver a message?"

"That's what we can't do," said the one with the truncheon. "No offense, mind. Orders."

"Mr. Chase's orders?"

"No," said Chase, coming up at that moment, "not my orders. What's this about? The boy merely wishes to assure himself that Miss Garrod is well. And who the devil are you two?"

"No visitors. No messages. The young lady is to be left entirely undisturbed," said the burly guard.

For once Lewis looked happy to see Chase. His brow lightened, and he reached out to grip Chase's coat sleeve. "They've locked her up, sir. We must get her out." He leaned around the burly man to deliver a rap at the door. "Marina, can you hear me?"

The vacant guard showed sudden signs of energy. Jumping up, he stepped closer to his companion, and they formed a barrier, elbows raised aggressively. "You watch it, boy," this man said, speaking for the first time. "Don't make any trouble, or we'll remove you."

"You just try it! Let her come and speak to me herself."

"She sees no one," said the burly guard.

Chase went still. "By whose orders do you confine Miss Garrod?"

"The Reverend Tallboys, sir," they chorused, responding to the unmistakable note of authority in his voice, and the burly guard added, "He said anyone who questioned the order was to speak to him directly."

"Where can I find him?"

"He's in Mr. Garrod's study, sir," the guard answered. He relaxed a little, letting his cudgel dangle from his hand, and gave a tentative smile.

A couple of local men, Chase thought, hired to isolate Marina Garrod from her friends. No doubt the rumors had been spreading since her appearance at the inquest, but wouldn't the family want discretion? Possibly the guards had been told she was distraught over her father's death and needed to be alone with her grief. They would have heard that her mental state was questionable.

"From the village, are you?" he asked the men.

"Yes, sir," they said.

"Stable hands?"

"How'd you know?" said the burly one.

"Your friend has a piece of straw sticking out of his boot," said Chase. Before Lewis could renew his protests, Chase said to him in an undertone, "Be patient. Let me find out what's going on."

"The young lady is ill and needs her rest," volunteered the more talkative guard, trying to be helpful.

Lewis hesitated. "Something's wrong, Mr. Chase. You'll bring me word as soon as you can?"

"Yes. Don't do anything stupid." Chase walked away.

Samuel Tallboys opened the door at Chase's knock. "Well," he said, smiling with all his teeth, "this is fortuitous. I needed a word with you, though my time is not my own this morning. The funeral, you understand. Come in, come in. I can spare you a few minutes." He waved a casual hand at an armchair in front of Garrod's desk. "Have a seat, sir."

Chase sat. Tallboys took his place behind the desk, smoothing the sleeve of his well-brushed black suit and straightening his pristine cuffs. As he reached into the drawer, he briefly admired his hand upon which a mourning ring of gold and jet gleamed. A moment later the hand reemerged with a bank draft, which he pushed across the polished surface toward Chase. "The balance of your fee, sir. I trust you find it satisfactory?"

Chase didn't pick up the check. "My fee? I thank you, sir, but I can't accept it for work undone. Mr. Garrod's killer has not been apprehended."

"Work undone? Those are the precise words used by Mrs. Wolfe when I tried to pay her for the magazine profile she was to have written. She refused."

"This surprises you? She feels as I do. It's not possible."

"Why not?" Tallboys said reasonably. "Though she was not able to complete the commission due to the tragedy that has overtaken us, she has lost several days of her valuable time and undergone an ordeal. We feel it is the least we can do. And the same is true for you. You mustn't think we blame you for what happened to Hugo. I am not certain it could have been prevented if the devil was bent on having his way. You may accept your fee in good conscience."

"What's this about? Why have you turned off the Bow Street constables and stopped access to Miss Garrod?"

Tallboys turned an aloof gaze on him. "You are too impatient." He pointed at the bank draft. "There is your money. Take it. This makes us quits, I believe."

"You are discharging me?"

"Your usefulness has come to an end, Mr. Chase. You were employed as escort for Miss Garrod, but these services are no longer required."

"In short, you are turning me off."

"I cannot help it if you choose to take it like that. Please understand. My responsibilities are immense at the present time. I must attend to an ever-increasing load of business in relation to the estate, consult with lawyers, be of comfort to my old friend's family, and care for his daughter. This in addition to my parish duties and my work as magistrate—" Tallboys broke off, drawing a hand over his eyes, overcome with emotion. When he pressed his head against the back of the chair, the fruity odor of the pomade from his curled wig reached Chase's nostrils.

"What about Miss Garrod? Allow me to speak to her."

"I'm afraid I cannot allow that. Poor, poor girl. Anyone must feel for her."

"Does Honeycutt know she is confined to her room? He told a room full of people yesterday that she is his affianced bride."

"Marriage." Tallboys shook his head. "That must be a consideration for the future. First things first, Mr. Chase. She must be made whole, purified, if you will, of her evil humors before she can become a suitable English wife."

"Be plain, Tallboys. What are your intentions for her?"

"Oh, you need have no fear on that score. She will receive the most tender attention." He looked at Chase sadly. "No one can be more eager to serve her than I. According to the terms of the will, I am to be joined with another in the guardianship of this child. It is a heavy charge, Chase. I don't mind owning that."

"You mean to bring in doctors to see her?"

"That has already been discussed. In any case, she is soon to depart."

"To…go…where?" said Chase, throwing as much force as he could into each word. A look of alarm crossed the clergyman's face, but he managed to scowl back from under his bristling white brows. Chase himself knew his attitude was all show. Tallboys had the law on his side. He had the right to send his ward to school, banish her to the country, send her abroad—anything he chose—and there would be nothing Chase could do.

Tallboys knew it too. "I don't owe you an explanation," he said mildly. "But as a courtesy, I'll tell you that we have made arrangements for her to go away for a few months until such time as she is more composed and can be trusted not to endanger herself or others."

"Preposterous. Miss Garrod is no danger to anyone. You do realize that the scene enacted for our benefit last night was faked. If you're the honest man you claim to be, you should ask yourself why Mrs. Yates bothered. Ask yourself, who benefits from Miss Garrod's disgrace? Ask yourself, who hopes to profit from her father's death?"

"Ah, but you see. I already know the answer to these questions. Though Hugo was in the habit of altering his arrangements frequently, one fact is beyond dispute. He was quite determined on making Marina his heiress. There is your motive, sir. Surely you sympathize with my wish to protect this family as much as possible. One person is dead, and I will not have the blood of others laid to my account."

Chase felt a muscle ticking at the side of his mouth. "You're wrong. Marina Garrod did not kill her father. The girl is as sane as you are—as I am. There is a conspiracy against her, and for all I know you are in the thick of it. Where are you sending her? To a private madhouse?"

"To the moon, sir. To the moon. Where better for a moon-struck girl?" He stood to signal the interview was over.

Chapter Twenty

"Who did it?" said Penelope. Sitting on a high-backed settle in the private parlor at the Windmill Inn, she addressed this question to John Chase, who rested an arm on the mantel as he kicked one booted foot against the fireboard. This board, designed to block the fireplace hole in summer, showed a painting of a large flowerpot that Chase probably scuffed without realizing. Edward Buckler didn't bother to point this out. He was perched on the window seat opposite, gazing at a sequence of hunting prints on the walls, which chronicled the destruction of a fox. He felt a paralyzing coldness within.

Chase said, "I have my own ideas about that. If more than one of them is involved, we know the reason."

"Greed," said Penelope.

He nodded. "They won't hesitate to destroy Miss Garrod's name even if they suspect, or know, that someone else is the real killer."

Sitting next to Penelope on the settle, Lewis Durant stirred, and her hand drifted over to pat him, though she kept her focus on Chase. "I agree," she said. "Money is at the root of this crime."

Chase gave the fireboard one last kick and went to throw himself into a chair at the small dining table. "A clever plot. One with few obvious mistakes." He leaned his elbows on the table and propped his chin in his hand. He described the gardener Higgins' testimony along with his own conclusions. "I asked the head gardener where Higgins was today. He's gone off to a plant nursery to collect some supplies. He'll be back soon. I must see this man."

"Even if Higgins gives you the name of the person who sent him to the boiler room, I don't see how that's proof of guilt," objected Penelope.

"You're right. That's been the trouble all along, hasn't it? Without a witness to place someone purchasing the poison or interfering with the teapoy, proof is hard to come by. What we need is a mass of circumstantial evidence—and knowledge of the will's contents."

Still, Buckler said nothing, but he wondered uneasily if Chase was aware of the reason for his silence. This reflection only increased his self-consciousness, his sense of being set apart from the people he cared for most, and his overwhelming fatigue. But at least he had no need to question whether Penelope understood him. He had been pretending not to notice the searching looks cast in his direction for the last quarter of an hour.

Lewis addressed Buckler. "What about Marina? Do they really mean to lock her up in a madhouse? Will you allow it, sir?"

Buckler didn't want to look into Lewis' pleading face; instead, he stared at the hideous print that showed a pack of dogs baying over a cornered fox, their teeth snapping inches away from its nose. After a pause, he said, "We don't know Tallboys' precise intentions. He may intend only a rest cure at some spa. She may have nothing more sinister than that to fear."

"I don't believe that," said Lewis. "They mean her harm. I'm sure of it."

"Why not murder her then?" asked Chase, his tone thoughtful. "Why go to the bother of sending her away if they need to eliminate her? Why not quietly ensure she takes an overdose of laudanum?"

"To get her on her own so that we can no longer protect her?" said Penelope.

"Marriage," said Buckler.

They stared at him. Chase's eyes kindled with interest. "What the deuce do you mean?"

A faint smile twitched at Buckler's mouth. "Garrod told you from the first that he wanted his daughter wed. No doubt his will reflects that ambition."

Penelope squeezed her brother's knee and released it. Rising, she crossed the room and stood near Buckler. "But if he thought her mentally incapable?" she argued. "He wouldn't make her the heiress, Edward. The family systematically fed her father's doubts about her and made her appear superstitious and unpredictable."

"He had a number of legal options. As to why the family wishes to isolate Miss Garrod, this may be a preparatory step to a hasty marriage once she has 'recovered' from her illness or a means of preventing any marriage at all. Or perhaps I'm wrong—and they lock her up because they do not wish to draw further attention from another death." Buckler contemplated Lewis. "They may have believed it necessary to remove her before she could fall in love or elope with someone else."

Penelope stepped closer. "Can they do this? Can they confine her against her will?"

The warmth of her arm pressed against his reminded Buckler that he must throw off his gloom. "They can. Tallboys is her legal guardian. He will have given his authorization, which is strengthened by his role as magistrate. The family may also have obtained a doctor's certificate."

"A medical certificate?" said Lewis. "What rot! No sane person can be treated like this in a free country. Sir, what's the writ, the one you and Mr. Thorogood used for that man who had been imprisoned? You can try something of the sort for Marina, can't you?" Again, he appealed to Buckler, and Buckler, seeing the concern behind the boy's anger, fumbled for an explanation that might satisfy him.

"A writ of *habeas corpus*. It is seldom successful, and we have no legal standing. We are not relatives or even close friends of the family. Tallboys may intend private confinement for a single 'lunatic,' which is not subject to the same regulation—"

Lewis cut him off. "There must be something we can do. You give up too easily."

"Lewis. Let Edward speak. You're being rude," cried Penelope.

"It's fine," said Buckler. The boy did not know about the fear that haunted him—the thought of that gently bred girl forced to live among strangers, perhaps treated cruelly, unable to make the smallest decision to govern her own life. He hid his shaking hands by thrusting them into his coat pockets, but he managed to answer with composure. "We may be able to get a judge to order an examination by a doctor of our choosing. This kind of thing does happen. Pretended friends, mercenary relations, and impatient heirs—they have all been known to arrange for the disappearance of people who stand in their way. There has been some progress: the registration of patients, visitation and licensing requirements, restrictions on the power of the madhouse keepers. Not enough. Secrecy and a family's right to privacy often make oversight difficult. The relations may use a false name for the victim, for instance. And once confined, the victim is denied writing materials and sometimes…restrained. What must a rational mind suffer under these conditions?"

He gave a harsh laugh and when no one seemed inclined to comment, he continued. "Many of our finest medical minds seem convinced that we have a positive epidemic of insanity in England, especially, some say, among the youth and the poets. This, they claim, can be traced to English indulgence in luxury, our spirit of competition, even to an abundance of…love or a passion that maddens the soul."

His voice choked on this last word. He saw that Penelope had tears on her cheeks, that Lewis seemed bewildered, that Chase did him the service of a friend by waiting calmly for him to finish while affecting not to notice anything wrong. It was this last kindness that steadied him. He got to his feet and wrapped an arm around Penelope. He kissed her cheek. "Enough talk. We must act before it is too late. John, will you see Tallboys again, or shall I? I'll force feed him some law, if you think that will help."

Chase frowned. "That won't do any good. I've an errand in town that I hope will uncover the purchase of the poison. With more information, I can convince Tallboys to delay."

"What makes you think he would stand against the family?" said Buckler. "If there's a conspiracy, he may be one of the guilty ones. Penelope tells me he seems damnably fond of Anne Yates and Beatrice Honeycutt. None of them can be trusted to stand Miss Garrod's friend."

Chase rose, thrust his hat on his head, and looked around for his walking stick. "What choice do we have? I must try."

Lewis said, "May I go with you, sir? I feel I must be doing something."

Penelope smiled at Chase. "Yes, John. Let us do something."

"Return to Laurentum and pack your things. Make your farewells in a leisurely fashion but arouse no suspicion. If I'm not back after an hour or so, go home and wait for me there."

"What about me?" said Lewis.

Chase directed a stern look at him. "Go with your sister. Watch Miss Garrod's door to see if any visitors are admitted. You may contrive to strike up a conversation with the guards. By God, Lewis, don't make me sorry I trusted you."

Lewis flushed a little. "I won't, sir."

"I appreciate that," said Chase curtly. Penelope said nothing more. She left Buckler and went to give her hand to Chase. She bid them both goodbye, and Buckler read the tenderness in her face for both of them. Putting on her bonnet, she paused in front of the mirror above the hearth to assess her reflection with a small grimace, as if readying herself for a performance. She followed Lewis from the room.

His heart aching, Buckler watched her until the door closed behind them. "What can I do?" he said when he and Chase were alone. "Give me something to do to help that unfortunate young woman."

Chase's eyes went to Buckler's black coat. "You will pay your respects to the memory of Hugo Garrod at the funeral. I imagine his lawyers will be present on this occasion." He consulted his watch and restored it to his waistcoat pocket. "Draw them aside and drop a word in their ear about Miss Garrod's plight. Make them listen. And find out if Ned Honeycutt knows about the plan to take Miss Garrod away. I'll join you at the house as soon as I can."

"Got it," said Buckler. Some of his depression lifted. Together they would achieve some good, he thought. His friend, eager to depart, was already in motion.

But as Chase reached for the latch, the door flew open. The surgeon Aurelius Caldwell stood on the threshold, his face beaming with enthusiasm. "The landlord told me I'd find you gentlemen here."

The graveside service over, Edward Buckler waited in the churchyard while a long line of carriages withdrew down the road back to London. He looked around. Some of the mourners lingered among the graves of the seventeenth-century victims of the Great Plague nestled among those of Roundhead soldiers killed in a battle fought near Clapham. Buckler had positioned himself next to Hugo Garrod's altar tomb, trying to catch a word here and there of the conversation between the Reverend Samuel Tallboys, Ned Honeycutt, and a trio of lawyers, two of whom were the men who had waited in vain to see Garrod in his final hours. Tallboys had put off his cassock and surplice and now stood arm-in-arm with Honeycutt. The younger man's face was pale and anxious, and Buckler had observed several stormy glances sent the clergyman's way. But Honeycutt stood patiently under his grip and spoke when called upon to his uncle's business acquaintances, friends, and the sprinkling of local gentry.

At another time, Buckler might have been eager to explore the churchyard's antiquities. This was not the modern parish church of Holy Trinity, where Garrod had taken seats for his family to attend divine worship. Instead, the ceremony had been held in the older church, a thirteenth-century structure taken down except for one of the aisles and the transept. Still used for burials, this church had drawn a sizeable crowd today.

Buckler tried to seem lost in respectful contemplation of the inscription on Garrod's black marble memorial tablet that must have been carved in advance. He hadn't been able to get close to Honeycutt during or after the service. Now he watched him step into the family coach followed by Tallboys. Leaning from the door, Tallboys maintained a stream of apologies to the men within earshot. He was sorry, he said, about the lack of a cold collation at Laurentum since the family still suffered from the effects of the tragedy, Miss Garrod, in particular, being in poor health. "You will excuse us, sirs," he repeated over and over as he shook hands.

"Shabby, isn't it?" Buckler heard a gentleman in a tall beaver hat whisper as he passed by. "When we've come out here to pay our respects."

"Who do you suppose gets all the money? Is it to be the colored girl, after all?" responded his friend in a voice he likely thought was hushed but wasn't.

"Shh…If so, they'll marry her off right quick, you mark my words," said the first.

"Pretty young lady," said the other, "but not just what would take my fancy."

"Lord no. A strange filly. No breeding, of course, on either side. Not sure I'd be tempted either, unless she came well gilded."

Buckler heard no more. He returned his attention to the tomb. Under an arch supported by white marble columns was a medallion carved in stone, which framed a recumbent white marble figure in Roman dress. The medallion showed Garrod in profile, a laurel wreath on his head and a solitary mourner at his feet: a woman with large, doe-like eyes and a mouth eloquent of sorrow. In humble posture, she inclined gracefully toward the deceased, extending a skull in one palm. The mourner, Buckler had seen at once, was intended for Marina Garrod, bound to her father in death, as he supposed Penelope was bound to the living father who attempted to control her life from Sicily. What would be the end of it for Marina? Whether or not Samuel Tallboys had any inkling of a conspiracy against Miss Garrod, he would do nothing to help her unless confronted with indisputable evidence. Buckler saw this clearly and knew that the same would be true of the lawyers—narrow, efficient men who would not see beyond their duty to their client. It was likely they would refuse to speak to him at all.

Watching the remaining mourners file by, Buckler's anger grew. Mixed with this anger was determination, a welcome feeling, for it did away with the sense of futility that had overcome him when Chase explained the girl's plight. *Thou knowest the secrets of our hearts; shut not thy merciful ears to our prayers but spare us, Lord most holy*, Tallboys had intoned during the service. What were the secrets of Hugo Garrod's heart? He had released his daughter from slavery, cherished her, given her ease and luxury. And yet in his sugar cane fields in Jamaica, the dark men and women toiled on; they filled his coffers with more and more and more wealth. If her father's heiress, Marina Garrod would own hundreds, perhaps thousands, of human beings. Buckler had read the abolitionists' pamphlets. Like everyone else in England, he had consumed the stories of cruelty—the nightmare journeys across the ocean, the shackles, the whippings, the daily indignities inflicted on these people. All of this ought to sicken the heart and torment the conscience. Were he honest, he'd admit that he read the pamphlets, put them aside, and went on with his life. But now he wondered: did Hugo Garrod deserve to be spared? Had anyone ever bothered to ask this question?

At long last Tallboys vanished into the coach, and the three lawyers, apparently having decided to stretch their legs, set off on foot for Laurentum. Buckler followed.

Chapter Twenty-one

"Let me tell you how it was, Mr. Chase," said Aurelius Caldwell, gesturing with his hands and pacing back and forth on the hearthrug. During Garrod's final illness, Chase had learned to consider the surgeon a sensible and reliable man. He still did. But it seemed that science enraptured Caldwell like nothing else. Though Chase had sent Buckler to catch the lawyers at the funeral, he needed to leave on his own errand.

"Explain yourself, sir." Chase pulled out his pocket watch and checked the time again, not concealing his impatience.

"Of course. You're a busy man. First, we noted that the powder was gritty and had a milky whiteness." Caldwell launched into a description that involved his friend the chemical gentleman tossing some of the sugar from the teapoy's cut-glass bowl onto the fire. "There it was," said Caldwell. "The distinctive garlic smell." When Chase looked blank, he hastened to add, "Assuredly, it was the garlic smell. Then we saw the most remarkable thing, sir. My colleague Mr. Holt—a talented man of science—took a few grains of the powder and set them atop a penny, which he balanced over a candle flame. Indisputable. Unequivocal. When cooled, the coin bore a silvery sheen laid down by the fumes. In short, we saw Addington's white flowers," he finished in triumph.

"Cut line, Caldwell. I'm in a hurry."

"I quite understand. We are fortunate in that the science has advanced since Mary Blandy poisoned her father's gruel, yet Holt thought it appropriate to begin with the older tests. Addington observed the white flowers when he threw the powder on a hot iron and held cold iron over the rising fumes. The deposit resembled a burst of blooms, you see." Caldwell saw that Chase was already at the door. "Shall I accompany you, sir? All will be made plain directly."

Chase motioned him into the corridor, smiling with a grim humor. "You can do more than that. Have you got your gig with you?"

The surgeon seemed taken aback, but even that could not stem the flow of words. After they had hurried through the coffee room and spilled out into the yard, Caldwell said, "My friend Holt was not satisfied there, no indeed. He next did the color test—the silver nitrate—which resulted in a glorious yellow cloud that turned the solution the most distinctive shade of yellow you've ever seen."

They mounted into the gig, the surgeon making no objection when Chase picked up the reins. The placid pony trotted down the lane as Caldwell resumed his report. "Unfortunately, the tests on the victim's stomach contents and the other samples of effluent I had collected were inconclusive." The surgeon's face fell for a moment, then brightened. "On the other hand, you'll be glad to hear that Holt is convinced in regard to the tests on the sugar. I trust his expertise absolutely; of that you may be confident, Mr. Chase. The tests are definitive."

"Of what exactly?" said Chase, slanting a sidelong look at the man's eager face with its pointed chin, ragged side-whiskers, and shiny, bald pate.

Caldwell grinned in delight. "Why, the poison was arsenic, just as I said it was."

"You or your friend will testify to this?"

"Glad to, sir. One or both of us. Whatever you like."

Chase absorbed the significance of this information. Would it be enough? Yes, he thought it would, for how could Tallboys claim that Marina had used a botanical poison to kill her father if Caldwell and his colleague were willing to swear the agent had been arsenic? Was this one of the reasons why the plans for her removal seemed rushed? Was she to be put out of reach before the test results could exonerate her? Now Chase faced a dilemma: should he hasten back to Laurentum with Caldwell's testimony or go to London to interview the druggist who had sold the tonic? Logic dictated the former—he had no solid indication that the druggist could tell him anything to the purpose. But if the druggist could...

Swiftly, Chase made his decision, his mind busy with the implications. A thought occurred to him. "What of Miss Garrod's composing draught?"

The pony whickered at its freedom, the dust swirling around them as they joined the London road. So far, his companion, intent on sharing his own news, had asked no questions. Fanning himself, Caldwell replied, "Oh, the draught is the usual sort of stuff, but it seems to contain more opiate than is wise." The surgeon gave a cough, frowning. "I must have a word with her guardians about that." Thankfully, his message delivered, Caldwell seemed content to sit quietly. But suddenly he sat up straighter on the bench. "Where in thunder are we going, sir?" he demanded.

◇◇◇

Wagons, carts, coaches, and gigs struggled over London Bridge, sometimes pulling in the wrong directions so that all traffic ground to a halt. Pedestrians in long ant trails crossed to and from the Surrey side of the Thames by footpaths. Whips cracked; wheels rumbled on stone; carters and hackney coachmen swore; the river roared and frothed under the human tumult. The noise was so deafening that Chase had to shout to make himself heard. "I need proof of Miss Garrod's innocence," he said.

"By tracing the purchase of the arsenic?" shouted back Aurelius Caldwell. "Excellent notion, if you can accomplish it. The druggists are not required to record such purchases. They do as they damned well please. Some refuse to sell poisons to those they don't know; others are not so choosy. Blasted scoundrels calling themselves chemists and druggists—not a one of them has a particle of real medical training." Once Caldwell had heard the story about Marina Garrod, the surgeon, with quick sympathy, had thrown himself into the spirit of the adventure. However, he must have been conscious of the risk to his professional practice and reputation should he make an enemy of a powerful family.

Chase spoke into his wind-reddened ear. "Are you willing to examine the patient? If you compose a report that she's lucid, locking her up would look bad for the family."

"Well," Caldwell replied, shrugging philosophically, "I suppose I am. But you must know, Mr. Chase, rich people are not so easily turned aside from their purposes. At the very least, I'll tell them what I think of giving strong opiates to young girls."

"They wanted her quiet and biddable." Chase thought of Marina as she faced the crowded coroner's court and smiled at the memory. "It didn't work."

"Got spirit, doesn't she?"

Caldwell sat back to nurse his own reflections, and they rattled off the bridge, barely avoiding another stoppage when the wheel of a southbound dray snapped and a bed piled high with cabbages tilted drunkenly over the pavement. Chase guided the gig around the vehicle and shook a fist at a rude driver who'd thought to seize the right of way from him, all the while telling himself that he was a fool to take the risk of being gone for several hours. Perhaps he should have stayed at Laurentum, though it was difficult to see precisely what he could have done there, given that he'd been sent about his business. At any rate, it was too late. Shaking off these thoughts, he kept his attention on the road.

As the gig traveled up Fish Street Hill, Chase and Caldwell inhaled the odors of horses, sewage, and fish mingling with the reek of the cows plodding to the slaughterhouses near Leadenhall Market. The gig joined the coaches that inched past the spire of St. Magnus and the soaring but ugly column of the Monument, which had been erected in commemoration of the Great Fire. A few minutes later Chase pulled up in a dingy court off Gracechurch Street close to the coaching inns, where the mail and stage-coaches departed. It had occurred to him that if someone from Laurentum had wanted to conceal a journey to purchase the poison, he or she might have boarded a public coach from Clapham to Gracechurch Street and found a local shop. Now Chase would discover if his instincts had steered him right. The shop featured a sign above the door that was lettered with the proprietor's name—*Obadiah P. Pope, Chemist and Druggist*—and decorated at either end with the same green sprig Chase had found on the medicine bottle with the torn-off label. A set of small-paned windows displayed a host of vessels and jars with painted labels, some with colored water. On one windowpane a notice announced: *Surgeon and Apothecary in Constant Attendance. Enquire Within.* Caldwell gave a fastidious sniff and followed Chase inside.

The chemist was a large, shambling man with stooped shoulders and heavy hands that trembled as he pressed them together in a nervous desire to please. He employed a shop-boy, whose shock of mud-colored, uncombed hair seemed to give him no end of bother, flopping across his forehead and into his eyes. Armed with a vigorously wielded broom, he sent his master occasional looks of scalding contempt.

Caldwell's lips tightened as he looked around. The half light woven through the bottles in the windows revealed a scratched mahogany counter behind which was a tall set of drawers with wooden knobs for the chemist's powders, roots, and herbs. Above these drawers were still more shelves of earthenware jars and bottles. The vessels all appeared to bear labels, but how the chemist ever found what he needed was a mystery. Here and there stacked on tables in the corners and heaped in piles on the floor were broken pots, pill jars and containers, boxes of lozenges and pastilles, even tarnished shoe buckles of various sizes. Arranged on the countertop next to a brass scale were bottles of eau de cologne and elderflower and rose water.

Chase presented his gold-crowned baton. "Mr. Pope? John Chase, Bow Street. I have some questions for you about a purchase of your restorative tonic. This your bottle?" He set the green glass vial on the counter.

Despite the innocuous nature of the question, the chemist seemed to shrink before their eyes. The hands that had been resting on the counter began to twitch. Becoming aware of this fact, Pope gripped his right hand over his left, slid out the left and thrust it down again on the right. The motion was repeated as his watery and almost colorless eyes studied Chase anxiously. He did not pick up the bottle.

"You wish to ask about a purchase," he said, offering this statement, as though Chase might have forgotten his own words. "My restorative tonic. My patrons do purchase it frequently." He cast a sidelong appeal at Caldwell.

"I am in a hurry," said Chase. "You won't waste my time like you did with the man I sent to inquire."

Pope blanched. "Waste your time? Oh, no, sir. I'm sure I won't. But I don't know what you mean."

"You do," said the shop-boy with evident pleasure. "The little man what was here yesterday. You was too scared to talk to him. Me, I would have given him a kick in the arse if I wanted 'im out of the shop, but not you. No, you just run like a rabbit into the back and hide till the fellow took hisself off."

The chemist made no effort to quell this disrespect, merely hunching his shoulders still more and sagging toward the counter. "Be quiet," said Chase sternly, and the boy moved away to resume his sweeping but remained close enough to hear every word of the conversation.

"Fetch your ledgers," Chase said to Pope. "I'm interested in your sales of the last few weeks. You sell any poisons?"

The shop-boy gave a loud snort. "Ledgers? You'll not get very far there, sir. Told him time and again that we'll be closing our doors if he don't learn to manage better. Does he care? He's too much the fool to know his own incompetence, no matter how many times I remind him. Not him. You ask him, and he'll say he stands well before the world. He thinks everyone likes him, he does. But he's a sniveling, crawling, mean-hearted little worm, he is."

"My friend told you to shut your mouth." Caldwell took a step toward him.

Hastily, the boy withdrew a few paces, but nothing could banish the sneer on his countenance. He subsided, however, continuing to watch the scene with interest.

"We are in a hurry," Chase said. "If you have no records, you must search your memory." He paused, then indicated the bottle. "Perhaps a week or two ago? Someone bought a bottle of this tonic? A stranger?"

The hands twisted and writhed, engaged in their own bizarre dance. "I don't remember anyone in particular. I sell this tonic to many people. It is popular, sir, especially with the ladies."

Chase held the chemist's eyes. "Can you recall any particular ladies, Mr. Pope?"

"A lady purchasing my tonic?" whined the chemist.

"A lady—or anyone. Anyone you remember." Suddenly he wanted to bloody the sniveler's nose, but he kept a tight rein on his temper. "How many bottles have you sold in the last fortnight?"

"How many bottles have I sold? It's difficult to say—maybe a dozen?"

"Right. To whom? Describe these customers." Chase held up a hand. "Not their names, sir, but their general appearance. Anything you can tell me about them, especially those who were strangers to you. I need to know what else they bought—especially that, Mr. Pope."

"God save me," said the shop-boy. "If you don't tell 'im about her, I will. I said it was a rum go, and I was right." He smirked at Chase. "There was a lady, sir."

"Old or young?"

"Well now, I didn't see her face, so you'd best ask 'im about that."

Obadiah P. Pope burst out with a stream of words, as if eager to get the ordeal over. "A respectable lady. Her dress, a gown of black silk. Her voice, refined. Worried about a young woman of her acquaintance, who required relief from distressful feelings. Confusion and giddiness. Troubling images presenting themselves to the mind. Insomnia. Pulse: quick and weak. The lady did me the honor to tell me the whole of the patient's symptoms." The chemist's voice broke off; then he added mournfully, "Young ladies are such hypochondriacal creatures. They must have a discharge of bile. Pure air. The healthy exercise of their muscles. They do keep themselves too confined, sir."

"You are a disgrace. What do you know about it?" snapped Caldwell. "You merely recite something you've read in a magazine. God, the harm the quacks like you do." He put his hands on the counter, drawing back in disgust as he felt its stickiness.

Chase addressed the shop-boy. "You weren't here?"

"No, sir," the boy replied, puffing out his narrow chest. "Himself had sent me on an errand, and I come in just as she was going out the door. But I know what she bought. If there's trouble here, you won't find me mixed up in it." He jerked a thumb at his master. "You won't credit what this one gets up to in my absence."

Pope wrung his hands. "What could I do? How was I to know? I made her a batch of my restorative tonic. No harm there. Tincture of Peruvian bark, one dessert spoonful. Ten drops of aromatic elixir of vitriol. An ounce of pure water. Sugar and ginger to taste."

Chase and Caldwell exchanged a glance. "He's right, Chase," said the surgeon. "Nothing out of the ordinary in that. You can buy such nostrums at any druggist."

"Ah, but you see, that wasn't all." Chase turned to Pope. "You sold her a packet of arsenic, didn't you?"

"A packet of arsenic," Pope echoed in desperation. With a heroic effort, he pushed the writhing hands down behind the counter. "She said the young lady had a rash. She meant to add some of the arsenic to water for a wash and mix the rest in lard for an ointment. Less caustic that way. I warned her, sir. I warned her, and I wrote 'POISON' on the wrapping." He shuffled back and forth on his feet and avoided looking at any of them. "I am not to blame. I serve the customers. How can I help it if they ask for it? She...she has used the arsenic to destroy herself?"

"No," said Chase wearily. "To murder."

Chapter Twenty-two

Penelope and Lewis entered Hugo Garrod's property at a side gate that led into one of the wooded walks formed of slender birch trees. The weather was gloomy, a summer shower threatening to descend. Lewis was quiet, apparently occupied with his own thoughts, and Penelope's heart sank to see again that closed expression that had so often daunted her since they had been living under the same roof. In the last few days she'd observed his animation when in the company of Marina Garrod. Penelope had grown, if not exactly to love the girl, at least to appreciate her resilience and strength of character. And Penelope had learned that guiding her brother would be a difficult task.

All her old worries about Lewis' future came swarming back as they trudged in silence. If he didn't want to go to university as their father commanded, he must be established in a profession, though what that was to be, and where the money would come from, she had no notion. She'd been wondering whether that profession could possibly be the law. But she knew Lewis had been disappointed in Buckler today. He had wanted Buckler to suggest a clever legal maneuver likely to achieve a brilliant success and a heroic rescue of a damsel in distress. Now it seemed a defeat to walk through these grounds, go tamely into the house, pack their bags, and go. She felt that too.

The sun peeked out from behind the clouds, and a ray of light gleamed in the rivulet that trickled along the path. Penelope's hopes quickened. Lewis was young. If his heart had been touched by Marina Garrod—so far above him in station—he would recover, and Penelope would find a way to solve their other problems. They emerged from the shrubbery, and the house appeared above them like a pearl in its elegant setting.

She broke the silence. "They want us gone, Lewis. We'll wait as long as we can for Mr. Chase. Then we'll gather our things and make our farewells. Agreed?"

He sent her an inscrutable glance. "Agreed."

"Lewis?"

"Go upstairs and pack, Penelope. I'll meet you in the hall."

"We promised Mr. Chase we wouldn't do anything foolish," she reminded him.

"And we won't." He smiled, and she was so sharply reminded of her father that her throat tightened. She gazed up into his face, trying to decide if he could have grown another inch in the last week, and saw that he was already a man. More of her burden lifted. She could not be his mother. She must instead be counselor and trusted friend and sister.

"What are you going to do?" Penelope asked.

He told her. "Lewis!" she said.

"Don't worry. I'll rejoin you soon. I promise."

She sighed. "Be careful."

Penelope thanked the footman for carrying her valise and fumbled in her reticule for a coin. It seemed absurd that she had been worrying about the proper gratuities to bestow on Garrod's servants, but so it was. She didn't think she had forgotten anyone who had waited upon her. She would keep the rest of her cash for the coachman who would drive her and Lewis back to town. When she got downstairs, she found Niven, the butler, waiting.

"It's been a pleasure to serve you, ma'am, even under these distressing circumstances," said Niven, bowing.

She smiled at him. "Thank you. May I say that you and your staff have been magnificent? It can't have been easy."

Something flickered in his eyes. She thought he likely knew more of Marina's plight than he would own to an outsider; no doubt all the servants did. "No, madam," he agreed. "Some of the younger housemaids have been quite upset, but we are returning to our usual routine."

Penelope studied him. Garrod's butler was typical of the breed. He had a forgettable face and a manner so assured as to be undentable. Even a flicker was a response from him. "Has a tray been brought to Miss Garrod this morning?" she asked.

There was a pause. He said, "No, ma'am. We've been told she is asleep and not to be disturbed."

They regarded one another somberly. "Will you give her my regards and thanks?" said Penelope, feeling awkward. "I can't be sorry to have come to Laurentum and made the acquaintance of the family. I hope they will soon find…peace."

"Oh, yes, ma'am. We all hope that." He glanced toward the staircase, obviously curious about where her brother could be, so she hurried into speech. "Can you tell me where Miss Honeycutt and Mrs. Yates are? I'd like to make my farewells in person."

"I believe Mrs. Yates is below-stairs, but Miss Honeycutt has gone to the hothouse to walk among the plants. Shall I call the coach for you and Mr. Durant, ma'am?"

"In half an hour," she replied coolly.

Thanking him, she went down the passage and into the drawing room. The curtains had been drawn to protect the furniture, and the room, though immaculate, looked somehow pathetic. She was remembering Hugo Garrod's immense pride in his house and gardens. He had created something beautiful at Laurentum, with attention to every detail, and now even the ormolu clock on the mantelpiece managed to look forlorn, as did the Sevres porcelain and the rich blue of the Axminster carpet showing the moon and a glittering constellation of stars. She did not linger but crossed the room and opened the door to the garden.

The sun strove through the clouds, too weak to warm the day. Rain spattered her gown as she followed the path, admiring the way the softer, gray light revealed the subtle hues of the greens, yellows, and browns in the flowerbeds. As she approached the hothouse, she encountered a bright-faced old man who materialized from a smaller side path, carrying a spade over his shoulder. On an impulse she stopped. "You're Higgins, aren't you?"

Lowering the spade, he touched his hat. "Yes'm. Do something for you?"

"Some information, if you please. You were the one who found the seeds of the exotic plant in the boiler room?"

He nodded, wary.

Penelope gave him a smile. "Mr. Garrod showed me and my brother the mechanism on the day of the party. My brother was terribly interested, though I confess it was all a little technical for my tastes."

"Yes, ma'am. It do take some learning to understand all that."

"Indeed. Mr. Garrod was justly proud of his modern improvements, wasn't he?"

The gardener's face fell, and Penelope caught the sheen of tears in his eyes. To give Garrod his due, he had earned the loyalty of his staff. He had drawn the servants into his schemes; he had inspired them to do all they could to make his dream perfect. She thought this odd, considering that the dream's riches could never drop down upon them. "He was a good master to you?" she said softly.

Stroking his chin, Higgins pondered the question. "That he was, ma'am," he said at last. "He liked things just so. Cut up rough if one of his people didn't follow orders or do his part. But he was fair, and he had a pleasant way about him. I'm old, see. Never expected he'd be in his grave before me."

"No one ever does expect someone younger to die, Mr. Higgins. I'm curious. Did Mr. Garrod mention a problem with the steam mechanism that heats the hothouse? I understand you were told to go down and inspect it on the day before the inquest?"

"Mrs. Yates mentioned the matter to me, ma'am. She was busy with the preparations for the funeral and came to discuss the flowers needed for the laying out o' the corpse. She recalled as how Mr. Garrod had told her the water pipe was leaking.

Imagine that, ma'am—he was worrying over such a thing while mortal ill. Surely that were his way. But he were mistaken. Not a thing wrong with that pipe or anything else. I made just a few adjustments, and it were tip-top."

"Mrs. Yates? Was she alone when she said this to you?"

Higgins' white eyebrows wiggled in surprise. "She was, ma'am. She were that fretted on the matter."

Thanking the gardener for his time, Penelope stepped into the hothouse. She heard voices but could not immediately see the speakers who stood behind several tall plants. After a moment, she picked out a voice that was pitched low and penetrating, familiar yet unfamiliar. It wasn't until it lifted into a higher register that she recognized it as that of Anne Yates. Then she identified the second voice: Beatrice Honeycutt. Penelope glanced down at her feet. Today she had worn her soft leather slippers instead of her half boots, not having expected to do any walking. As she crept closer, she gripped the folds of her dress to stop it from rustling against the urns on the walkway, her pulse quickening with excitement and fear.

"What are you doing in here, Beatrice?" Mrs. Yates scolded. "I need you in the house."

Beatrice was harder to hear, her responses high and pleading, but Penelope caught her next words. "…promised she would not be harmed. It's not right, ma'am."

"She won't be, you foolish girl. You didn't answer my questions. Was Marina sleeping when you left her? Is there any sign of that John Chase? Did you tell the servants that he must not be allowed on the property?"

"No…when…"

"Beatrice! Go back at once. Did you tell Todd to give Marina more laudanum?"

"….we dare not…dangerous for her."

Mrs. Yates became caressing. "Oh, my dear, it will soon be over. Marina will receive excellent care, and you'll assume your rightful place in the world. You and Ned both. You'll have years to bless me once matters are settled."

Beatrice's reply was lost as a groundskeeper, passing outside, whistled a tune and called out a remark. Penelope heard Mrs. Yates say, "Where is Mrs. Wolfe, and where is that rogue, Lewis Durant? Have they gone at last?"

To Penelope's frustration, the two women moved into a more open position next to the pelargoniums, where she could not follow, but she remembered the boiler room under this building and the gratings through which she'd heard voices during Garrod's tour. If she could get into that room, she might be able to hear more. She retreated like a ghost, pausing at the side door to listen. The voices had moved even farther away. Penelope edged the door open and slipped around the rear of the hothouse to approach the cellar doors. They were stiff, but she dragged one door open so that she could wedge her body onto the stairs. She left the door ajar behind her so that some gardener would not come along and shut her inside. There was no lock, and she felt reasonably sure she'd be able to get out in any event.

The heat in this underground place struck her like a blow. Sweat broke out all over her body. In a hunched position she moved forward cautiously, her hand groping the wall for balance. When she stood on the floor, she looked around. There was the massive boiler with its cistern. There was the furnace, which on this chilly summer's day had a crackling fire burning inside it. As she advanced several paces, her slippers left black smudges on the stone. Her gaze traveled, first to the little window above the cistern, which allowed light to trickle in, then to the gratings. She could hear the voices, but the bubbling of the boiler made it hard to distinguish the words. Then she remembered the ladder used to service the cistern and dragged it to the back wall as quietly as she could. Climbing up, she shoved her hair out of the way and put her ear to one of the grates.

"Ned and Mr. Tallboys will return soon," Mrs. Yates was saying. "I want the coach away before they come if possible. If not, leave Ned and the lawyers to me. You stay with Marina.

When the keepers arrive, I'll bring them upstairs to you. Go now." It seemed the women had altered their position, for Mrs. Yates' next few sentences were lost. As Penelope craned her neck and shifted her body to thrust her head next to another grate, her foot slipped from the rung, and the ladder scraped against the wall. She froze. But the voices overhead grew stronger again and continued without interruption. Penelope drew a breath of relief. She hadn't been detected.

Beatrice said shrilly, "Why didn't you arrange for the mad-house keepers to come after the reading of the will? The lawyers will object to your plan."

"No, my dear, they won't. Marina won't be seeing them. She is unwell today. The lawyers will understand that we have nothing to hide in our arrangements, that we act for the good of the family."

"But how long will Marina be gone, ma'am? This seems wrong. Let me speak to Mr. Tallboys myself."

Anne Yates laughed, a chilling sound that made Penelope grateful to be hidden from view. "Why do that? He knows all about it. He thinks it was his idea to lock her up." After a pause, she added, "Besides it's only until she is better. What can you be thinking of me, Beatrice? You are not yourself. Your nerves are disordered. You know what Marina has done. What if she were to play more of her tricks or, worse, harm someone else? What other option do we have but to put a stop to her wickedness before we are all disgraced?"

This time the silence stretched for so long that Penelope thought the conversation must be over. Finally, Beatrice said, "Aunt, you must listen to me." The footsteps retreated, their voices fading. Though Penelope shifted her position and strained her ears, she heard no more.

Assuming that the women would make their way out of the hothouse, she decided to allow them a head start. After a minute or two, she descended the ladder. She must find Lewis and go to the inn to wait for Chase and Buckler. With her testimony and perhaps Beatrice's, who seemed to be having second thoughts about her cousin's treatment, Marina's removal could be delayed if not stopped altogether. But as Penelope went to the stairs, the door above her head slammed shut. The clang of metal striking metal hit her ears.

Penelope called, "Someone's here. Don't go away."

She pushed both hands against the door but could not budge it. Suddenly she understood the significance of that clanging sound. Someone had jammed the handles by thrusting an object between them. She called again, her heart pounding, her body breaking out in a fresh sweat. Already her breath came in gasps. She had been so focused on listening to the women's conversation. Now she noticed that there was a sharp metallic smell; the air seemed denser and smokier. Surely that apparatus ran too hot.

As if this weren't enough, water began to surge into the iron cistern, pouring from the pipe above her head. Someone had opened the valve. Not sure what to do, she retreated to the stairs. It was probably only her imagination, but the whoosh of the water seemed louder, and the boiler creaked ominously. She felt panic hum through her veins, making it almost impossible to think. How long would it take for the water to overflow the cistern and flood the cellar? Not long. It poured and poured and poured. It reached the top and began to flow down the sides and pool on the floor.

At that moment, she felt the prick of eyes upon her and looked up. A face peered down at her through the window. One glimpse was enough to sear the image in Penelope's brain. Anne Yates gazed on her with a pitiless stare. It seemed unfocused, as if the woman had moved beyond her normal self and could no longer trifle with ordinary human concerns. Penelope opened her mouth to shout at that face but, before she had formed the words, it vanished.

Chapter Twenty-three

Buckler watched the mourning coach carrying Honeycutt and the Reverend Tallboys trundle past him up the road and roll into Laurentum. Ahead of him, the trio of lawyers walked up the broad drive lined by oak trees. One of them, the youngest of the three, clutched a leather portfolio under his arm and walked a step or two behind his seniors. Buckler increased his pace, wanting to catch them before they reached the house. But when he was at their heels, the middle-aged solicitor with the careworn aspect glanced over his shoulder.

"May we assist you, sir?" the lawyer said, not sounding as if he wished to do anything of the sort.

"A word with you." Buckler doffed his hat and bowed, in the process catching the eye of the younger man, who looked him full in the face and froze. The young lawyer was a short, rotund man in a black suit and crooked spectacles. He sported an air of dignity and moved stiffly as though he'd spent too much of his life bent over books.

"I recognize this chap. I've seen him argue in the Old Bailey," this lawyer said to the others. To Buckler he said, "Edward Buckler, isn't it? Thought I caught a glimpse of you in church." Observing his middle-aged colleague's raised brows, he added, "He's the barrister who defended Collatinus, Mr. Dudley."

Dudley's thin lips pursed. "Is he indeed, Mr. Rourke?" He gave Buckler a cool look. "Well, what can we do for you, sir?"

Buckler glanced at the third lawyer, an aged man in a pow-dered bob-wig and three-cornered hat. He had a deeply scored countenance and eyes almost hidden in a welter of flesh. His skin was white, his lips bloodless, his nose majestic. Buckler, having seen at once that he was the one in charge, addressed the next speech to him. "Are you aware that Miss Garrod will soon be taken from her home?"

"Taken from her home?" echoed the young lawyer, rudely inserting himself. "Why, what can you mean, and what's it to do with you? We're on urgent business today, Buckler."

"I assume you're here for the reading of the will, and I concur the matter is urgent. As to who I am, you may say I'm a friend to the young lady. She's been unjustly implicated in murder, by her own family. Someone means to thwart your client's wish to make Miss Garrod his heiress." He hesitated, then said, watching for a telltale shift, "To inherit only under certain conditions?"

Dudley snapped, "No concern of yours, sir. Allow us to proceed." But Buckler had noted the flash of confirmation from him and the younger lawyer called Rourke. The old lawyer's expression remained perfectly bland.

Rourke leaned over and whispered in Dudley's ear, something Buckler was presumably not intended to hear. *Associates with low lawyers and thieves' attorneys. Bit of a loose fish, they say...*

Frowning and shaking his head, Dudley said, "You waste our time, Buckler. We'll bid you good day." He resumed his stately progress up the drive, his colleagues falling in with him.

"Miss Garrod is friendless and alone," Buckler called after them. "Do me the justice to at least listen to me. I've been stay-ing in the house and know far more than you can. She has been drugged, confined to her room, and denied access to her friends. I fear she will soon be locked up in a lunatic asylum. I merely ask you to delay. Inquire. Speak to her privately and ascertain her welfare. A Bow Street Runner will add his voice to mine."

The lawyers stopped and turned around. Dudley said, "A Runner? It is our duty to help our client's family hush the gossip, not encourage it. There is nothing in our instructions to authorize the employment and payment of any thief taker." He used the derogatory term for the men attached to Bow Street, which was also applied to private individuals who pursued thieves and other criminals for financial reward.

"Mr. Garrod hired him to investigate some nasty tricks being played on his daughter. He now investigates the poisoning," said Buckler desperately. "He is persuaded that the motive for the crime lies in the settlement of the estate."

Rourke's dislike got the better of him. "We've heard the rumors. The girl is touched in the upper works. If the family has decided to seek medical treatment for her, how should that be any bread and butter of yours? She is a minor under the care of respectable people. There is a blood tie, even if they may not approve of her. Dashed smoky affair all the way around. Who can wonder if the family is unnerved?"

"You forget yourself, Mr. Rourke," said Dudley repressively and told the young man what he thought of his indiscretion in a few choice words. Rourke blushed and subsided, though he shot Buckler a murderous glare that promised repayment should opportunity arise.

At that moment they heard the rumble of carriage wheels, and a second coach passed under the stone archway that marked the entrance to the property. Imperturbably, the old lawyer, who had remained silent throughout the encounter, drew to one side of the road to allow it to pass. Rourke and Dudley joined their colleague as Buckler tried to get a look at the coach's occupants. It was a large landau, painted a shiny black, unmarked. At first Buckler's hopes had leapt high when he thought it must be John Chase returning from his errand. Instead he saw a coachman, who stared straight ahead, and caught a glimpse of two strangers, both looking curiously out the window at the group on the sweep. Buckler had an impression of hard, determined men, as one of them put an arm out the window to wave them out of the way.

"That must be the madhouse keepers." Buckler heard the tremor in his own voice and cursed inwardly, ashamed of his emotion. But the thought of those men taking Marina Garrod away made him sick. Where was Chase? What was to be done if he did not return? If Marina disappeared, their chances of finding her would be remote. Without a court order, an institution would not be required to disclose the names of its inmates, and there were private madhouses all over the country, some holding only a few patients. Buckler and his friends would never find her.

Dudley had raised a handkerchief to shield his nose from the dust. "We'll bid you good day, sir."

"Think of the money at stake," Buckler said. "Think how greed may warp the heart and turn people cruel and unscrupulous. At least make inquiries on Miss Garrod's behalf. I must try to stop those men."

"You are out of order, sir," said Rourke.

"I agree," said Dudley, but he didn't seem entirely convinced of his own judgment. He said to the old lawyer, "What is your opinion, Mr. Endershaw?"

The man in the wig came to life. He raised one languid hand, his shrewd gaze fixed on Buckler's tense face. "Be calm, sir. We shall make inquiries."

Buckler thanked him with real gratitude. As they walked on, he stayed with the lawyers, deciding he'd have a better chance of gaining access to the house in their company. By the time they reached the portico, the mysterious coach had drawn up at the foot of the marble steps next to the mourning carriage, which a groom was leading to the coach-house. The driver of the second coach was still in his place on the box. There was no sign of the two strangers.

In the hall the butler Niven hovered. He greeted the lawyers with his customary smoothness and took their hats and coats. "You are expected in the library, sirs," he said. "Will you come this way?" As he spoke, the sound of raised voices floated down from above, and Buckler stiffened, imagining he'd heard Lewis' among them. The three lawyers looked at each other. Niven glanced uncertainly at Buckler and opened his mouth to speak.

Buckler, pretending he hadn't heard the noise, interrupted him. "Where is Mr. Honeycutt? I'm sure he is busy this afternoon, but please inform him I'd like to speak to him." Buckler had decided that Honeycutt might be the best one to corner since Tallboys was unassailable in his role of guardian, not to mention pompous and self-satisfied. At least Honeycutt had defended Marina at the inquest and had confessed himself eager to marry her. He might be a party to a plot against her; then again he might not. Buckler could only make the attempt.

"Mr. Honeycutt will be down in a moment. He went to wash his hands and refresh himself before the reading of the will."

Ah, thought Buckler, he's likely taking a nip for courage before he finally learns his fate, but what was going on upstairs, and where was Penelope? "Mrs. Wolfe? Is she in her room?"

The butler replied, "She went to make her farewells to Miss Beatrice in the glasshouse, sir." He added in a wooden tone, "I had expected her back by now. She had requested that the coach be brought round for her departure within the half-hour. I hope she found Miss Beatrice."

At that moment Beatrice herself emerged from the drawing room. When she saw Buckler, she stopped short and said in some alarm, "Mr. Buckler. I thought you'd left us."

He searched his mind for an excuse. "Pardon the intrusion, Miss Honeycutt. I've just come from the memorial service. I needed to assure myself that Mrs. Wolfe has no further commands for me. Have you been with her?"

An extraordinary series of emotions flashed across Beatrice's face. She raised her chin defensively, her pale blue eyes blinked, and her broad, white forehead wrinkled in distress. "I think she may be in the hothouse, Mr. Buckler. You should go and fetch her at once. Excuse me, gentlemen. I am needed elsewhere." She hurried toward the stairs.

"Is there a problem, ma'am?" Buckler said.

"Go, Mr. Buckler," she said, without looking back. She fled.

Though Niven stared after his mistress, the butler seemed to rouse himself. "This way, sirs," he said again to the lawyers. The old lawyer called Endershaw wore an arrested expression, and he pointed his nose in Buckler's direction with his first direct look.

But he consented to accompany Niven and his colleagues to the library. Left alone, Buckler didn't hesitate. Something in Beatrice Honeycutt's voice had frightened him. She had been warning him—but of what? He didn't wait to consider this question but retraced her footsteps through the drawing room, out the French window, and down the path, almost before he realized what he was doing. Something was very wrong. Every instinct he possessed told him to find Penelope. He broke into a run.

On the way back from Gracechurch Street, John Chase and his companion grew increasingly confidential. Chase found that he liked the surgeon and was grateful for his help, though the man's impulsive good will rather took him aback. Caldwell was eager to testify at the reconvened inquest and at future criminal trials. The surgeon repeatedly expressed his shock at the chemist's testimony that an older, motherly lady had purchased the arsenic. But Chase had not been surprised.

His suspicions had pointed to Anne Yates ever since the prior night when he'd spent all those lonely hours in the corridor with nothing to do but think. Chase had assembled a few pertinent facts: she'd had access to the drawing room on the morning when, presumably, the stolen key had been used to tamper with the sugar in the teapoy. She'd also been in the hothouse to set up for the party and had had an opportunity to drop the key to make it seem Garrod had simply misplaced it. Later that night, she had avoided drinking the poisoned brew. Chase hadn't seriously considered the housekeeper before because he thought it unlikely Garrod could have made her his heiress. Garrod would want a younger person—someone who could bear children to carry on the family name. This had always been a case about money, Chase had believed. But another idea had belatedly come to him. What if he'd got the motive partially wrong?

Barely attending to the surgeon's chatter, he halted the gig at Laurentum's entrance porch. A coachman walked his horses on the drive. Was that the lawyers' landau or the coach that was to take Penelope and Lewis back to town? Chase subjected the vehicle and its driver to a quick scrutiny but could determine little other than that the coachman seemed bored. He tossed the reins to Caldwell and used his walking stick to cushion his jump to the pavement. Still, his knee made its unhappiness at this maneuver known.

"Stay here until I call you," he told the surgeon.

Caldwell nodded at the driver of the coach, who eyed them with suspicion. "Who's that? Shall I inquire?"

"You do that," said Chase.

He went up the steps and into the hall, not bothering to ring the bell. Though the hall was deserted, he was greeted by a clamor from the floor above. Pausing to listen, he heard Lewis shout, "Get away from her! Don't touch her."

Chase ascended the stairs, taking them two at a time and gripping the banister to haul himself up. When he gained the landing, he turned toward the voices, which came from Marina's bedchamber. On the threshold stood the lady's maid Todd with the guards hired from the village. Todd saw him and burst out, "The young gentleman has run mad, sir. He won't let anyone near Miss Garrod."

Ignoring her, Chase strode into the room. The first person he saw was Lewis, who stood, feet planted in a firm stance, next to Marina's bed. His expression was determined, his eyes sparking fury. Behind him Marina sat up among a tangle of bedclothes, one bare calf draping over the side of the bed. Her long hair covered much of her face, but the one visible eye seemed bleary and dazed. Chase saw at a glance that she was making an effort to gather her faculties. She was busy pinching her own arm, no doubt bruising the tender skin.

Samuel Tallboys confronted Lewis with two strangers at his side. These men had spun round at Chase's entrance, one of them moving to the center of the room to block his advance. Respectably dressed in brown pantaloons and tan coats, they had brought a litter to carry their patient, which rested on the carpet next to the second keeper. The man who blocked Chase's way studied his face, as if trying to determine whether he was friend or foe. Apparently, he chose the latter option, for he said, "You've no call to be here, sir, unless you mean to take *him* away with you." He poked a rude finger at Lewis. "The boy hinders us in the execution of our duty."

Tallboys, showing a livid countenance to Chase, snarled, "We don't want any trouble, but this is unacceptable. Get Durant out of here, Chase, or I'll have you and your friends arrested and confined in the Clapham lock-up. Don't think I won't do it. Don't you see that you only frighten the girl and make everything worse? Take the boy away."

Lewis cried, "Thank God, you're here, Mr. Chase. I was afraid I wouldn't be able to stop them. Miss Garrod doesn't want to go with these men, but he"—here he paused to glare at Tallboys— "refuses to listen to reason."

Chase sidestepped the keeper in his path and went to the open window, which admitted the cool air. A ladder had been leaned against the frame. "Resourceful of you, Lewis, and I suppose of Miss Garrod too, since it was she who must have opened the window. Where did you get the ladder?"

Lewis waved this aside. "Found it in a shed. They've drugged her again, sir. I had the deuce of a time rousing her."

"I see that. She is half asleep still."

Hearing this exchange, the girl on the bed made a valiant effort to throw off her drowsiness. "It's all right, Lewis. I feel a little strange, but I'll be fine." She pushed herself up so that her other leg joined the first on the carpet. But it trembled and failed to find purchase, boneless.

"Stay where you are, Marina," said Lewis.

The keeper had followed Chase to the window. "I'll tell you one more time, sir. You have no right to interfere."

Ignoring him, Chase addressed Tallboys. "I have evidence that Miss Garrod is innocent of all charges. Do me the courtesy to hear what I have to say."

Tallboys straightened to his full height and grew stern. "Evidence, you say? I don't believe it for a moment. Your superiors at Bow Street will hear of your conduct, Chase. I will send the letter this very day."

"Unless you want to make a gift of your family's private affairs to these strangers, send them away. If that's what you want, I've no objection, nor will they. They can dine out on this story for years to come."

"Get out, Chase," said Tallboys.

"So that you and the rest of Hugo Garrod's loving relatives can feather your nests at the cost of this girl's life? I think not."

"How dare you? Today of all days when I am harassed with cares. A funeral service to deliver. Lawyers to meet." The clergyman took a step closer to Marina and held out a placatory hand. "And this unfortunate creature left to my charge. How dare you question my motives and interfere in plans that are for everyone's benefit?"

"Will you listen or not?"

Tallboys swept out his arm and turned a bristling gaze on the two keepers, who had been listening to this exchange, open mouthed. "That's enough," he said grandly. "Keepers, remove this man, and when you're done, get rid of the boy too."

This apparently was no uncommon occurrence in the keepers' line of work. A martial light coming into their eyes, they closed on Chase, one to either side. They were big men, young and muscular and no doubt used to opposition, which they probably enjoyed. Chase knew the type. They would fight with little temper and without quickened breath, their goal to incapacitate with minimal fuss. In the doorway, the two guards from the village glanced at each other but didn't budge.

"Mr. Chase!" Lewis reached back to grip Marina's shoulder. Swaying a little, she now had hold of one of his coattails, so he couldn't have moved even if he tried.

Chase reached into his pocket for his pistol. Calmly, he leveled it at the breast of the man who had first challenged him. "That's quite enough out of you," he said politely. "Get back."

Before anyone could move, Ned Honeycutt swept into the room. "What is going on here?" He moved closer to the bed, a powerful smell of cologne and spirits following him. He cast a puzzled glance around and then noticed the pistol in Chase's hand. Tallboys stared at Honeycutt, horrified.

"Who are these men?" said Honeycutt to Chase. At his tone of command, the keepers launched into explanations, but Chase spoke over them.

"You mean you didn't know? They are come to lock up your cousin in a lunatic asylum."

"Lock her up? What do you mean by that?" Honeycutt's gaze swung toward Tallboys. "I see you've been up to tricks. I was afraid you couldn't be trusted. Out to deprive me of my inheritance and my affianced bride in one fell swoop, are you?"

"Ned," sputtered Tallboys.

"Well, what am I to think?" Honeycutt caught sight of Lewis for the first time. "What are you doing here, Durant?"

"If you really were Marina's betrothed, I am doing your job, which is to protect her. But she has no intention of marrying you."

Honeycutt's smile was dangerous. "No, I think she means to break my heart," he said sadly.

"You've been drinking, sir," said Tallboys, trying and failing to regain his authority. He retreated toward the door, his eyes darting continually toward the pistol in Chase's hand.

Honeycutt strolled toward the bed. "Don't poker up, Durant. I mean the girl no harm, as she'll tell you herself. Whose idea was it to have her committed?" he inquired in a conversational tone.

Chase spoke. "That was Mrs. Yates, wasn't it?"

Tallboys gaped at him. "I don't know what you're implying, Chase."

He kept the pistol steady on the two keepers. "Yes, you do. Ask these men to go back to their carriage and await further instructions."

Tallboys hesitated. He looked at Chase, then at the pair on the bed. Lewis had sat down next to Marina to hold her hand and stroke her bruised arm. She leaned against him trustingly, as Honeycutt scowled on them both. But before anyone could move or speak, they heard a boom like a thunderclap or the volley of a ship's cannon. The windows rattled in their frames, and shouts broke out in the garden.

Chase was already at the door. "Lewis, take Marina to the library and stay there with her."

All color had drained from Lewis' face. "Mr. Chase," he said, his voice hoarse, "where is my sister?"

Chapter Twenty-four

Approaching from the path, Buckler avoided the full blast at the rear of the hothouse. But he felt the earth shake, and an iron plate the size of a door was tossed into the sky to slice through a huge plume of steam before plummeting back to earth. The steam hovered for an instant before it began to dissipate, sparkling with innumerable slivers of glass. He heard a loud crack as more panes of glass shattered.

Buckler ran up to a group of servants, who stared open mouthed at the building. "I'm looking for a woman," he said, breathless. "A guest here—Mrs. Wolfe. Know where she is?"

An old man in a battered hat came forward. "I saw her go in, sir," he said, pronouncing each word at a measured pace. "She went to speak to Miss Beatrice."

"Miss Honeycutt has returned to the house. Where is Mrs. Wolfe? Hurry, man, tell me."

"I don't know, sir. She likely came out again, least I hope she did. Hey," he exclaimed as Buckler rushed off, "you can't go in there. Ain't safe."

Buckler yanked open the door. This end of the structure seemed mostly intact, though the walkway was littered with piles of glass and fallen timbers. Several of the trellises leaned drunkenly, and there were heaps of dirt and broken pots where plants had been shaken from their perches. He skirted these obstacles as he ran toward the source of the explosion, trying to recall what he knew of the layout. After a moment, he stopped, appalled. Ahead of him lay a crater in the floor where the dais had been, and next to that an enormous pile of rubble blocked access to the rear of the structure. This was where Garrod and his family had taken tea on the night of the poisoning. What had once been a garden was now a waste—a waste of shredded metal and shattered bricks and chunks of stone. The detritus included the murdered plants: broken branches, green stalks, and crushed blooms, all jumbled together in a surfeit of destruction. A charred, metallic smell hung heavy in the air.

"Penelope," Buckler shouted. He tried to think what he must do next, but a sick fear had him in thrall, and he was telling himself that it couldn't be, must never be, if he was to keep his sanity. It was a feeling like none he'd ever experienced, in which it seemed that life was choked to quiet, waiting to learn if the blight had struck. He felt the sickness in every part of his body, as he called Penelope's name again, louder this time, at the top of his voice.

Then he heard her answer.

◇◇◇

In the minutes before the explosion, Penelope had not been idle. She sloshed through the cold, knee-deep water to retrieve the ladder from the back wall and dragged it back to the base of the cistern. Each time a drop of spray hit the boiler, it hissed at her like an angry dragon, but she blocked the noise from her mind. She also ignored the water gushing from the pipe above her head and flowing in a sheet over the sides of the cistern, though it made her climb difficult. Lifting her soaked dress, she scrambled up the ladder.

At the top she contemplated the window. On the opposite side of the tank, her hope of an exit was only about five feet away, yet it looked impossibly distant. Still, knowing she had no choice but to cross the gap, she measured the distance with her eyes. Her ladder didn't extend to the top of the cistern, and she didn't trust her ability to balance on the narrow rim, even assuming she could jump without mishap. She decided she would have to descend into the cistern and climb up the other side. Clinging to the ladder with one hand, she used the other to struggle out of her dress and let it fall into the rising water. She threw her slippers after it and hesitated a moment to gather her courage. When she was ready, she dropped into the tank.

She sank, and for one panicked moment, as she scrabbled for the bottom, she was sure she would drown. But her feet touched and she stood upright. Shoving off as hard as she could with both legs, she splashed out and extended her arms to grope for a handhold. She missed. She plunged back into the cistern, gasping for breath and inhaling a mouthful of brackish water. She shoved off again, and this time when she jumped, she was able to grab the window ledge. Grimly, she held on, fighting against the current that flowed from the pipe, trying not to flinch when the boiler emitted another hiss. A cloud of steam billowed from below. As her feet started to slip, she curled her toes and dug them into the iron, relieved that the surface was rough and could offer her feet traction. Then she walked up the side, her arms feeling as if they would be wrenched from their sockets. With one final, groaning effort, she pulled herself level with the window. Breathing hard, she lay along the ledge and fumbled for the latch.

It wasn't locked. With all her might, she forced the sash open about halfway and wiggled through. Fresh air washed over her, and she felt the cushion of grass under her knees. She was outside the hothouse. She'd made it. But there came an ominous crash as the trusses that supported the cistern gave way. Penelope stumbled to her feet and ran down the incline. Behind her the glasshouse erupted, and the force of the explosion hurled her forward and knocked her legs out from under her. She fell to the ground, covering her head. Glass rained down, a hail of wreckage.

She lay soaked and shivering in the grass, like a castaway who had crawled to shore. Oddly, she was thinking of her mother, a woman, like Marina, who had been elevated to an entire new world by a man, in this case Penelope's father. Alessandra Lucchesi Sandford had died when Penelope was ten years old. Her mother had been required to give up her faith and her low connections in order to become an English lady, a task at which she had never succeeded to her husband's satisfaction. Her daughter remembered her as a small, dark woman, perpetually nervous, furtively religious, and tragically alone.

"Penelope!" It was Buckler's voice. When she raised her head, he was not in sight, though, not twenty feet away, she spotted the dome of the boiler that, like her, had come to rest in the grass. Shaking with relief, she drew breath and called to Buckler, and a moment later she heard his footsteps pounding down the path. He rounded the summit of the hillock and raced toward her. Then he was moving his hands over her body and patting her with urgent pressure on her legs, arms, and face. She saw his tears and felt a burst of joy.

"Edward," she said, laughing. "Stop it. I'm not hurt."

"There's blood on your shift. Where does it come from?"

"I've cut myself. There's glass everywhere."

In response, he sat down on the ground and pulled her into his lap, his arms closing around her. "My God, Penelope. You scared me half to death. Were you in the hothouse when it blew?"

"Right before the explosion I was in the boiler room underneath, but I managed to climb out in time."

The arms tightened. "You idiot," he said.

"Edward, I know who the murderer is. We must find John before she gets away. She heard me eavesdropping on her and Miss Honeycutt. She did something to the pipe so that the water flooded the cellar and the boiler exploded. She may try to get away—"

"Hush," he said and kissed her.

Penelope suddenly remembered that she was clad only in her shift. Her nipples, stiff with cold and excitement, pressed against his chest, and the warmth of his mouth on hers shook her to the core. She twined her arms around his neck and kissed him back, their tongues mating urgently. Penelope groaned when he drew back.

"What are we doing?" he said, sweeping a hand through his hair in distraction so that it poked up like the bristles of a hedgehog. "I'm sorry, love. I think I must be mad. Come on, let's get you back to the house before someone sees you in this fetching attire." As he spoke, his eyes traveled down her body, lingering despite the briskness of his tone.

Penelope sat up. "No," she said. "You are not mad and nor am I." She cupped her hands around his cheeks and looked into his eyes. "You aren't mad, Edward, and I don't want to wait anymore. I love you, and I no longer care what the world thinks. I will live with you and be your love. I will walk with you and talk with you and dine with you and laugh with you. I will play hostess to your gentlemen acquaintances since their wives will never approve of us. And I will comfort you when you are sad, especially that." She kissed him gently on the lips. "What will you do for me, sir?"

"Will you let me prove myself worthy of you?"

"Assuredly. You will battle injustice and earn a heap of treasure to pile in my lap."

"Will you let me cherish you?"

"You shall tuck me up when I have a cold in the head. You shall even darn my stockings if you want to."

"No, my dear. I'll buy you new ones." He glanced significantly at her feet. "Will you trust me with Lewis and Sarah? To treat them as my own?"

"I will and I won't mind the gray hairs they give you."

"If there should be children of our own, Penelope?" he said, his voice low.

"Should God please to send them to us, we will love them and do our best for them, like most parents."

Another tear leaked from his eye, rolled past his reddened nose, and plopped off his chin. He brushed it away impatiently. "Penelope? You do know it's impossible. Do you think I'd disgrace you and bring the world's scorn down on your head? Do you think I'd see Sarah's or Lewis' prospects ruined?"

"And yours. Never mind all that. We will find a way. I will show you that I mean that. Not here, not now, of course. But my knight is to have his reward at long last and damn the consequences." Laughing, she swung her feet to the grass. "Ugh, there's glass everywhere, and I've lost my slippers."

Buckler sighed. "I suppose I'll have to carry you."

◇◇◇

When John Chase ran out of the hothouse, he caught sight of Buckler and Penelope toiling up the slope. He set off toward them, his heart in his mouth. Penelope had her head tucked into the curve of Buckler's shoulder and her eyes closed. Her feet, covered in tattered stockings, bounced to the rhythm of his stride.

Chase reached them. His hand went out to grip Buckler's shoulder. "Is she hurt?"

Penelope lifted her head. "A few cuts and bruises, John; that's all." She saw his expression and added, "Don't look like that. I'm fine, as you see."

"I don't see that. You look terrible. What's happened?" He wrapped his large hands around hers, feeling the slickness of blood. He pulled away to brush the grit of glass from her fingers. Then he bent to kiss her cheek.

She smiled at him. "Was anyone inside the hothouse?"

"One man at the opposite end is all. He wasn't hurt. We were lucky. What were you doing in there, Penelope?"

Buckler grunted a little and shifted her weight. "Can we have this conversation later?"

Chase knew better than to offer to share his burden. His friend cradled Penelope, looking as if he'd bite anyone who offered help. What did Buckler have to look so pleased about? As Chase accompanied them up the path to the house, he said gruffly, "Where is your valise, Penelope? You'll want to wash and change your clothing." He could have said more. He could have told her how he felt shaky with relief that she wasn't seriously hurt or how he'd been frightened and was downright happy to be walking freely in the open air with both his friends. He didn't say these things. At any rate, she knew them, and there was still work to do.

"Can you manage from here, Buckler?" he said. "I must find Mrs. Yates."

Penelope stiffened. "She locked me in the boiler room and flooded the cistern. She played the tricks on Marina and poisoned her own brother. You'll stop her, John, before she can do more harm?"

"I'm going now."

◇◇◇

Leaving them, Chase circled around the side of the house and walked through the kitchen garden. All was peaceful here, the neat rows of plants still glistening from the earlier rain. None of the servants seemed to be around, probably because they had gathered outside to examine the damage to the hothouse. He went down the steps and in the kitchen door. The cook, busy with her dinner preparations, had little time to spare, especially since her helpers had deserted her. She was hunched over a sauce and muttering to herself, but she nodded in the direction of the housekeeper's room when Chase asked for Mrs. Yates.

He opened the door to this room without knocking and went in. Anne Yates sat in her horsehair armchair, her feet on a small stool, her head reclining against the cushions. It seemed she had just settled down to rest, for a cup of tea steamed gently at her side. She looked up as Chase entered and met his gaze without shrinking.

"I expected you," she said.

"Are you ready to accompany me to the library?"

"In a few minutes. Why don't you sit down, and I'll tell you all about it?" She smiled at him invitingly, indicated the matching armchair, and raised the cup to her lips.

"No, ma'am." Chase reached out to take the saucer from her hand. "You won't be needing that."

He went to the window, opened it, and poured out the contents of her cup. When he faced her again, he saw that she watched him, her eyes faintly quizzical, her hands folded in her ample lap.

◇◇◇

John Chase and Aurelius Caldwell went to examine the gaping hole, which was all that remained of the boiler room. The gardeners' chief concern was to protect the specimens in the hothouse from further damage. A cohort of estate workers used wheelbarrows and carts to relocate the plants that could easily be moved, while other helpers, some from the village, swept up the branches, green stalks as fat as a man's arm, piles of earth, and scattered blossoms of every hue, along with the fragments of crockery, steel, and wood. The glass lay thick on the ground, in pieces ranging from the tiniest specks glinting like fairy dust to jagged shards that could have taken off someone's head.

A cold fury swept over Chase, as he realized how terrified Penelope must have been, followed by a surge of pride in her resourcefulness. Of course, it had been foolish to hide in the first place, as he had every intention of telling her. Ned Honeycutt, entirely sober now, directed the cleanup for a while before he went to see about summoning a glazier and a builder for the repairs.

Observing Honeycutt's relish for these responsibilities, Chase reflected that Hugo Garrod was at least partially at fault for his nephew's conduct, for Honeycutt had been indulged in his youth and allowed to develop bad habits. It would have been kinder to disinherit him years ago and make him work for his bread. In this new, energetic mood, Honeycutt had dismissed the madhouse keepers and Marina's hired guards. He had also challenged Tallboys for not having informed him about the plan to commit his cousin. Eyeing Beatrice and Mrs. Yates uncertainly, Tallboys nervously allowed that he had failed in his duty in not making his own assessment of Miss Garrod's state. He would do better by his old friend.

Beatrice had said nothing. Nor had Mrs. Yates who had been put under guard in the library.

Chapter Twenty-five

When Chase was finished in the hothouse, he crossed the drive, still accompanied by Caldwell. The surgeon had examined Marina Garrod, administering a mild stimulant to counteract the opium. He had promised to look in on her later and to watch for any after-effects from the discontinuation of the drug.

Since no one had been seriously injured, Caldwell felt free to indulge his scientific curiosity. "I had a word with the head-gardener Mr. Amos. Amos says he thinks the apparatus had been strained by overuse. Mr. Garrod had asked the staff to run it more frequently while he was entertaining guests—and then in all the chaos following the poisoning, some normal oversight had gone neglected. The water level in the boiler may have got dangerously low."

"Would that be enough to cause the blast?" asked Chase.

"Perhaps not. But there may have been other factors. Mrs. Yates asked one of the under-gardeners to check the apparatus, and this man apparently took it on himself to adjust the valves. Of course, the fellow denies he did anything wrong, so I suppose we'll never know."

That meant Mrs. Yates could likely not be blamed for causing the explosion. Had the murderer hoped Penelope would be drowned, or had she only meant to frighten her? Chase halted for a moment, leaning on his walking stick. "But what about the water flooding the cellar? What role did that play?"

"Impossible to say for certain." Caldwell glanced up at the villa rising above the terrace. In this area there was little evidence of the disaster, only sparkles of glass that dusted the shrubs at the side of the path. Caldwell's voice was reflective when he continued. "Amos had expressed concerns about the construction of the boiler, but Mr. Garrod would hear none of that. It's possible there was a flaw in the workmanship from the start. More likely, when the cistern collapsed, the influx of cold water striking the overheated sides of the boiler ruptured it and caused a sudden and dangerous change in the internal pressure. That's the theory that makes the most sense to me."

They made their farewells, with promises exchanged to dine together at some future date, and Chase entered the hall. The efficient butler had dispersed the awed servants, but Niven himself waited to speak to him.

"Mr. Buckler is upstairs with Mrs. Wolfe?" Chase asked.

"Yes, sir. She, Mr. Durant, and Mr. Buckler are taking coffee in Miss Honeycutt's boudoir." He paused. "You'll tell Mrs. Wolfe how glad the staff are that she was unharmed?"

Chase nodded and started to move away.

"Mr. Chase?" said the butler. "How is Miss Garrod? I have been concerned for her. We all have."

He believed Niven. There was kindness in the man's face as well as a hint of diffidence that had not been there before. "She is well," Chase said. "I'll tell her you asked after her."

In the library, Chase dismissed the footman guarding Mrs. Yates and went to stand behind Marina's chair. Mr. Endershaw and his colleagues had established themselves at the mahogany table. On this table were placed a silver tray that held a coffee urn, a cream jug, a sugar bowl with nippers, a set of china cups, and a plate of cakes. Mr. Rourke, the youngest lawyer, had been upset by the explosion; he had to be called to order several times, but he became more cheerful when he saw the iced cakes, greedily consuming three or four. At a look from the solicitor named

Dudley, he hastily wiped his hand on a napkin and went back to staring at his feet.

The other eyes in the room were on the portfolio from which Dudley now extracted a parchment tied up in red ribbon. With reverent fingers, he handed the parchment to his superior, and Endershaw unrolled it.

Abruptly and shockingly, Ned Honeycutt said, "Aunt Anne, why don't you speak? What's happening here?"

Mrs. Yates did not respond. Under her crisp cap, her gray hair appeared dulled like a worn coin; her cheeks were ashen; her expression opaque. Still, she looked neither defeated nor ashamed but composed and resigned.

Tallboys jerked to his feet and went to her. "My dear madam. There must be some mistake. I simply cannot believe..." He stuttered to a halt and looked imploringly into her face. "My dear Mrs. Yates," he protested. For an answer she returned her attention to the life-sized portrait of Hugo Garrod that hung over the mantelpiece. It showed the plantation owner and merchant, clothed in a burgundy velvet suit and white silk stockings, one hand resting upon the chart that mapped his commercial empire. In the background of the painting, a ship had anchored next to the West India docks.

Chase said, "Be patient, Tallboys. All will be explained. Let's get on with it. Is this will of recent date, Mr. Endershaw?"

"Mr. Garrod added a codicil one week ago." The aged lawyer gave him a level glance. "Certain provisions gave us cause for concern. I believe my thought was that the codicil was a whim he would repent, as he had done several times before. He generally did come around to agreeing with our advice."

"He did repent," said Chase.

"I suspected as much, given that he summoned us to his deathbed, though he was too weak to alter his arrangements. But I suspect that at least one of these provisions need not concern us any longer, for reasons you will no doubt explain to us, sir. By the by, it is unorthodox to have an individual present who is not a named beneficiary. Can I assume, Miss Garrod, that you wish Mr. Chase to remain during the reading of your father's will?" Endershaw gave a courteous bow in Marina's direction, which earned him a small smile.

She said, "Mr. Chase has been my staunch friend. Let him stay."

Unlike the other occupants of the room, Marina eagerly drank her coffee. When she stretched out her hand to pick up the cup, it was seen that she wore the bracelet of John Crow beads. She seemed much more alert, her eyes alive with challenge. She had changed into an elegant black gown, and Penelope had helped her style her hair in a knot at the back of her slender neck. Now she stared at her aunt over her cup, as if determined not to cower.

The reading of the will commenced with a long list of charitable bequests and legacies left to Garrod's "faithful servants." Finally, Endershaw reached the part that concerned Tallboys. "To the Reverend Samuel Tallboys," he read, "in grateful recognition of our long friendship and his obliging me by serving as trustee, guardian to my daughter, and one of my executors, I leave my prayer book and two thousand pounds." At this news, Tallboys could not hide his emotion. He fumbled for his handkerchief and blew his nose.

Endershaw surveyed the room. "It may be worthwhile to note that my colleague Mr. Dudley will serve as a second executor and was originally one of Mr. Garrod's trustees." The solicitor Dudley inclined his well-barbered head.

Endershaw raised the document and continued. Ned Honeycutt was left the funds to purchase a mourning ring, an annuity of six hundred pounds, and a lump sum of five thousand pounds. He was also instructed to submit, within sixty days of the proving of the will, an account of his creditors. Hearing that his debts would be settled, Ned relaxed slightly, but his expression hardened again when it was Beatrice's turn. Garrod bequeathed her the diamond ring he wore on his little finger and his set of corals, plus an annuity of three hundred pounds and a small sum in ready money.

Chase's impatience grew as the lawyer, refusing to be hurried, worked his way through the document. Nor was he alone.

Honeycutt could barely restrain himself, and his sister looked wan and afraid. Of all the family, Mrs. Yates and Marina seemed the least concerned. Chase thought at first that Marina might be impatient to escape the tedious proceedings but soon realized she had built a wall to shield herself from more hurt. These people were the only relatives she had in England, and there wasn't a single one among them who truly loved her or could be trusted not to cheat her. Mrs. Yates, who had murdered this girl's father and plotted to hide her away in a madhouse, exerted an iron control and a chill that lacked human feeling.

Finally, Endershaw came to the codicil. In a dry, precise voice, he read:

> *"Inasmuch as I have manumitted the mulatta Joanna and her child Marina, known as Marina Elizabeth Garrod, and having obtained for said Marina Garrod a privilege grant entitling her to the same rights and privileges as English subjects born of White Persons, as if she were descended of and from white ancestors—*
>
> *"And inasmuch as Marina Elizabeth Garrod has been reared in the Christian religion and educated in this country, I give the remainder of my personal estate, property, goods, chattel, and effects, here and in the colony of Jamaica, to be held in trust for her sole and separate use, independent of any husband she may take, and after that in trust for her children, under CONDITIONS here to be specified."*

Endershaw paused, saying, "Miss Garrod, have you understood me thus far?"

"Perfectly," she said.

The lawyer nodded.

Honeycutt asked, trying for nonchalance and failing: "Dare I hope the condition is that you must wed me, Marina?"

Her dark eyes flashed. "I'd sooner be your scullery maid."

"If I have to, I'll fight this will in Chancery Court," said Honeycutt to the solicitor.

Endershaw shrugged. "You are certainly free to make the attempt, sir, but I would counsel against it. You will only tie up the estate for years."

"Name the conditions." Honeycutt leaned over, gripping the table and jostling one of the coffee cups so that liquid slopped against the rim.

The solicitor adjusted his spectacles. Then he continued reading:

> "*CONDITION THE FIRST: that Marina Garrod is never to return to Jamaica or any part of the West Indies.*
>
> "*CONDITION THE SECOND: that she is not to manumit any enslaved persons on my plantations.*"

Endershaw's eyes went to the young girl, who watched him with a touching gravity. He said, "We did inform Mr. Garrod that it is uncertain whether this condition could ever be enforceable. For one thing, laws do change with the times. However, Mr. Garrod insisted upon its inclusion as a father's last wish." When no one commented, he resumed:

> "*CONDITION THE THIRD: that Marina Garrod marry in England, within one year of probate, with the full approval of the trustees herein appointed, she to retain a life interest in this estate, which is held in trust for her lawfully begotten issue.*"

"Marry whom?" Honeycutt exclaimed, his face darkened with rage. "It says nothing more particular than that? It was always understood—"

"It doesn't say she can't marry you, Ned," said Beatrice.

"Be silent, sir," said Tallboys. "Let Mr. Endershaw speak."

Honeycutt slapped his hand on the table. "I won't be silenced. I said, is that *all?*"

Rourke and Dudley flinched, but Endershaw merely lifted one finger and laid it over the parchment to mark his place. "My dear sir," he replied with weary disdain, "no, that is not all. Allow me to proceed, if you please."

Now Endershaw's attention focused on Anne Yates. "We come to the further provisions of this codicil." He read in a colorless voice: "*I hereby appoint my esteemed sister Anne Yates to be joined with Samuel Tallboys as guardian for my daughter Marina in the joint care of her person, until she reaches her majority, weds with the approval of her trustees, or for so long as is needed in the case of her incapacity. Further, Anne Yates is joined with Samuel Tallboys as trustee of the residue of my estate, both real and personal, to have and to hold the same, with power to receive the income, dividends, and profits therefrom, and to apply the income as far as shall be necessary to my daughter for her comfort and support until she should marry. In consideration of my sister taking on the responsibilities herein detailed, I bequeath to her an annuity of one thousand pounds for life.*"

"My aunt to control the life interest?" said Honeycutt.

Endershaw set aside the parchment. "With Mr. Tallboys."

"We know what that would mean," said Honeycutt bitterly. "Aunt Anne and my sister know how to turn Tallboys up sweet."

Ignoring the clergyman's exclamation, Beatrice rose from her chair and went to Mrs. Yates. "When did my uncle tell you he had added this codicil?"

When she failed to get Mrs. Yates' attention, Beatrice addressed Endershaw. "Let me understand you. Marina must marry within one year to inherit?"

"Yes, Miss Honeycutt. To secure her life interest she must wed. The trust provides that this interest is to be considered a 'separate estate,' though I warned Mr. Garrod that many a husband may be tempted to mount legal challenges to this provision unless the arrangement be made explicit in the marriage settlements."

Beatrice spoke calmly. "What if she remains a spinster? Or fails to bear living children? Or if she should die or become…ill?"

Endershaw answered her. "If she does not wed, she will be left to the charity of Mr. Garrod's trustees. Furthermore, in deficit of lawful issue born to Miss Garrod, the estate would be held in trust for the firstborn male of either you or your brother Mr. Honeycutt, until that child should reach the age of twenty five. Failing male issue in your line, the money would descend to any female children. Mr. Garrod was quite explicit on this point. He intended to guard the interests of the next generation."

Marina went to stand in the middle of the hearthrug. There was anguish in her voice, and she looked at Chase as though he might be able to tell her what to do next. "We've heard enough. My father is dead, and no one feels the slightest grief for him. I wish he had left me in Jamaica. At least there I had a mother."

Shaking his head in regret, Endershaw rolled up the parchment. Tallboys uttered another expostulation that was ignored, his hands visibly trembling. Ned Honeycutt strode to the window, keeping his back turned. Beatrice returned to her seat and put her head in her hands. Anne Yates sat in her chair, stone-faced and impervious.

Chase approached Marina and conducted her back to her seat. "We're not finished, Miss Garrod," he said. To the lawyers, he added, "But I suppose your business here is complete, sirs?"

"For the present," said Endershaw. He nodded toward Mrs. Yates. "It is apparent that the court will need to appoint a new trustee, but I will leave that to you to explain to the family, Mr. Chase." He snapped his fingers at Rourke, who hastened to retrieve the will and restore it to its portfolio. The lawyers bowed themselves out.

"Must we go on, Mr. Chase?" said Tallboys. "I think we all understand the terrible truth. It is unseemly to dwell on it more, particularly in a house of mourning. We've undergone a most distressing and fatiguing day. Whatever you have to say can wait." As he spoke, he watched Anne Yates. He had every right to hate her for having duped him into authorizing Marina's confinement, yet there remained some impulse to protect. He wanted to spare the housekeeper, or perhaps to spare Marina.

"I've sent for another magistrate," said Chase. "Given your close relationship to the prisoner, you can no longer act officially. After the inquest resumes to hear the new evidence about the purchase of the arsenic, Mrs. Yates must be committed for trial."

Tallboys took this without a murmur. The family waited in taut silence. When the lady's maid Emma Todd, her face blotched and tear-stained, entered the room, she cast one quick, scared glance around and seated herself in the chair Chase indicated.

Removing his notebook from his pocket and donning his spectacles, Chase rose to his feet and began. "We won't keep you long, Todd. First, who directed you to give Miss Garrod the composing draught?"

"Mrs. Yates."

"Every night?"

"Not always, sir."

"The same dosage?"

"Sometimes she'd say I was to give Miss Garrod a little extra."

"Did she ever explain why this medicine was prescribed?"

"Miss Garrod needed to be kept quiet like. But then the girl started to wander from her bed, and I thought maybe Mrs. Yates would bid me leave off with the dosing, but she didn't."

"Why do you suppose that was?"

Todd's gaze had been lowered, but now she forced her eyes up to meet his. "Sometimes body and spirit would be worn out utterly, and Miss Marina would sleep for hours. At other times, the laudanum excited her. I think...I think it was intended she be driven out into the night to pursue the will-o'-the wisp."

"The light in the garden. What do you know of that?"

"Nothing, Mr. Chase. But I'm sure that was Mrs. Yeats' doing. I saw it once myself from the window. If anyone else saw it, he'd have thought it was Miss Marina herself playing her tricks."

"And the John Crow beads?"

"Why, that necklace was left on Miss Marina's pillow. No one would admit to putting it there. She could have taken it from her father's curio cabinet herself. But I'd seen Mrs. Yates coming out of her bedchamber that day when no one else was around.

Later I told Miss Marina to remove the ornament, but she got ever so angry with me when I snapped the string accidentally. I only meant to help, sir."

Chase paced the carpet a short distance and turned back. "You never told anyone of your suspicions? You didn't speak to Mr. Garrod or Mr. Honeycutt, for example?"

"I couldn't. I was afraid I'd be dismissed. You must believe me, sir."

Marina said fiercely, "That's a lie, Todd. I saw my aunt slip money in your hand one day. She paid you to spy on me, and I won't have you near me anymore."

Breaking out in a storm of tears, the lady's maid rushed to her mistress and tried to seize her hands, but the Reverend Tallboys barked out a command for her to leave the room. Sobbing, Todd complied.

When she was gone, Chase continued. "It was clear to me from the first that the malicious tricks were the work of someone in Miss Garrod's intimate circle. Someone, moreover, with knowledge of Obeah. Mr. Garrod had told me his daughter feared a curse. This was precisely what she was meant to believe— that she could not outrun a heritage that made her unworthy to be her father's child, that she could not cleanse herself of her mother's blood. She was to be driven mad, encouraged to think she'd brought a taint with her to England. It was to seem that in her madness she performed these tricks herself and didn't even know it.

"Then there was the fact that Mr. Garrod was so eager to see his daughter wed. This suggested that her marriage would play a central role in the disposal of his property, so I wondered what would happen if Miss Garrod didn't marry or didn't marry fast enough to suit her father. Two possibilities occurred to me. Either someone killed her father before he could make a new will or after he'd made a will that he'd threatened to change. Mr. Garrod played a dangerous game. He was impatient; he wanted his daughter settled in life. He was waiting to see if Honeycutt made any headway with the heiress since the London season had been a failure. If not, he meant to tell his nephew and Miss Garrod that they'd better get themselves engaged. I'm certain he shared his plans with his sister Anne Yates, respecting as he did her influence on her 'children.'"

Chase said to Honeycutt, who had remained standing by the window, "I suspected that you, sir, had been playing the tricks to destroy Miss Garrod's chances and prevent her from marrying one of her other suitors. But after her father died, I began to see that you weren't the culprit. If you'd been named your uncle's heir and killed him to preserve that status, there was no reason for you to torment Miss Garrod further or have her locked away. If you weren't the heir, surely you'd want ready access to her so that you could try to convince her to wed you, which you stated several times was your goal. Perhaps you suspected your aunt or your sister of playing these tricks—but you made the mistake of assuming they acted for your benefit."

"They all lied to me." Honeycutt addressed Tallboys. "You lied, too, you scoundrel. You never told me your plans for my cousin."

"I…I'm sorry, Ned," said Tallboys. "Mrs. Yates advised that we save you the pain, and the girl's removal was to be temporary just until she recovered her senses. At any rate, I thought that—"

"Miss Garrod had poisoned her father," cut in Chase. "And you, Honeycutt," he added before he could be interrupted, "entertained the same possibility, as did your sister, though I suspect Miss Honeycutt, at least, had a good notion of the truth. Marina's guilt wouldn't have stopped you from marrying her if you'd been given the chance. But Mrs. Yates had other ideas. She would have let the year allotted in the will for Miss Garrod to marry elapse, thus effectively disinheriting her."

Chase turned to Beatrice, his disgust evident. "Perhaps at first you did work to ensure your brother's inheritance. You knew something about the tricks all along, but you believed them intended to keep your uncle's money in the family." He paused. "Did Mrs. Yates tell you of her plot to murder your uncle, ma'am?"

"My God, no! I too believed her when she said it was Marina revenging herself on us. It was only after I had time to think and she asked me to help persuade Mr. Tallboys to agree to the committal that I began to realize..."

"When it was too late for you to retreat," said Chase. "Maybe you were too scared, if so much can be said on your behalf. I will say for you that you did not try to silence your uncle on his deathbed. You wanted to hear what he would say. He knew the killer had to be someone in his family—the nephew or the niece who stood to profit if his daughter did not wed. Or his sister who had made their interests her own. I'm quite sure he didn't suspect his daughter."

"Marina," cried Beatrice, jumping up from her seat to kneel by her cousin's chair, "can you ever forgive me? Yes, I suspected our aunt, but I didn't know, not for certain. I tried to talk to her today, stop her. You can ask Mrs. Wolfe. I think she heard us. Oh, Marina. It's true I envied your good fortune, but I swear I never meant you any harm." Marina hesitated for a moment and deliberately averted her face.

"Return to your seat, Miss Honeycutt," said Chase. Beatrice obeyed, her air of hopelessness making her appear suddenly much older. Chase looked at Marina, trying to convey reassurance. "Mrs. Yates miscalculated. Miss Garrod knew she wasn't mad. She fought back. Even I, hired to protect her, didn't believe in her at first because I couldn't see why she wouldn't have confided in someone. But I suppose the habit of silence, engrained from her early years, was too strong." His eyes sought and held Marina's in mute apology.

Marina nodded. "I'll speak now, Mr. Chase. Aunt Anne, the way you crept into my room and leaned over me with those scissors in your hand last night..." She shuddered.

Mrs. Yates said nothing, and it was Chase who spoke. "Did you mean to terrify her in the dark, ma'am, so that she would be goaded into attacking you? You wished to reinforce the general belief in Miss Garrod's lunacy to justify having her put away in a private madhouse. You needed to prevent her from marrying anyone, even your nephew Ned Honeycutt, so that you could control Laurentum and Hugo Garrod's vast wealth. You knew Mr. Tallboys would not hinder you in your ambitions."

Honeycutt went to the cabinet and poured himself a drink. He flung himself back into his chair and tossed down the brandy. "I've been a fool. My loving family has done its best to destroy me."

"Ned…" protested his sister, but he refused to acknowledge her.

Chase said sarcastically, "Oh, I suspect that once Miss Garrod was either dead or confined to an institution for life, Mrs. Yates would have played matchmaker for you, Honeycutt. Found you a suitable bride to bear suitable babies. But that was for the future."

He paused, dismayed to feel his throat closing with emotion. "The worst of the evil inflicted on Miss Garrod involved the bracelet made of *Abrus precatorius* seeds. The John Crow bean, a token of her island home and a sly reference to her mother's name—Joanna." Chase glanced at Marina's wrist as he spoke, and everyone in the room followed his gaze. The bracelet with its beads of red and black was out of place in this conventional English library with its towering shelves and luxurious tables and sofas. Marina held up her arm.

"Todd has told you that the ornament was broken. But Miss Garrod restrung it and wore it in defiance of her tormenter."

Chase went to stand in front of Mrs. Yates' chair. "The scope of this woman's malice is unfathomable. Imagine what this child endured all these months. Then after Mrs. Yates had committed murder, she crushed a few of these poisonous beads and hid them in the boiler room so that it would appear her niece had used them. To make sure this 'evidence' was discovered in time, she instructed the gardener to inspect the mechanism. Her plan worked. The coroner's jury might have come in with a finding of murder against Miss Garrod and sent her to stand her trial had not my friend, Mr. Buckler, intervened and had we not convinced the coroner to adjourn the proceedings."

"What was the poison?" demanded Honeycutt. "Did my aunt use the savage beads?"

"She did not. She put arsenic in the sugar."

Beatrice gasped. "I had hoped the poisoning was the impulse of a moment, or intended merely to sicken the victims. But if it was arsenic, that means—"

"The murder was premeditated, yes. I have located the chemist who sold the poison, and he is prepared to identify its purchaser." Chase flipped through the pages of his notebook, deliberately prolonging the moment. "Here it is," he murmured. "*She was an old lady in a black silk gown, a respectable matron or an upper servant.*

"I've also learned that Mrs. Yates was absent from Laurentum for several hours on that day. There is, by the way, a public coach one can take to the city just a few steps from Laurentum's front door. It is through an innocent bottle of tonic that the druggist who sold the arsenic has been traced." He looked at the housekeeper. "Why didn't you discard this bottle somewhere it wouldn't be found? I suppose you thought tearing off the label was enough."

Mrs. Yates' composure wavered; her eyes flew to Chase's, seeming to burn from within with repressed fury and pain. He had no intention of showing any mercy. He wanted to find out if Anne Yates could be made to abandon her pose of gentility, could be made to hurt a little as she had hurt others, could be made to bare her foulness to the world. He could see a muscle twitching in her cheek, and her lips looked dry like paper.

He shook his head theatrically. "I needn't trouble us much further here. There's the key to the teapoy, which Mrs. Yates stole from the drawing room on the morning of the party and later left on the floor of the hothouse. There's the fact that she did not drink the tea and made sure that Honeycutt would be absent from the hothouse so that he would be safe. She also relied upon Mr. Tallboys' oft-stated resolve that he would not consume the costliest sugar. There too she miscalculated, but she was lucky in that her co-trustee, whom she knew she could manipulate, survived."

When Chase saw realization striking Beatrice, he added grimly, "Yes, Miss Honeycutt. Your Aunt Anne was willing to risk your life. You were young. She probably hoped you would survive, but she didn't think anyone could ever suspect her, the person who had raised you and been a mother to you, of being the poisoner. She gambled with your life."

Tears poured down Beatrice's face. "May I withdraw, Mr. Chase?"

Mrs. Yates stared at Chase's waistcoat, as if fascinated by his buttons. "In a moment, Miss Honeycutt," he said. "Do you wish to withdraw too, ma'am?" he asked the poisoner. "Do you have anything you'd like to say first?"

Anne Yates lifted her brows at him and moved her foot a fraction of an inch so that it aligned perfectly with the other. He began to wonder if he'd been overconfident. The cringing chemist would make a poor witness—a clever defense-barrister might shake his identification of Yates as the woman who had purchased the arsenic. Also, arsenic could be put to so many household uses. Again, a clever barrister could suggest she had meant it to kill rats or something of that nature. No one had actually seen her put the poison in the sugar.

Chase threw all his anger and his disdain into his next speech: "A word or two more, and we are done. We must acknowledge today's incident that nearly proved fatal to my friend. Mrs. Yates and Miss Honeycutt heard a noise from the boiler room and understood that someone had been eavesdropping on them. Miss Honeycutt did not wait to see what happened or try to prevent her aunt's next act. No, she ran away, though she did send Mr. Buckler to the hothouse to rescue Mrs. Wolfe. Anne Yates jammed the cellar door and opened the valve of the pipe so that the cellar was flooded." Saying this made his voice turn husky again, and Chase felt chagrin at his lack of control. But that was hardly the point, was it? He felt a driving need that this woman should own her guilt.

"I cannot say if Mrs. Yates knew the boiler would explode, but I think she did," he said.

She spoke at last. "No…I didn't know."

Chase reached down behind his chair and pulled up something he'd hidden there. "I returned to the housekeeper's room an hour ago and found this at the back of one of the cupboards. Mr. Tallboys has identified it. It's an Obeah bundle, isn't it, ma'am? You used these foul ingredients to play your games with Miss Garrod. I presume you learned these tricks when you lived in Jamaica?"

Chase began to deal out the contents of the scrap of cloth onto the table. Fishbones. Some musty smelling black dirt. Eggshells. The teeth of a cat. Three glossy black feathers.

When Marina saw the feathers, she gave a cry. She made her way across the room to stand with Chase, saying in a passionate tone, "How could you, Aunt? How could you do this to me?"

An ugly animal-sound burst from the housekeeper's throat. "I want to die. Why did you stop me, Chase?" Her mouth stretched wide, and her fingernails, curling like claws, came up to scratch her wrinkled cheeks. "My children…I did it all for you."

"It wasn't really about the money, after all." Chase lifted the woman's hands from her face and restrained them in a tight grip.

Mrs. Yates stood in the role of mother to Marina, to Beatrice, to Ned. This mother had decided that, in Marina's case, the human material she molded was simply too flawed. To defend, as she saw it, the family name, she had been a realist. She would torment the girl, sabotage her London debut, deprive her of position as an heiress and in society. She would poison the mind—and the body—of her brother to ensure what she deemed the appropriate settlement of the estate. Above all, she would not indulge Hugo Garrod's dynastic dreams for his mixed-blood, illegitimate daughter.

Chapter Twenty-six

Marina bid a tearful goodbye to Lewis, swearing to persuade her guardian to allow Lewis to call in future, though whether such visits would ever be permitted seemed dubious. The young people wore defiant expressions and seemed inclined to put the rest of the world at a distance. Waiting until his sister and Buckler had stepped into the coach, Lewis bowed over Marina's hand for the last time.

"I will never forget your goodness to me," Marina said. He straightened, and their eyes clung.

"It was nothing, Miss Garrod." Lewis forced himself to look away to address Tallboys, who waited on the portico steps. "Your servant, sir."

The clergyman inclined his head. "Let me add my thanks, Mr. Durant. Let it never be said that I do not value loyalty and friendship as I should." He beckoned to his ward. "Come, Marina. Our guests are eager to depart."

When Penelope stepped into the sitting room, Sarah ran into her mother's arms. "Mama, you're home!" she cried. Looking at the child afresh, Buckler saw that she had lost much of her baby fat. Her thin, wiry arms were clasped around her mother's neck, and she was dropping little kisses on Penelope's cheeks and chin. After a moment, she raised her face with its huge, dark eyes to examine her mother more closely. Apparently satisfied, she wiggled free. Maggie, Jamie, and Frank clustered round Penelope, Maggie breaking into a stream of chatter and her sons jumping up and down. Frank tugged at Penelope's skirt, while Jamie put his thumb in his mouth and stared at her. After Penelope released Sarah, Lewis greeted his niece by lifting her into the air and making her shriek with pleasure. Maggie's boys, who worshipped Penelope's brother, were soon drawing him aside to show off their treasures. Frank had a ball he wanted to demonstrate to the peril of a vase that sat on the sofa table, and Jamie a scrawled picture that was supposed to be a dog.

Buckler had not moved from the threshold. He felt a lightness of heart that made him grin like a fool, mingled with the terrifying sensation that he had come home, even though no one but Penelope knew it yet. Not that these lodgings in a mean street off Golden Square could ever be a real home to any of them. The house itself had once been splendid enough, but, now let in suites of rooms, it had deteriorated into damp and dingy shabbiness.

As they'd ascended the broad staircase with its blocked-up windows, Buckler's imagination had been busy with schemes to relocate the whole family. A place where the air was clean and the children could play out of doors, but not so far away that he could not easily manage his business. There were difficulties ahead—enormous ones. He would investigate Penelope's precise legal position with her marriage, and arrange a bond that would secure her an income for life, no matter what happened to him.

He watched her with the children. She'd been so young when she wed Jeremy Wolfe, just eighteen. She'd never told him the full story of her marriage, but he was certain she hadn't had her father's permission, and he thought she might have married abroad. Could there be a loophole that would free her? If not, could he bring himself to put her at risk if their relationship became what he so ardently desired? Later. He would ask himself the hard questions later and make sure Penelope asked them too.

When the clamor had subsided, she glanced over her shoulder, smiling. "Edward, say hello to Sarah."

He went to the child and held out his hand in greeting.

>>>

It was John Chase's turn to take leave. He'd escorted the maid Todd, lugging her valise, to the main road and had written the report laying out the evidence against Mrs. Yates for use in the coroner's court and beyond. He'd supervised Tallboys in preparing a statement for her to sign in which she formally resigned as trustee. He'd also consulted with the magistrate, who would oversee the initial inquiry into her crimes, and seen the poisoner confined in the village lockup. Tallboys and Honeycutt, asking that she be provided with every comfort, had arranged for an attorney to wait upon her. Tallboys had inquired if Chase would remain for dinner, but he'd declined, eager to get home. In the morning he would see the chief magistrate at Bow Street, but for tonight he was tired and wanted to be alone.

Tallboys now seemed to distrust his powers of management—a reaction that made him more likeable and that probably wouldn't last. He asked Chase what should be done with the Honeycutts, if Marina should persist in her antagonism toward them.

"Send them about their business," recommended Chase. "The will leaves them provided for. Why should Miss Garrod be expected to house and feed them if you, her guardian, doesn't choose?"

"You don't think—" Breaking off, he shot Chase a doubting look, then said, "Would it be possible, do you suppose, that Mrs. Yates might go away somewhere and live quietly? She must have been mad to play those heathen tricks and murder her own brother. The scandal, Mr. Chase. It will be dreadful for Miss Garrod."

And for you, thought Chase. "Not possible. Mrs. Yates must stand her trial. I'll see that she does myself. I think you know that she is entirely sane, sir."

The clergyman heaved a bottomless sigh. "And what if a suitable candidate can't be found for the girl's hand in time? Miss Garrod will be left to my charge forever if she does not satisfy the terms of the trust."

"Leave that problem for another day," said Chase.

Marina Garrod took his arm and accompanied him right to the carriage door, waving Mr. Tallboys off when he tried to dog her heels.

"Mr. Chase," she said when they faced one another in the warm glow of early evening, "it is not too much to say that you have saved my life—you and your friends—but chiefly you. I was unhappy when my father employed you. I thought you were another spy. I never thought you would be my friend."

"But your father did. He chose me because I owed your mother my life. Mr. Garrod hoped I was the kind of man who wishes to repay old debts, and he was right in that. Now, though, I would act for your sake alone, out of my great admiration for you. It has been an honor to serve you, ma'am." This was not the speech he usually delivered to his clients, but he felt it warranted in this case. And meant it, every word. It had been iniquitous of Garrod to make his daughter's marriage a condition of her inheritance, but Chase believed she would somehow continue to manage her relatives, and he did not envy Mr. Tallboys in his task.

"I would hate never to see you again." Marina paused, then added lightly, "Perhaps I will one day give a grand party. Will you come watch over the jewels of the guests?"

He bowed, taking her hand. "Glad to, Miss Garrod."

"I want you to know that in any house of mine, you will be an invited guest. Standing around and terrifying the servants will not be allowed. I will even expect you to dance with me."

"If these creaky bones decide to cooperate, I am your man."

They smiled at one another, and Chase released her.

He was about to mount the steps into the coach when she called him back. "Mr. Chase, do you think I might write a letter to my mother in Jamaica? Will they let me?"

"Insist on it," he told her. "Mark my words. From this day forward, your family will strive to please you. When you write to Joanna, give her my regards."

"Anyone who wishes to please me will help me defeat the infamous provision in my father's will that forbids the emancipation of his slaves. Mr. Durant and I have already discussed the matter." She paused, looking thoughtful. "Do you suppose Mr. Buckler can advise me?"

Chase almost laughed aloud but didn't want to hurt her feelings. The thought of Tallboys forced to deal with a budding abolitionist was delicious to him, and, should she persevere in these aims, Buckler would be jolted from his bookish retreat yet again. Or maybe that retreat had become a thing of the past, in any case. Chase had noticed the perfect harmony that existed between his friends and was both happy for them and determined to reserve his judgment of this development for the future. Marina awaited his response. He said, "I am sure Mr. Buckler will be glad to assist you, and if you need me for anything, you'll let me know. Goodbye for the present, Miss Garrod."

"Goodbye, Mr. Chase."

As the carriage rolled away, he put out his head and waved a hand to her. She waved back. He watched her until the coach turned onto the main road.

At home, he let himself into the entrance hall. He heard the clatter of the dinner dishes coming from the dining room as he sneaked up the stairs, wishing to avoid seeing anyone. On the landing, however, he met Sybil Fakenham.

"You're back," she said, seemingly without much interest. But the curiosity was strong in her eyes, and he knew he'd likely be receiving a late-night visit.

"Why aren't you at dinner? Still at daggers-drawn with Mrs. Beeks?"

"We've reached a stalemate, though hostile forces are ever ready for attack."

"Declare a peace treaty. You won't be around long enough to wage a war."

"Oh, am I going somewhere?" Her sharp nose wrinkled at him.

"You are going to be lady's maid to a young woman. It's all arranged. Miss Garrod needs a friend in her household, so I'll ask you to keep that tongue of yours between your teeth and make yourself useful to her. They expect you tomorrow. It's a good position, Sybil." He named the salary that Tallboys had quoted him.

Her eyes widened. "I'll start packing my bags. Mr. Chase, there's something you should know."

"Later," he said, so exhausted that he stumbled a little as he approached his door. He hadn't had a full night's rest in five days. "Tell Mrs. Beeks not to disturb me with a tray for several hours at least."

He went into his bedchamber and closed the door. He removed his boots, ripped the cravat from his neck, and shrugged off his coat. Just as he was about to throw himself on the bed, he saw it, a white rectangle in the middle of his desk. It was impossible to see more, for the room darkened rapidly as night descended. Chase walked to the desk and picked up the letter. Showing foreign postmarks, creases, and water spots, it was addressed in a firm, young hand, which he recognized at once. It was from his son. His fatigue forgotten, he strode to the mantelpiece to retrieve the tinderbox. He lit a candle and sat down in his armchair to read Jonathan's letter.

Acknowledgments

I must start by thanking my friend Dan Kelleher for helping me understand boiler explosions. Dan, chemistry teacher extraordinaire, pointed out problems with my scenario and suggested clarifications. In a historical novel, there's always the question of what actually happened versus what my early nineteenth-century characters *believed* had occurred, especially since steam technology as applied to greenhouses was newfangled in Regency England. I truly appreciate Dan's help.

Margaret and Peter Mason generously gave their time to read a draft of the manuscript and offer perceptive comments. It is in no small part due to their efforts that I was able to catch a number of silly mistakes. Thank you, Margaret and Peter!

As always, I thank my husband, Michael, who helped me with boilers, laudanum, greenhouses, and about a thousand other plotting and character matters. Let's just say that he comes along with me on the journey of every book.

Finally, I am grateful to everyone at Poisoned Pen Press for shepherding this manuscript through production. Thank you, especially, to Barbara Peters, Annette Rogers, Beth Deveny, Rob Rosenwald, and Pete Zrioka.

Historical Notes

In 1791 the abolitionist William Fox exhorted Britons to acknowledge the cruelty of racial and geographic boundaries that seek to separate person from person, soul from soul: "Can our pride suggest that the rights of men are limited to any nation, or to any colour? Or, were anyone to treat a fellow creature in this country as we do the unhappy Africans in the West Indies; struck with horror, we should be zealous to deliver the oppressed, and punish the oppressor" (as quoted in Debbie Lee's *Slavery and the Romantic Imagination*, 14).

Lee refers to slavery as "the great moral question" of the late Georgian era. Another related development of the time was, of course, the impulse toward freedom represented by the various revolutions sweeping the globe, including the one that gave birth to America, and that created the first black republic in the French colony of St. Domingue (Haiti). Slavery was not a faraway evil easily ignored by Britons. It was hotly contested, its moral dimensions explored in pamphlets and in poignant images of suffering humanity. While many people who profited from the institution battled to uphold it, others, "struck with horror," argued, with increasing success, that slavery was antithetical to British values. Still, after the abolition of the slave trade in 1807, slavery itself endured for several more decades in the British empire. And none of the oppressors were ever punished. Instead, the government provided thousands of English men and women with financial compensation when they were forced to free their slaves.

Exposure to the issue of slavery in Georgian England brought with it anxieties about the danger of permeable boundaries in a global society (sound familiar?). And this exposure to new ideas, other cultures, and other races evoked a corresponding concern about protecting the purity of the domestic hearth and of national identity. Nor was the fear that sacred boundaries could be dissolved limited to race; the anxiety also extended to gender, social, and cultural norms. Thus, my character Marina Garrod is perceived as a threat to her family on every level. She is not a true English rose in that she carries Africa in her blood, a heritage made visible in her complexion. She is illegitimate and lacks breeding. Moreover, as the presumed heiress to a large fortune, her father has tapped this "half lady" to become the mother of a dynastic line. Lastly, through her mother, she is linked to Obeah, an African folk religion that can be seen as a vehicle of hidden power and revolt. In a society that prided itself on refinement and enlightenment, and that valued the transmission of family name, lands, and wealth to the next generation, Marina does not belong.

A quick note on Obeah and John Crow: I intend to publish a separate essay on this subject on my website, for there is no room here to discuss the fascinating connections between Obeah, the vulture John Crow, the John Canoe dancers, poisons, and *Abrus precatorius* or the jequirity bean (wild licorice). Some fuzziness exists as to when these symbolic links were forged. My main source—an essay by John Rashford, "Plants, Spirits and the Meaning of 'John' in Jamaica," which was published in the *Jamaica Journal* in 1984—mentions that the first record of the Jamaican turkey buzzard being called "John Crow" did not occur until 1826. But I have found indications that this may have happened earlier, and certainly, ideas can brew in the popular culture for some time before they are written down. A source of 1811 refers to the beads of wild licorice as being popular with Jamaican slaves for jewelry.

I am indebted to Rashford and to many other scholars of the Caribbean and the West Indians in London, and regret that I can mention only a few more in these already lengthy notes. First and foremost, I must acknowledge Nick Hibbert Steele. Nick—a descendant of George Hibbert, the model for my character Hugo Garrod—provided resources from his personal library and his valuable insights. Very kindly, he read the manuscript in order to help me catch any historical inaccuracies. I should emphasize that Hugo Garrod is *not* George Hibbert. Though Hibbert's family wealth derived from Jamaica, Hibbert never went to the island and had no mixed-race children. He did live in Clapham among abolitionists such as William Wilberforce, and he kept a famous garden filled with botanical exotica (in particular, the Proteas mentioned in this novel). I have borrowed some of Hibbert's biographical details for the purposes of this story.

Next is Dan Livesay, whose dissertation titled *Children of Uncertain Fortune: Mixed Race Migration from the West Indies to Britain, 1750-1820*, was essential to this project. Dan's work chronicles the precarious lives of mixed-race children who relocated to Britain. White relatives sometimes mounted legal challenges to the inheritances left to these children or tried to rebrand them with the mark of slavery. For example, Dan explores the life of Barbadian planter Joshua Steele. Steele died, leaving his mixed-race children, Catherine and Edward, a sizeable inheritance. When Catherine and Edward were sent to school in England, Steele's sister, Mary Ann, successfully proved that the children were not properly manumitted, a tactic she used to make herself heiress of the estate and guardian of the minors. She did settle money on them but not as much as had been allocated in her brother's will. Dan makes the point that Catherine and Edward were left in a subservient position and were prevented from being independent people of color. I thank Dan Livesay not only for his scholarship but also for his encouraging response to my email. Thanks also to Brooke Newman, professor of history at Virginia Commonwealth University, and Dr. Ian Barrett of King's College, London, for their assistance.

I should mention the work of Deirdre Coleman and Felicity Nussbaum. In particular, Coleman's essay "Janet Schaw and the Complexions of Empire" helped me develop a mystery built around the notion of deadly convention. My idea was that my murderer should be a woman who poisons her brother (with arsenic that has tainted the purest sugar) because she feels he has brought a contaminating influence into her respectable family. In short, she wants those boundaries, those walls, to be raised up so that the Other can be excluded. Her obsession with purity, whiteness, and Englishness becomes a sickness of the spirit that pollutes her relationships with all of her adopted children and turns her into a civilized savage determined to create her own domestic empire.

I like to ponder the connections between my twenty-first-century novel and an anonymous work of 1808 titled simply *The Woman of Colour: A Tale*. In his excellent introduction to this work, Lyndon J. Dominique states that the novel is important "not only because it is the first long prose fiction in British literature to prominently feature a racially conscious mulatto heroine, but also because, conceivably, a woman of color could have written it" (18). How curious and disturbing it is, then, that this novel was ignored for almost two hundred years! *The Woman of Colour* introduces Olivia Fairfield, the natural daughter of a Jamaican planter and a slave on his plantation. Similar to my character Marina Garrod, she is expected to marry her cousin, as a condition of her lover inheriting her father's estate. Olivia travels to England, where she is the victim of rank prejudice and fraud. But she is not afraid to express her fellow feeling with African slaves or her contempt for slavery. She skillfully uses the weapon of protest cloaked in propriety to battle her tormenters.

In *On a Desert Shore*, Marina escapes confinement in a madhouse. However, she is still subject to her father's patriarchal control, which he has the power to exert beyond the grave. And yet she is as inclined as Olivia to speak her mind and to enact her own will. In writing this novel, I grew very fond of Marina, in part because she reminds me of the many impassioned and outspoken young women of all backgrounds with whom I have worked in my teaching career.

A last word about the title of this book. Marina is shipwrecked "on a desert shore" in an alien land that does not welcome her, even though she is half English and has been mostly raised in England. But to me the title also suggests what William Wordsworth calls "the still, sad music of humanity" or Matthew Arnold refers to as the "turbid ebb and flow of human misery," the tide that comes in year after year and century after century. Why do we keep singing the same old song? I think it's because we cling to our proud systems, which are based on the lust of greed and the urge to dominate.

September 29, 2015

To receive a free catalog of Poisoned Pen Press titles, please provide your name, address, and email address in one of the following ways:

Phone: 1-800-421-3976
Facsimile: 1-480-949-1707
Email: info@poisonedpenpress.com
Website: www.poisonedpenpress.com

Poisoned Pen Press
6962 E. First Ave. Ste 103
Scottsdale, AZ 85251

CPSIA information can be obtained at www.ICGtesting.com
Printed in the USA
BVOW05s1337300116

434401BV00002B/2/P